Loving someone is something you never forget how to do . . .

Zoe Hornsby has enough on her plate. Her pet grooming business tucked inside her friends' veterinarian clinic is busy, and all her free time outside of work is dedicated to caring for her mother's ailing mind. Dating is certainly not on her agenda. For all she cares, the town gossips of Redwood Ridge, Oregon, can set their matchmaking sights on someone else. Because no way would she consider sexy veterinarian Drake O'Grady her perfect guy. Once upon a time, she may have harbored a little crush, but he'd only had eyes for her best friend. And the crazy attraction building between her and Drake now? Down boy, down.

After Drake lost his wife to cancer, he's finally clawed his way out of grief and beginning to feel more like a part of the human race. But he's appalled to learn his prying family thinks he's ready to jump in the dating pool. And the woman they thrust at him couldn't be more inappropriate. As his dead wife's best friend, Zoe is off limits. Even if they seem to share a common sadness, she is too potent a personality to get romantically tangled with. Yet she's making his heart beat and blood roar like he never thought it could again. And he doesn't want to just exist anymore . . .

Visit us at www.kensingtonbooks.com

Books by Kelly Moran

Redwood Ridge
Puppy Love
Tracking You
New Tricks

Published by Kensington Publishing Corporation

New Tricks

Redwood Ridge

Kelly Moran

LYRICAL PRESS
Kensington Publishing Corp.
www.kensingtonbooks.com

First Electronic Edition: September 2017
eISBN-13: 978-1-5161-0275-4
eISBN-10: 1-5161-0275-4

First Print Edition: September 2017
ISBN-13: 978-1-5161-0278-5
ISBN-10: 1-5161-0278-9

Printed in the United States of America

To my father-in-law, Mike, who was taken from us too soon. And for all those who've lost a loved one to cancer or are caregivers for someone they love. Bless you.

Acknowledgements

A big thank you to the team at Brentwood Animal Hospital, especially Lynn, who made sure I got the veterinarian thing down right. Any errors are my own.

Chapter 1

"I'm going to kill you."

Drake O'Grady stopped dead in his tracks and pulled his cell away from his ear to glance at the screen.

Yep. It was definitely Zoe Hornsby who had called him, but that wasn't her voice. Not that she hadn't threatened to kill him before. She was usually more subtle about it than coming right out with it, though. Feisty, opinionated, and with a spine of steel, she was just attractive and smart enough to be a pain in his ass.

Wiping sweat from his brow with his forearm, he put the phone back to his ear and called her name. When she didn't respond, he sighed and glanced around, flustered. Always—*always*—she flustered him. Her favorite hobby.

Deep in a pocket of dense woods, he stood outside his cabin and caught his breath after a three-mile run. All he wanted was a shower, a beer, and two hours of ESPN. He inhaled brine from the Pacific a few miles away that mingled with pine and moss from the forest. Dusk had come and gone, and the residual humidity made oxygen exchange nearly impossible.

Or maybe that was worry. His heart tripped behind his ribs in the off-chance Zoe didn't have things under control. It sounded like he was on speaker phone. Crashes and screams and glass shattering emitted through the ear piece. Which meant Zoe's mom was having a rough night. And judging by Zoe's lack of response, she'd...

"Pocket-dialed me again." Drake glanced at his faithful German Shepherd, Moses, sitting by his feet, tongue lagging from their nightly run. If dogs could shrug, his just did.

Though he and Zoe had been friendly since they were both in diapers, and they worked together at the animal clinic where she was a groomer and he a veterinarian, he hated to get involved. Zoe was fiercely independent and she'd been handling her mother's early onset dementia diagnosis the past few years better than a saint.

"Mama, please."

Drake's gut clenched at the weary tone in Zoe's voice. Heart pounding, he teetered in the decision to butt in or not. She'd probably maim him for the effort. Damn it, anyway. Unable to stand it, he whistled for Moses and opened the front door to let the dog inside.

"I'll be right back. Don't drink all the beer while I'm gone."

Bark.

"I heard that."

T-shirt soaked with sweat and muscles protesting the lack of cool-down stretches, he climbed behind the wheel of his truck. Disconnecting the call, he stared out his windshield, ground his molars, and shoved the vehicle in gear. He'd be in and out of her place in ten minutes. Then he could continue his fun-filled Friday night. Alone.

He drove the long, winding private road past his brothers' Flynn and Cade's houses, then his mother's, and continued to the main strip in their small town of Redwood Ridge. Folks were out enjoying the Oregon summer, eating ice cream and walking the cobblestone sidewalks. Old world lampposts lit the way, emitting a yellowish glow against the stars.

Truck at a crawling speed, he strummed his fingers on the wheel, avoiding eye contact with passersby. Eye contact meant encouragement to...chat. He shuddered.

After a few blocks and a handful of quick turns, he was in Zoe's subdivision. This older part of town consisted of gingerbread houses and postage-stamp yards teeming with flower boxes. Fireflies blinked over the neatly trimmed lawns. He pulled into her driveway, cut the engine, and strode up the porch steps.

In and out.

Screeching came from the other side of the door, and he rubbed the back of his neck while he waited for her to answer his knock. As he was about to pound again, the door swung wide.

All five foot four of her stood framed in the doorway. She was a bitty thing, though one would never recognize that fact with all her attitude. Wearing a pair of jean cut-offs and a white tank top, she cocked her hip.

And Jesus. Was a bra too much to ask? Avoiding the nipples poking out to bid him hello, he kept his gaze trained on her hazel eyes. Sometimes green, sometimes gray or blue, they were outlined by dark lashes and too big for her narrow face. Her once light brown, shoulder-length hair was pinned up in a messy knot, and was now a ridiculous shade of pink. For a year, she'd been dyeing it unnatural colors. Why, he hadn't a clue.

"It's not a good time, Drake."

To emphasize her point, something crashed inside the house.

"No kidding."

"Zoe? Zoe, honey." From the house beside Zoe's, her neighbor stepped out the front door, leaned over the porch rail, and wrung a towel in her hands. Distressed guilt was fraught all over her young face. "I just got the kids to sleep. Is there any hope your mom will calm down soon?"

Crash.

Closing her eyes, Zoe sighed. Shoulders deflating, she poked her head out her own front door. "I'm sorry, Mary. I'm trying."

"I know. I know you are, honey." She bit her lip. "Can I do anything?"

Drake would give her neighbors this, at least. They were good people who helped as much as they could. Except the deep caverns under Zoe's eyes and the fact she seemed thinner than ever could attest that no amount of aid was enough. Her mother had been declining at a rapid rate this past year, and Zoe was doing everything in her power to keep her at home. And killing herself in the process.

"Thank you. I'm okay." She crossed her arms and waited to speak until the other woman had gone back inside. "The pharmacy screwed up our refill request and I had to wait an hour. Thus, she's getting the sedative later than usual. With her sundowning as bad as it is, she's past confused and irate. I can't get her to take the pills."

He nodded. Sundowning—a common term for people with Alzheimer's and dementia—had been Zoe's worst enemy. Confusion tended to increase later in the day, ergo the term. Stepping around her, he walked inside, taking in a tossed coffee table and lamp on the bare wood floor. Around the divider island, her kitchen floor was littered with spaghetti.

She followed his gaze. "That's what kicked off the festivities. She claimed I was trying to poison her. Feng shui via pasta. Has a nice look."

At least she still had her sense of humor.

She scrubbed a hand over her tired face. "What are you doing here anyway?"

"You called me."

Her brow wrinkled in that adorable defiant way it used to as a child. "I did not."

"Pretty sure you did." Since they were about to get into a he said/she said battle of kindergarten wits, he grabbed her shoulders, spun her around, and fished her cell out of her back pocket. He held up her phone and raised his brows.

"I pocket-dialed you again. Sorry." She took the phone back and set it down. A blush crept up her neck, and he felt like a dickhead for embarrassing her. It was a rare sight, indeed. She squared her shoulders as if channeling her last diva reserve. "Unless it was an excuse for you to touch my ass."

And there was the Zoe who made his temples throb and his left eye twitch.

He narrowed his eyes in warning even though she was only baiting him. "I have never touched your ass."

"You just did."

"To get your..." He drew a slow, deep inhale for patience. "Why do I bother?"

An eye roll, and she waved off the argument. "Relax. It's the most action I've seen in awhile. I should thank you."

He snapped his jaw shut to avoid putting his foot in his mouth. Four years... For four years he'd been living in an almost near state of numb autopilot. A ghost among the living. His wife Heather's death from ovarian cancer had left a gaping hole where love used to be, had killed hope. And in all that time since, the woman before him had been the only one to arouse any kind of emotion.

Irritation mostly, but emotion just the same.

Catherine came into view from down the short hallway. A wrinkled nightgown was all she wore and it slipped off one shoulder. Her hair was the same shade of Zoe's natural color and they shared similar waifish body types. Before the disease had taken her mind, Catherine had raised Zoe alone, making her the independent, self-assured woman she was today. Add to that, they'd been more friends than mother-daughter.

Hollow bewilderment and a trace of fear were all that radiated in Cat's eyes now. His stomach bottomed out at the shell she'd become. If he was this wrecked after five seconds in the same room, he could only imagine how it was affecting Zoe. He'd watched Heather slowly fade, get sicker, and it was the hardest damn thing he'd ever done.

"Oh crap." Zoe grabbed his arms, startling him. She stepped in front of him and blocked his route to her mother.

Catherine raised her arm.

"Duck—" A book flew across the room and into Zoe's back. She sucked in a harsh breath and pinched her eyes closed, then dropped her forehead to his chest. "Damn, that hurt. She's been throwing things all night."

He froze, shocked out of his shoes that Catherine had shown any signs of violence. She'd yelled and rearranged a room burglary-style, but he'd never witnessed aggression like this directed at her daughter. He stared at the paperback that landed at his feet.

Zoe's light scent of lavender filled his nose, swirled around them, and reminded him of their position. He held his hands up in surrender at her unexpected touch. It had been a long time since he'd had even accidental contact. He tried to regulate his breathing, get a grip on just *what* his reaction was, then snapped out of it.

Anger sent his pulse hammering. Holding her at arm's length, he ground his jaw. "Did you just shield me? What the hell, Zoe?" He raked his gaze over her pained expression. "Are you all right?" The way her fingers dug into his forearms said no.

"I'm fine." Slowly, she straightened with a wince. "Mama, look who came for a visit."

Knowing his role, he offered a smile and took a step away. "Hey, Cat. I'm home." For whatever reason, she was more comfortable with men than women. The past year especially, she'd regressed to a time in her memory before Zoe, and often thought Drake—or any other male she came in contact with—was her uncle.

Cat's confused gaze leveled on him and softened. "Jimmy?"

He eyed Zoe and spoke out of the corner of his mouth. "Who's that?" Cat's brother's name was Ed.

"I think it's my dad," she whispered.

He faced her fully, not liking the mask she'd donned to hide her true feelings. "I thought you never met your father." Far as he knew, Zoe didn't even know the guy's name.

"I haven't. He took off while she was pregnant and didn't come back. But by the way she brings up his name and the things she says, it's a logical leap."

He nodded, wondering what to do now. "Where are her meds?"

"On the kitchen table in a cup."

"Jimmy? Is that you?"

Smiling, he stepped over to Cat and cupped her shoulders. "It's me. It's very late. How about I tuck you in and we can talk tomorrow?"

She appeared to be thinking it over, her gaze darting around. "I guess that would be okay." She glared at Zoe through hell-hath-no-fury eyes. "Who's this tramp?"

The moment the words must've sunk in, Zoe swallowed hard and hung her head. "I'm your new neighbor. I just dropped off a plate of cookies." Her voice broke near the end and she cleared her throat. "I'll leave you alone."

With dejection radiating off her in waves, she shuffled into the kitchen. It took everything inside him to keep up the charade and not follow. Everyday. She did this day in and day out.

He took the cup of pills off the kitchen table and, with a hand at Cat's elbow, walked her to the bedroom. She'd torn the place apart. Dresser drawers were pulled out, clothing everywhere. The bedding was in a pile in the corner.

Quickly, he righted what he could and convinced her to swallow the meds. After he got her tucked in, he sat at her hip for a moment to ensure she stayed there. Zoe needed a few damn minutes of peace.

"I can't believe you're here, Jimmy. I missed you."

The only thing harder than watching someone in this state had to be living in it. His throat tight, he smiled. "Me, too. You should get some rest."

Her lids drooped. "I think we should name the baby Diane. Or maybe Zoe." She yawned, eyes shut.

Guess that meant this Jimmy guy was Zoe's dad. It took a special breed of asshole to leave a pregnant woman and never look back. No child support. No birthday cards. And now she was stuck, alone, taking care of her mother.

"Zoe's a wonderful name." She was a hell of a person as well, much as they got under one another's skin.

Once he made his way down the hall, he noted Zoe had the spaghetti mess cleaned up and the coffee table righted. It was a cute little house. She'd grown up here and moved back in after her mother's diagnosis. But the place didn't fit Zoe's personality, not like her old apartment. Blue and pink striped drapes, floral-print couches, scarred pine tables.

He found her at the kitchen table, picking at a bowl of pasta. "She's asleep."

"Thank you." Refusing to look at him, she stared at the food. Silence stretched. "Are you hungry?"

"No." He pulled out a chair and sat next to her.

"The spaghetti is from the pot, not the floor." A dare lit her eyes.

He shook his head, his attempt at a smile failing miserably.

How many times had she been there for him, and he couldn't think of a proper thing to say. She'd been Heather's best friend and a damn good one to him. He wasn't a guy of many words, but Zoe was the only person who rendered him speechless. Always had, in fact. Not quite nerves, per se, but something uncanny anyway.

Crossing his fingers, he stacked his hands on top of his head. "I believe you're right about Jimmy being your father." He paused. "Have you ever tried looking for him?"

A noise resembling a dry laugh burst from her lips. "I have no interest. He couldn't bother to stick. I don't need him."

Drake whole-heartedly agreed.

Her cat bumped his leg and, happy to have something to focus on, he picked up the white ball of fur to set in his lap. Cotton, she'd name the thing. Poor guy had probably been hiding during all the commotion. "He's due for a distemper vaccination soon, isn't he?"

"Probably. I'll have Avery put him on Cade's schedule."

Avery was their office manager and his youngest brother's wife. Cade did most of the in-house clients at their veterinarian clinic. Flynn, his other brother, made house calls and traveled. Drake was the surgery vet, though he saw patients two days a week for appointments, like Flynn.

"I'll bring a vaccination over next week." She had enough on her plate.

"Do an exam, too."

Her gaze whipped to his. Held.

He didn't know what to make of her expression or the way it made his stomach shift, so he eyed the cat. Cotton batted his arm in a silent demand for attention. Complying, Drake stroked the furball, letting the rumble of his purr settle him.

Zoe pushed her bowl away, not eating a bite. "I'm going to need to soundproof the house at this rate. Mama's getting louder. And worse. I'm lucky the neighbors haven't called the cops yet."

Jesus. "Zoe—"

"Don't." Her full lips thinned into a line. "Not you, too. I promised her I'd keep her at home. You did for Heather."

They hadn't outright said her name in so long it jarred him for a beat. "Heather had terminal cancer. Your mom's body is fine. It's her mind that's gone. One of these days, she could really…"

"What? Hurt me? She'd never—"

"She threw a book at you tonight." He closed his eyes to calm his temper, cool his tone. This situation wasn't Zoe's fault anymore than it was Cat's. Fifty-five years old, and her life was gone. "She's not the same woman who raised you. This person doesn't know you. She's confused, scared. Not even she could've known how bad it would get."

Abruptly standing, she sent the chair across the floor. Her back to him, she walked her bowl to the sink. "I can't put her away, Drake."

No, she wouldn't. Not even at the risk to herself. Loyal to a fault. He couldn't blame her. If it were his mother, he'd do the same thing. He hated seeing her like this, though. Tough as nails Zoe Hornsby, reduced to a wilted balloon.

"I should go." He rose and set the cat on the floor, surprised he didn't really want to leave. "I'll see you at the game tomorrow." Their clinic had teamed up years ago with some of the doctors and nurses from urgent care to start a softball league every summer. Tomorrow, they played the firefighters and police officers.

Her gaze skimmed over him as if seeing him for the first time all evening.

"Why are you wet and sweaty?"

"Your call interrupted my nightly run."

"Oh. You're welcome, then."

Smartass. "You know, some exercise might do you some good."

Her hands fisted on her hips. "Are you calling me fat?"

Considering he could bench press her with one arm...no. She had a great body, if not on the slim side. Olive skin tone, compliments of her gypsy heritage. A few freckles on her pert nose. Long legs, slight hourglass curve to her waist, breasts that would fit perfectly—

What the hell?

He shook his head. "I meant that exercise raises endorphins and improves your mood." Pausing, he wondered what in Almighty's name he was doing. "You could come jogging with me in the evenings."

Indignation infused every inch of her expression. "And you call yourself my friend. Get out of my house. And don't come back without cupcakes or tequila."

Ah, yes. There was the real Zoe. Much better. It was awfully damn hard to fight a grin. Regardless, he managed and went home.

Chapter 2

Zoe took a few practice swings on the third base sideline before the game. It was hotter than Haiti, but she couldn't wait to play. Their Saturday softball games were just about her only reprieve besides work. Drake's aunt Rosa watched Mama for her, and smacking a ball around was great therapy.

Sex would be better, but it was too much effort to bother. Flirting, dating, sealing the deal. Who had the time?

Breathing in the scent of fresh cut grass and sunshine, she glanced at the other players warming up. Eye candy, for sure. It was as if being hot were a prerequisite for the firefighters and police officers on the opposing team. She'd grown up with most of them, had even dated a few, but looking was no hardship. Neither team had very many women, and not that she went for that sort of thing, but they weren't an eyesore either.

Residents were filling the small set of bleachers on either side of the field. In the distance, the base of the Klamath Mountains was a pretty backsplash to Redwood Ridge's park. The roar of the rocky Pacific coastline hummed in the background. Hotdog and popcorn vendors were busy between bleacher sections.

"Whoa, easy there."

Zoe caught her bat up short and faced Parker Maloney. The Ridge's finest PD display right there, and now the sheriff. Dark hair, shocking green eyes, he was built like a rugged cowboy but had the look of a wicked Irish hellion. Next to him was Jason Burkwell of the fire department—a blond, blue-eyed cutie with a jaw full of scruff and a grin that promised fun. His tee was stretched over sculpted manliness she wished she had the inclination to explore. She hadn't had fun in ages.

She grinned. "Checking out the competition?"

Jason's gaze slid south over her white shirt, past the quarter-length black sleeves, and kept going to her white capris. "I'll forfeit if you run away with me. I'd be happy to show you my fire hose."

Parker shook his head. "Original, man. Real original."

"Be still my heart." Zoe waved her hand in front of her face, adoring their teasing banter. They were great guys who'd been in her high school graduating class. Harmless flirting had always been a part of their makeup. "Parker, can we borrow your handcuffs?"

"I think not."

She frowned. "Sigh. Such a party pooper."

Jason adjusted his hat. "How's your mom doing?"

Mood kill. "Not great, but thanks for asking." A rewind of last night played through her head and she sighed. Drake had been a godsend, not that she'd tell him so. Her lumbar still hurt from the back-versus-book debacle. Mama had one hell of an arm. Book for the win.

"Sorry to hear that." Jason's gaze made its way over her shoulder and narrowed. He tilted his head. "Is there a reason Drake O'Grady is shooting daggers our way?"

Was he? Her stupid, stupid heart pounded. It took obscene effort not to turn and look. Interesting development, but why? And if Drake were, say, upset by her chatting it up with the Ridge's hotties, it would maybe—a little—have her grinning inside.

Idiot, party of one.

"Not a clue." She hoped her voice sounded as nonchalant as she tried to make it.

"You two aren't a thing, right?" Jason's focus remained across the field. "I didn't know he was ready to date again, but it's been some time since Heather died."

"I assure you, we aren't a thing, and that I'm aware, he's not seeing anyone." If Drake were ever ready to meet someone and fall again, he'd go for anyone but her. History and circumstances had already proven that fact.

Parker glanced behind her. "Well, he either very much dislikes us talking or we have a bull's-eye on our faces."

There had to be another explanation. She'd probably pissed him off last night or he was put out by her having called in the first place. Drake didn't care one iota who she dated, hung out with, or talked to.

Then her stomach twisted with another thought. Maybe he felt sorry for her after what he'd seen at her house. Drake loved with his whole self. He didn't know any other way. Whether it be family or friends, if one were lucky enough to be a part of his inner circle, they were privy to his severely protective and giving nature. No matter their differences, Drake loved her in his own way.

Refusing to focus on the matter, her gaze swept the field and landed on the mound. "Who's the guy pitching?" She'd never seen him before.

Parker grunted. "Rick Addison. New deputy down from Portland. Bit of a douche if you ask me."

Zoe leaned on her bat. "I'll take him down a few pegs when I hit everything he throws."

"I've got a beer with your name on it at Shooters if you do." Jason crossed his arms. "I don't care if we lose because of it."

She shrugged. "You'll lose anyway."

"Damn right." Cade strode over. And speaking of eye candy...

Dark blond hair, gray-blue eyes, and reformed playboy of the Ridge. Or Drake's little brother, as she referred to him.

He grinned at the guys. "If you're trying to distract our best player here, it won't work." He looked at Zoe. "We're ready to start."

Nodding, she waved bye and let Cade lead her away with his arm around her shoulders.

"Still breaking hearts all over town, I see."

She jabbed him with an elbow. "Someone has to now that you're married."

Cade stepped away and whistled for Avery, then asked her to bring Hailey to the field. Hand in hand, Avery stepped off the bleachers and passed her eight-year-old off to him. Hailey squealed and flapped her hands, indicating she was excited. As the girl was a non-verbal autistic, Zoe had learned to read her mannerisms.

Drake leaned on the chest-high chain-link fence separating the field from the dugout bench as if completely unaware anything was going on around him. Forearms braced on the top rail, he watched Zoe head over, eyes hooded and expression blank. The position stretched his jersey across his wide shoulders, narrow waist, and defined biceps. A slight five-o'clock shadow dusted his jaw. Thick black hair poked out from under his cap and eyes the shade of forbidden chocolate trekked her destination until she stood in front of him.

Fifteen years had passed since the dreadful, awful day she'd realized her crush. In that time, he'd dated, married, and buried her best friend. Never so much as hinted he knew Zoe was a female, regardless of whether he considered her an attractive one. One would think she'd have gotten a clue.

In her defense, she hadn't pined for what could never be, nor what had never been hers in the first place. Back then, she'd cried a couple times over the teenage angst like any proper sixteen-year-old. Alone, of course. No one had suspected her feelings. And in a handful of instances since, she'd snapped the lid tight on any fantasies when she'd caught herself daydreaming.

Damn, the man still made her pulse frantic and her heart trip in rhythm, though. It just wasn't freaking fair. And why was he staring at her?

Clearing her throat, she glanced behind her at the pitcher's mound where Cade had Hailey in front of him, ball in hand. "What are they doing?"

"Hailey's throwing out the first pitch." His voice was a deep, reverberating rumble that had the capacity to shake her foundation to rubble. He rarely raised it and even more rarely used it, but his tone got her between the ribs every time.

When she faced him again, his gaze was still on her. And, yeah. Something was off about him today. "Is everything okay?"

"Why wouldn't it be?"

Maybe because there were upwards of a hundred people in the stands, players on the field, and the team behind him, and all he was doing was watching her. If she didn't know him so well, she'd swear there was... interest on his part. But that was stupid. Chances were, he was replaying a surgery inside his head.

He jerked his chin toward infield. "Didn't realize you still hung out with Jason and Parker."

Oh hell. Had she entered a *Dr. Who* episode or something?

In response, she walked around the fence and plopped on the bench next to Flynn. Like his brothers, Flynn was an attractive guy with reddish blond hair and hazel eyes. Since the middle O'Grady was deaf, she signed and spoke simultaneously. "That's so cute they're letting Hailey throw the first pitch."

He nodded, grinning. *"It was Drake's idea,"* he signed.

He leaned over his other side and gave Gabby a quick kiss. She also worked at the clinic as Flynn's tech. They'd been dating since this past spring and were so cute together it made Zoe's teeth ache.

Jealousy, meet thy minion.

She refocused her attention to the mound. With Cade's help, Hailey brought her arm back and let the ball loose. It sailed wide left of the plate, but made it to the catcher's mitt without a bounce. The crowd applauded, Avery loudest of all, and Hailey squealed.

Zoe grinned and clapped, pride filling her chest. She may only be an honorary auntie, but that was one great kid.

Gabby jumped to her feet, cheering, her blonde ponytail swinging. "She's got quite the arm."

Drake grunted. "We'll have to recruit her for the team next year."

When had he sat next to her, darn it? And those black nylon shorts hugging his muscular thighs should be against the law. His forearm brushed hers and she sucked a shallow breath. The heat from his body was twice at hot as the air and his scent rose over that of the park. She could never quite nail what his scent was, but warm male, testosterone, and forbidden fit the bill.

Once the game was finally underway, Zoe relaxed. Their batting rotation catered to their strengths by having two O'Gradys up first, followed by Zoe, and Cade hitting cleanup. A few of the doctors and nurses from urgent care filled the middle lineup with Gabby wrapping it up. Her first time at bat, Zoe struck out, which severely pissed her off, and they took the field.

By the top of the ninth inning, they were down two-to-one and she was considering taking her fist to the pitcher's face. Parker had been right. The guy was a douche. He'd spent most of the game heckling her team.

Drake was on second base after being walked and Flynn was on first with a single. Two outs. Zoe strode to the plate and took her stance, eyes narrowed on the jerk in question.

Instead of winding up, the pitcher turned to face outfield. "Bring it in, bring it in. Woman at bat."

Oh hell no, he didn't.

Drake's shoulders moved with a sigh as if resigned to a fight breaking out. Flynn merely lifted his brows like the pitcher had fallen out of the stupid tree. The other team said it best when none of them moved an inch, giving Zoe the respect she deserved and Rick-the-Dick pitcher a blind eye.

She was about to show him what a woman and a bat could do to his testicles when Cade's voice sounded behind her. "Save it for the ball, Zoe. You got this."

She turned and offered Cade a knowing grin, then took her stance again. The ball sailed right toward her head and she ate dirt. The crowd gasped.

Cade stomped around the fence and Drake shot off second base, rage in both their eyes. But she got up and called them back, refusing to dust herself off. This was a friendly small town softball game, for christsakes. Halfway between second and the mound, Drake froze at her command, fists clenched.

"Let her show him, big brother." Cade nodded, then Drake and Zoe resumed positions. "Jerk won't know what's coming."

"I'm shaking in my cup," the pitcher droned.

Zoe rolled her eyes. "That would require you having the goods to wear a cup."

That had the whole infield laughing and Rick's jaw clenching. He wound up and let loose.

She swung. Her bat connected, and she knew from impact it was hard enough to bring Drake in to tie the game. Dropping the bat, she shot toward first base as the line-drive sailed past the shortstop and into left field. Drake scored and Flynn rounded third. Zoe tagged first and headed to second. The throw to the plate came late and Flynn slid in, safe.

"Yeah!" From her position on top of the second base bag, she wiped her sweaty brow with her palm and grinned. Her team cheered from the bench and she took a bow.

Leaving shortstop, Jason moved toward her and held up his fist. "Nice hit. I owe you a beer."

She bumped knuckles with him. "Thank you."

Rick didn't say another word, and the other team was unable to score at the bottom of the inning. Accepting the win, they shook hands and collected equipment.

But apparently Rick hadn't learned his lesson. As he walked past their bench, a bag in hand, he shoulder-checked Cade. "I'll throw her a real pitch next match."

Cade tilted his gaze heavenward. "You're nuts. She bested you. Man up."

Rick eyed Zoe. "Speaking of nuts, I hear it runs in the family. What's that they call your mom? Crazy Cat?"

A feral roar in her throat, she launched at him, but Cade caught her mid-flight. "Cool it. He's not worth it, yeah?"

In the next breath, Jason's fist collided with the pitcher's face. He went down, ass over elbow. Huffing, Jason shook out his hand, wiggling his fingers. "I suggest you stay down."

A crowd was beginning to gather. Murmurs from behind grew louder, and tension from the players on both sides shot cosmic waves into the stratosphere—all directed at Rick.

Zoe shook with rage until she could barely see straight. Cade merely held her tighter to keep her from earning twenty-to-life.

Wiping his lip and face mottled to a shade of tomato, Rick glared at Parker. "I want to press charges. He punched me."

Parker shrugged, removed his ball cap, and scratched his head. "I'm afraid I didn't see anything. If there weren't any witnesses"—he glanced around, but no one spoke up—"it might be a case of your word against his."

Rick growled. With a slow nod, he got to his feet. "I see how it is here in Podunk. She's got the sheriff between her legs. Then again, from what I've heard, half the department's been there, too."

"Son of a bitch." Drake shoved his way between Jason and Parker, murder in his eyes. Fist connected with face, and the pitcher hit dirt a second time. Drake straightened and rolled his shoulders, breaths heaving. "I believe you were told to stay down."

Zoe's jaw dropped in shock. A quick glance at Cade proved he was just as floored by Drake's actions.

"Well," Parker said. "I'm afraid I didn't see that either. Good game, guys."

Chapter 3

"I can't believe you wouldn't let me hit him." In the Adirondack chair beside Drake's in Flynn's backyard, Zoe took a healthy gulp of beer. She looked at Drake like he were the one at fault. "You got to punch the guy and it wasn't even your mother he insulted."

Drake bit the inside of his cheek and stared at his own longneck bottle. His temporary moment of insanity had little to do with the opposing pitcher's remark about Cat and everything to do with what he'd said about Zoe. One second Drake was irritated and ready to leave the field, the next his knuckles were throbbing.

They'd had a cookout at Flynn's after the game, rehashing the events, and were now sitting in a semi-circle, shooting the shit as dusk descended. Off near the tree line by the riverbed, Avery's daughter Hailey was playing with the gaggle of dogs. Cade's black lab, Freeman, and Avery's yellow lab puppy, Seraph, were chasing her. Flynn's golden retriever, Fletch, barked at Drake's new rescue from a dog fighting ring, Cyprus. His other dog, Moses, was lying in the tall bed of wildflowers, watching the girl. Rain and pine scented the air as fireflies blinked.

He should be calm. Friends, family, a lazy evening. Instead, he couldn't figure out where all this restless energy was coming from.

Cade clinked his bottle with Zoe's from her other side. "Relax. We'll save your bail money for another time, yeah?"

Drake frowned. The way Parker had been flirting with her before the game, she wouldn't need bail money. The sheriff would just let her walk. And then Jason could get on his trusty fire ladder and rescue her cat from a tree. Or something.

Jesus. Drake swiped a hand down his face. What the actual hell was wrong with him?

The icepack he'd set on his chair earlier dropped onto his knuckles, startling him. He looked over to find Zoe's pointed stare on his hand.

"Keep it iced. You're a surgeon. You need those hands."

Her pissed off version of a mother hen routine grated his nerves raw. She'd replaced the icepack more than twenty times since they'd finished eating. "It's fine."

"Well, my heart's still all aflutter from that masculine display." Brent, their vet tech, patted his chest and batted his eyelashes, then let out a gay *rawr* of prowess that was his customary verbiage. "I about jumped your bones right there on the field."

Cade choked on his beer.

"What?" Brent insisted. "I'd bow my head in shame, but I'm not, well…ashamed."

Drake let the comment roll off his shoulders, used to Brent's antics after years of working with the guy. Feeding into him would only encourage him anyhow. He laid his head back on the chair, staring at the stars peeking through the pinkish-gray sky, and listened to the rhythmic hoot from an owl. A slight breeze gave some relief to the humidity.

"Maybe you should x-ray your hand at the clinic." Avery smiled at him. "Just to be sure."

Cade had struck gold with her. Avery had beat their clinic into organized submission and made Drake enjoy leaving his house again. Something about her calm control spoke to the lonely part of him. And she was the perfect fit for his little brother. Love looked good on Cade.

Gabby tilted her head. "She's right. It couldn't hurt."

And again, Flynn was one lucky bastard, too. Gabby's sweet personality, combined with the way she straddled the line between doting on his brother and giving him space, made her the right yin to Flynn's yang. It had taken them a bit to break through the friendship line to love, but they'd done it.

Drake wiggled his fingers. It hurt like a bitch, but nothing was broken. "I'm good, kid. Thanks." Avery was still eyeing him through those concerned golden brown orbs, so he schooled his expression blank. "I repeat, I'm fine."

"Yeah, doll." Brent patted her arm. "Besides, if he's not okay, a certain vet tech could play nursemaid. And by that, I mean me."

Flynn was the one to choke on his drink this time.

Maybe it was the beer, maybe it was the ridiculousness of the conversation, but Drake laughed. "Does playing nursemaid involve you in a costume? Because then I'm out."

Zoe gasped. "Did you just make a funny?"

He eyed her with a baleful side-glance. One day, he'd really shock the crap out of her and shut up that smart mouth of hers. He froze and closed his eyes as visions of *her* in a naughty nurse outfit shoved to mind.

Just what had they laced his beer with tonight?

"You know, that reminds me." Gabby looked pointedly at Brent. "Why does Avery get a cool nickname like doll, Zoe gets firecracker, and I'm stuck with *sugarbuns?*"

Brent offered a dramatic sigh. "Because Avery is a doll with those round cheeks and her old soul. Zoe's is self-explanatory. She's a firecracker. And you are sweet as sugar, plus your buns fill jeans like the second coming."

"True story," Flynn signed.

"Aw." Gabby grinned, obviously mollified.

"I don't know." Cade shrugged. "My wife's got a pretty great backside, and if I remember correctly, you could bounce a quarter off Zoe's ass."

Drake's gaze whipped to his brother's, unadulterated irritation making his pulse pound.

"Ha." Zoe's grin could've slayed monsters into submission. Drake's heart rate shot to stroke level just being in the vicinity. "That's right. College drinking party. You bet that frat house you couldn't do it."

Cade nodded. "And we won a case of Budweiser."

With a contented hum, Zoe sat back. "Good times."

"Hold it. Just…hold it." Brent's gaze darted between them. "Cade and Zoe used to date?"

"Hell no. She's like my sister, man."

"A sister with a great ass." Zoe clinked her bottle with Cade's.

There had to be a very dark, very deep hole Drake could crawl into to avoid this conversation. He was sure of it. One just had to search hard enough—

"Ask Drake." Zoe tilted her head in his direction. "He touched my ass last night."

Drake ground his molars to dust. "I did not touch…your…ass." And for the love of all that was holy, could everyone stop saying the word Zoe and ass in the same sentence? Please.

Flynn's eyebrows lifted and he offered Drake an *oh, really* stare. Cade wasn't much better with his expression dialed to *this is interesting.*

His niece, Hailey, saving grace that she was, bounded over and plopped near Zoe's chair by her feet. Squealing, she reached for Zoe's hair and drew back, flapping her hands excitedly.

"You like my hair?" Zoe ducked her head, and the girl patted the pink strands.

The color—any unnatural shade she'd dyed it this past year—irked him. She had such lovely light brown hair that revealed golden highlights in the sun. Why she'd choose to ruin that was beyond him. It was cut to her shoulders, but back in high school, it had trailed down her back in loose waves. He'd sat behind her in quite a few classes and stared at the soft strands.

Catching himself staring, he jerked his gaze away, only to lock eyes with Brent, who looked like he was suddenly in plot mode.

"Maybe your mom will let you color yours, too." Zoe tugged lightly on the ends of Hailey's ponytail.

Zoe's relaxed smile reminded him of a time when her personality had been more relaxed, as well. Before her mother's diagnosis and Heather's death, she'd been carefree. She'd always had attitude in spades and a backbone of titanium, but it was as if life had hardened the softer edges and she'd hardened right along with it.

The girl he'd known, had grown up with, would bend over backward to do anything for, and defend to the ends of the earth, those she befriended. She still would. Yet the smile that could kill any bad day hadn't made much of an appearance as of late. He found himself missing it, missing her. Like someone had extinguished the sun, and she was gone. They'd spent a lot of time together, with or without Heather. Once upon a time, she could've had him laughing to a state of tears. He could barely remember the sound.

Loss and melancholy tugged his chest as he watched her profile. He wasn't listening to the words, but she was talking to Hailey with animation in her tone. The sharp point of her pert nose, the dip of her chin, the curve of her brow, the long column of her throat…those full lips—all familiar. Yet something shifted inside him near the region of his ribs and began to heat as if he'd never seen her before.

"Absolutely not." Avery shook her head with a laugh.

Drake sucked in a much needed lungful of air and looked at the horizon. Cedar, redwood, and pine were black shadows against an inky sky. Moonlight shimmered off the riverbed. The base of the Klamath Mountains dipped and peaked past the skyline. Sights he'd known all his life, yet appeared altered. Or maybe it was him who'd changed.

"Oh, come on," Zoe insisted. "Just one streak of color? Look how excited she is."

Avery's gaze darted between her daughter and Zoe, her lips thin. "Fine. But just one small streak and it goes back to normal after summer vacation."

Zoe bounced and Hailey squealed.

Gabby cleared her throat. "Flynn and I have some news." She paused, then held up her left hand, where a…ring donned her finger.

Flynn's grin said it all. "She said yes." Due to being deaf, he didn't speak often, but thanks to the beautiful blonde next to him who'd been encouraging him to be more himself, Drake was getting used to the odd dialect as normal.

And damn, wasn't that the best news?

Avery flew out of her chair and hugged Gabby. Cade did the same.

Shaking his head, Drake rose to his feet. Throat tight, he pulled Flynn in for a hug and eased back so his brother could read his lips. "About time. I'm happy for you." He'd watched these two skirt around their true feelings for years. His chest swelled to capacity. And Gabby? No one was more ideal for Flynn. Someone who didn't see his handicap, but the man instead. Drake held her to him and whispered in her ear. "Thank you."

Well wishes and exchanges of congratulations went around. In no time, Brent and Avery were talking wedding venues. Drake sat back, taking it all in. Life didn't always suck, that was for sure. He lost interest in the conversation when words like *pink* and *tulle* got thrown in the mix.

Hailey, having found a new best friend, reclined against Zoe's leg in front of the Adirondack chair with her iPad in hand. Which didn't escape Avery's attention. She watched the pair with affection. "Cade and I are hitched. Gabby and Flynn are headed down the aisle. Are you next, Zoe?"

Zoe frowned. "Bite your tongue."

"Oh, please." Gabby brushed hair away from her face. "You're obviously wonderful with kids. Find a guy, settle down, raise a litter."

With a shake of her head, Zoe dismissed them. "Can't you see it now? I'm walking hand-in-hand with my daughter through a department store toy section. She stops by a shelf and says, *Mommy, does Barbie come with Ken?* And I'd say, *No, honey. She comes with G.I. Joe. She fakes it with Ken.* Then child protective services steps in and I'm forced to remind you I told you so."

"I don't get it." Brent slapped his thigh. "That's exactly why you'd make a great mom."

"Um…" Cade scratched his head. "I think we should take Zoe and Brent off babysitting detail." He eyed Hailey, who appeared to be paying them no mind.

Drake's brain detached from his mouth. "You used to want children."

Zoe stiffened, not meeting his gaze. "I used to want a lot of things."

Silence hung, then they all talked at once.

As the others chatted about Zoe and marriage and kids, and while she rebuked all their encouragement, something dangerously close to despair coiled in Drake's gut. Visions of her in white, walking toward some unknown future husband, caused panic to trip his pulse. Which made no damn sense.

Then her words sank in, and he swore his heart broke right there in his brother's backyard. For as long as he'd known her, like him, she'd always wanted the family thing. Spouse. Children. A realistic, Zoe-version of a fairy tale, but an ever-after just the same. Just when, exactly, had she stopped hoping for that? It felt an awful lot like she'd given up.

He studied her flushed cheeks and despondent gaze, the way her shoulders sagged and how she rubbed her forehead as if she had a migraine looming. Her defenses were locked in place, like he'd seen her erect a number of times the past few years when the subject of anything remotely personal arose. It was true. She'd lost hope. Had thrown away her dreams.

Zoe, who'd stand up to anyone with her morals and fierce friend code. Zoe, who had more life and gumption in her pinkie than the whole of humanity did in their entire beings. Zoe, who gave her mother everything she had left, even when that mom didn't recognize her. Zoe, who'd stayed up all night, every night, texting with him after Heather died so he wouldn't be alone in the dark. Zoe, of the fire and brimstone she showed the world, masking the honey and saccharine underneath like it was a weakness.

Dear Christ. She'd been perfect. Where had she gone? And could he get her back?

He froze, a chill of warning skating over his skin. Wait. Him? Why would it be up to him to remind her of who she used to be? Or that she could still have what she'd once wanted?

With a shaking hand, he set his beer aside before it spilled. Any more of the lager—or these thoughts—and he might get sick.

"Okay, okay." Cade held up his hands in surrender. "Leave her alone. Maybe we should start talking about her ass again."

No. Nope. He was done. Jesus, Mary, and Joseph. And all the patron saints. Hell, add in Noah and the Ark. Drake shoved from his chair and strode into the house.

Leaning against the counter in Flynn's dark kitchen, he laced his fingers and stacked his hands on his head. Closing his eyes, he let the cool air wash over his heated skin and enjoyed the quiet hum of nothing. He should've called for his dogs before coming in. Then he could just leave. Now he'd have to go back out there if he wanted to head home. Which he did. Right?

Zoe's image popped to mind and he growled.

After he didn't know how long, Gabby, Flynn, and Cade came into the kitchen and hit the lights, searing his retinas. Drake's dogs, along with Flynn's, followed them inside. Gabby gave Flynn a quick kiss and went down the hall.

Drake watched her disappear, then eyed his brothers. "Did Avery take

Hailey home? Brent leave?" And...Zoe? Why did it seem odd to bring up her name all of a sudden?

"Yeah." Cade pulled out a chair and sat at the table.

Flynn followed suit. *"Sit. What's wrong with you tonight?"*

Noticed that, did they?

"Nothing. Just tired, I guess." Or restless, irritable, thinking crazy thoughts, and going out of his ever-loving mind. He pulled out a chair and dropped into it.

Cade shifted his gaze from Flynn to Drake. "Is all this relationship conversation upsetting you?"

He hadn't wanted to talk about Heather's death back then, and he didn't really want to now. Sure, he'd mentioned a few things to Avery, and it maybe hadn't been such a chore. But doing so with his brothers was akin to reopening the wound he'd tried damn hard to seal. Besides, Zoe was about the only person he went down that dark hidey hole with.

When he didn't respond, Flynn ran a hand over his hair. *"Gabby wanted to tell everyone about the engagement at once. Perhaps we should've waited."*

Anger. Yes, anger he could deal with. "Shut the hell up." Drake leaned forward. "If you ever imply you need to tiptoe around me, I'll knock you upside the head. I'm happy for you." He glanced at Cade. "Both of you." Drawing a calming breath, he rolled his shoulders.

"We know you are, but it's got to be hard, yeah? Hearing all of us make plans, move on."

"It's exactly what you should be doing." After four years, Drake should be doing it, too. The fact that he'd been thinking about trying the same, well... Those were his demons and guilt to live with, not his brothers'.

Cade and Flynn exchanged a cryptic look before Cade's gaze resettled on Drake. "No tiptoeing then." He paused, and Drake was struck by how similar his little brother's eyes were to Dad's. It was going on ten years they'd lost him to a heart attack. Much had happened since then. "Have you thought about dating again?"

Drake barely reined in a flinch. Crossing his arms, he sighed. "The thought's crossed my mind." More and more by the day, in fact.

It wasn't necessarily that he was over Heather's death, but he'd certainly accepted she was gone. Her absence had grown less painful as the days and nights passed until here he sat, wondering how to breathe without grief again. They'd had plans, a life together, and death had ripped those pages from his book. She wouldn't have wanted him to remain stagnant while the rest of the world kept rotating. But she'd been his one, his only. In more ways than the obvious.

Perhaps that was the biggest hang-up. He and Heather had been a couple since junior year of high school. He'd never been with anyone else. He wouldn't know how to date if someone downloaded an instructional manual directly to his cerebral cortex.

When he looked up again, Cade and Flynn were staring at him like he'd spoken in tongues. "What?"

"Nothing." Flynn shrugged and looked at Cade as if seeking guidance.

"We're just...glad you're..."

"Ready," Cade finished. "Are you? Ready, I mean?"

Deciding he'd rather have teeth pulled than partake in this discussion, Drake stood. "Yes. I don't know. I'm getting there. Good enough?"

Cade hastily got to his feet, worry in his eyes. "I'm sorry if we pushed. We're concerned, that's all."

Damn it. He completely understood. And he'd been too self-absorbed if they felt they couldn't talk to him. "I love you both. You know that, right?" If life had taught him anything, it was that tomorrow was never a given, so he told those he loved as often as the situation allowed.

In response, Cade hugged him and Flynn patted his shoulder.

And since Drake had reached his social limit for the week, he called his dogs and went the half-block home. Once inside, he set his keys down and glanced around.

He and his brothers had built their homes on land Dad had purchased years before he'd died. Deep on the edge of the forest surrounding town, the area was private and called to their roots. All were log cabin in stature with stone fireplaces, hardwood floors, wall-to-wall windows, and exposed beams. But where Cade had a loft-style and Flynn a ranch, Drake's was a two-story and the largest of the three. Because he and Heather had planned to fill it with kids.

Not one thing had been changed since she'd died. The wall color, the furniture, even the pictures lining the mantle—exactly as it had been the day they'd buried her. Heather had chosen most of the elements and he'd never given them a second thought.

Shutting off the lights, he let the dogs out one last time, headed upstairs and showered, then dropped on his bed in a pair of boxers and eyed the ceiling. Habit had him reaching for his cell phone.

The night of the funeral, he'd done this very thing. He'd laid in bed, wrecked, alone, and fighting not to lose it. To this day, he didn't know why he'd typed that text to Zoe, but somehow the meager lifeline had saved him.

I miss her so much I can't breathe.

She'd responded in seconds. *Me, too.*

That had started what turned out to be an almost nightly occurrence of communication. They typed what they couldn't say aloud. Everything from random thoughts to secret admissions. And they never spoke of it, any of it, to each other or another soul. The words stayed locked inside the cellular void as if never put out there in the first place.

His thumbs went to work. *I think I need to redecorate the house.*

Her response took mere seconds as if she were waiting for him to start. *What brought this on?*

He sighed. *Change. Can't move on if everything looks the same.*

She didn't ask the obvious like everyone else would've. In the time since Heather died, and out of all the people in his life, Zoe trusted him to know his pace and she didn't push. She reacted. That was all. Just reacted. *Which room first?*

Chapter 4

In the teeny grooming room in the back of the Animal Instincts clinic, Zoe rinsed suds from a French poodle in the waist-high sink and eyed Rosa. Drake's aunt and their former office manager had a wicked gleam in her eye as her thumbs flittered over her cell screen.

Cade liked to refer to his mom and two aunts as the Battleaxes, since their sole mission was to interject themselves into others' lives and often play matchmaker. Or God. Zoe still had no clue why the woman was here, but she'd been at it for an hour. Texting. Smirking. Probably starting World War III via Twitter.

Zoe drained the sink basin and towel-dried the dog as her phone chimed on her desk. "Could you check that, Rosa?" It was probably nothing, but best to play it safe in case the call was about her mom.

She patted the stairs that led to the grooming table, encouraging Paris the poodle to jump down and move over. Thankfully, the dog had always been one of her best clients—calm and friendly. She hopped right up and planted her butt with a regal tilt to her head.

As Zoe brought out the hand dryer, Rosa checked Zoe's cell. A frown marred the other woman's brows before they lifted as if to say, *oh really*. She scrolled for a beat and set the phone aside. Zoe waited, but Rosa said nothing.

"Well?"

Rosa shrugged. "Not an emergency. See you later." And with that, she sauntered out of the room, short red hair unmoving, zebra-printed butt swaying.

Zoe eyed Paris. "What was that about?"

With no forthcoming insight from the dog, she dried wet fur, brushed tight curls, and tied a pink bandana around the collar. Since she'd already trimmed the nails, Paris was all set to go home. Thankfully, this was Zoe's last client of the day. If she timed things right, she'd have forty-five minutes before the adult daycare van brought Mama home.

Whatever would she do with herself?

Once she had Paris reunited with her owner in the lobby, Zoe made her way back to the grooming room and checked her phone. The text earlier had been from Drake.

I'll bring the vaccination over tonight and do Cotton's exam, if that's okay?

She shot off a quick reply of confirmation, then frowned. Rosa had scrolled through the phone for a few moments. The text chats with Drake were very private and had been ongoing since the night Heather had died. No way Rosa had enough time to read more than a little, but Zoe's stomach cramped with worry. The most recent note had been about redecorating and he'd mentioned he'd bought paint. Not exactly federal secrets, but still.

Sighing, she turned to grab cleaning supplies and got to work scrubbing the tub, wiping the counters, and soaking the brushes. When finished, she stared at the mural she'd designed on the far wall of dogs swimming in a pond with a few cats looking on from a tree branch. She'd painted it, along with the ones in the lobby and kennel room, about six years ago when the O'Grady boys had remodeled. Things had been so much easier back then. Happier. Heather had been alive and Zoe's mama still had her mind.

Her small eight-by-ten workroom with the cheery walls and blue tile floor only served to remind her how little she'd been able to focus on her art the past couple years. Sad truth was, the clinic had been a reprieve from the craziness at home. What she'd give to have two hours with a real canvas and a paintbrush again.

Or an evening to herself to go on a date. She hadn't exactly been promiscuous, but she'd had her share of lovers. A lifetime ago, she'd been known as the "good time." She didn't miss the guys, but she did miss the intimacy. These days, she was lucky to have five minutes to wash her hair.

Shaking her head, she made her way around a waiting chair and froze. Something skittered across her corner desk. A mouse? Maybe. It had moved too fast to make out. She hesitantly stepped closer. Whatever it was crawled off a stack of files and partly up the wall.

Not a mouse, but a…*spider*.

Her limbs locked and her lungs collapsed. Terror seized her chest. And that monster was no ordinary spider. Hell to the no. It was easily the size of her hand, furry, and…and…

Eyes glued to the nightmare, Zoe screamed bloody murder, then screamed some more. Shrieking wails that rattled her teeth and cracked her throat and could've landed her a starring role in a B horror movie. With a seizure dance and a burst of courage, she ran for the door. And plowed into Drake. He grabbed her shoulders, blocking the exit. "Hey, what's—"

Heart pounding, she launched at him, climbed his body like the rope in gym class, and did her best impersonation of a python by wrapping her limbs around him in a death grip. She fisted his black surgical scrubs, shaking. "Kill it, Drake. Kill it dead. Hurry."

"Kill what? And I can't breathe, Zoe. Loosen the choke hold."

She tightened her hold on him, not caring one iota how weak and girly she must seem. "You don't need to breathe. Look at the wall. Above my desk. Kill it, kill it, kill it…"

With a hearty sigh against her shoulder, he turned, cursed a wicked streak, and stumbled back into the wall. An uneven exhale ruffled her hair. "How in the hell did a tarantula get in here? They're not even indigenous to the area."

"Tell him that." As if that was even the point. She chanced a peek over her shoulder just in time to see it crawl a few more inches up the wall. It could've been crawling over her the way her skin itched. This time she screamed loud enough to have Drake jerking and tensing against her.

His arms hugged her to him. "Maybe if we back out slowly, we can escape. Set the room on fire or something."

Since she had her legs around his waist and her arms around his neck, his words were mumbled against her collarbone and she couldn't gauge whether he was being sarcastic or not.

The door banged against the wall and Cade strode in. He eyed the two of them, lifted his brows, and…smirked. The jerk.

Breath in her throat, she peered at him over Drake's head of dark hair. "Cade, you have a gun in your office, don't you? Shoot it. Now."

He set his hands on his hips, frustration marring his forehead. "No, I don't have a gun in my—" His gaze followed Drake's and landed on the beast. "Holy shit." He fell on his ass, crab-crawled over to her and Drake, and hastily got to his feet. "What the hell?"

"We're trying to figure that out." Drake nudged her arm down a fraction.

With a trembling hand, Cade scratched his head. "A gun couldn't take out that thing. Perhaps a cannon, yeah? Do they make cannons anymore?"

Zoe was dangerously close to hyperventilating. Her lungs had shrunken to prunes and her throat was tighter than Spanx. "One of you grow a pair and do something."

Shoving her hair out of his face, Drake grunted. "This from the woman who climbed me like a tree."

"I'm about to become your new tattoo." No way were her feet touching the floor until there was irrefutable proof the eight-legged freak was dead.

"I'm not kidding. If you don't do something—"

"What is all the yelling about?" Gabby strode in wearing pink scrubs and worry lines on her forehead. "You guys are scaring the patients." She took in the scene with a confused twist of her mouth and adjusted her ponytail.

Cade pointed to the wall.

Gabby turned and patted her chest. "Oh, thank goodness. There you are."

"Gabs, don't go near it. It could eat you in one bite." Cade shifted from foot to foot as if wanting to protect her and completely unable.

"Nonsense. He's been de-sacced. His bite isn't poisonous." Then she…she…picked up the monster beast spider and held it in the palm of her hand, causing Zoe to emit a full-body shudder. "I've been looking everywhere for you."

"Friend of yours, Gabby?" Drake asked, his chest rumbling Zoe's. His arms banded tighter around her as if concerned she'd slip.

"This is Cupid. He's boarding with us this week." Gabby blew a strand of blonde hair away from her face. "I must not have put his aquarium lid back on tight enough after I fed him this morning."

Cupid? What kind of twisted individual had a tarantula as a pet and then named it Cupid?

Cade's jaw fell. "Did you feed it a cat? Small children?"

"Don't you listen to him," Gabby cooed, bringing her face so close to the thing, Zoe gagged. "You're a perfectly nice wittle spidey, aren't you?"

"Oh my God," Zoe squeaked. "Make her stop, Drake. Make her stop."

With a roll of her eyes, Gabby huffed. "Honestly, you guys are being such babies."

Cade shoved his hands through his hair, eyes wide. "That's right. Slap a diaper on my ass and shove a bottle in my mouth. I'm a damn baby. Just get that thing out of here." His hands smacked his thighs. "And duct tape the lid shut this time."

Gabby shook her head and looked at them pitifully.

After she'd left the room, Cade side-stepped to the door and peeked around the corner. "It's gone." He blew out a breath and disappeared from view. "Gabs, don't think for one second I'm not telling Flynn about this. He should know his fiancée cuddles arachnids, yeah?"

Silence hung once she and Drake were alone, and he must've realized a 7.0 on the Richter scale had nothing on Zoe's tremors because his hands gently skimmed her back in soothing circles. "You okay?"

"No." She kept her face buried in his neck, partly due to the fact he smelled great, partly out of sheer relief, and mostly because she forgot how good it felt to be held.

"Are you going to be okay soon?"

"No." Sometime in the next millennium, she'd quit shaking. "That thing is in the boarding room right next door. It'll be in my nightmares for a month. It was *in here*. We should fumigate this room with toxic gas."

"That can be arranged."

"Twice."

"Whatever you want."

She shuddered. Again. "I want a tranquilizer the size of a Big Mac and a bleach bath. In that order."

His chuckle sent a warm breath across her cheek. She was so unaccustomed to the sound that she eased back and whipped her gaze to his. Damn, she'd forgotten about the dimple on his left cheek. Humor lit his dark gaze, causing tiny fans of laugh lines to form around his eyes.

"Are you laughing at me?" God, it had been so long since she'd heard him laugh. Rusty, low, and deep, it wove through her chest and settled in her core.

"My apologies." His grin slipped a fraction, but the warmth was still there. Gently, he tucked a strand of hair behind her ear, his gaze following the movement. "I forget sometimes that you're human. Hard to believe you're afraid of anything."

That sounded like a compliment. "Well, I am. I'm afraid of spiders." Embarrassed, she rolled her shoulders and eyed the floor, wanting to get down. Until visions of Cupid the Beast swam to mind.

"Let's sit while you get your breath back."

He moved to a corner chair and sank into it, her in his lap. His hands settled on her waist and she was reminded of how often they used to have incidental contact. All the O'Gradys were very hands-on. Touches of comfort. Hugs. But the longer they stayed as they were, the more she became aware of him. His direct gaze trained on her face. The light dusting of dark whiskers on his jaw. The purely male scent of him. His wide shoulders and the way he rocked a pair of scrubs. The muscles of his thighs under her and the corded tendon on his neck.

Desire coiled in her belly and spread. Guilt quickly chased the feeling and left conflicted uncertainty in its place. Unsure what to do, she stared at his chest.

He tensed beneath her like he'd hit rigor mortis. His lids fell closed in a flutter as he appeared to try to regulate his breathing. As if unaware of what he was doing, his thumbs stroked her ribs over her shirt and his fingers clenched. Little by little, his air exchange increased until he was all but panting. With his eyes still closed, a frown wrinkled his forehead and his jaw ticked.

"Guess I'm not the only one afraid of spiders," she whispered.

"It's not that." His eyes popped open and landed on where he held her. Quickly, he dropped his hands to his sides and fisted them. He cleared his throat, but his voice remained tortured. "We're in…very close proximity."

The breath seeped from her lungs. Mortification fumed her cheeks.

God. Oh God. She'd made him severely uncomfortable. And why wouldn't that be the case? His dead wife's best friend had scaled his body, clung like a desperate hooker, and then forced him to play upon his caring tendencies when she'd refused to put on her big girl panties.

"I'm…" Stupid. So stupid. Scrambling off his lap, she stumbled and righted herself. "I'm sorry."

"That's not what I meant."

Heart twisting, skin cold, she darted a glance around the room, needing to look anywhere but at him. She rubbed her hands over her arms. "Lock up, would you?"

"Zoe—"

"I have to go." Far, far away. Where she could crawl under a rock until one of them forgot this ever happened. Which would most likely be in the realm of never.

Tears burning her eyes, stomach like lead, she swiftly walked down the hall to the reception desk.

Gossip, their clinic cockatoo, ruffled his white feathers. *Squawk.* "Walk this way."

Normally, she found the fact that the bird only spoke in song titles or lyrics endearing, but she was so over this day. Faking a smile, she filled out a billing sheet for her last client and dropped it in the proper basket.

Avery finished with a call and regarded Zoe. "You all right? I heard about the mammoth spider incident."

"I'm good." Zoe ran her fingers over She-rah, where the clinic cat sat on her perch atop the printer. The cat allowed the petting with a queen-like narrowing of her yellow eyes. "I'll see you tomorrow."

Avery nodded just as Zoe's grooming room door slammed closed. Heavy footsteps headed their way. Since she couldn't handle Drake after what had happened, not without some Smirnoff, Zoe back-pedaled to shift around the desk.

Except she didn't watch where she was going and stepped on Thor's tail. One-hundred and twenty pounds of skittish Great Dane leapt to its feet and scrambled out from under Avery's desk. Before Zoe could react, the chickenshit dog lunged and she went down. Her ankle rolled as her back hit the floor. Thor cowered over her and licked her face.

Zoe stared at the ceiling. Sighed. And here she thought she wasn't getting any action. She might have a heart attack if the dog ever stopped being afraid of its own shadow. "Hi, Thor. I'm sorry about your tail."

Woof.

"You're heavy."

Woof.

"My face is properly clean now."

Woof.

Brent's shoes stopped by Zoe's head. "For the love of Cher. You can't be this hard up for a man."

She eyed Cade's tech. "You know, I used to appreciate our friendship so much that if we ever got in a cat fight, I would've totally avoided your face. I'm changing my mind."

Avery's worried expression blocked Zoe's view of the florescent lights. "Crap on a cracker. Are you all right?"

"Yep. A little help here."

"Thor, come." Drake's command shattered what little confidence Zoe had left. What was a miniscule thing like self-esteem anyway?

The dog climbed off her, and she groaned. Rolling to her side, she got to her feet. A fiery lick of pain infused her left ankle, not allowing her to bear much weight. Lovely. Just what she didn't need. And it didn't escape Drake's attention she'd hurt herself.

"Come into the x-ray room. We'll take a look and make sure nothing's broken."

Like her ego? That was pretty fractured.

He wrapped his large hand around her upper arm, and she had to bite her tongue not to lose her shit.

"I'm fine." Swiping her purse from the desk, she hobbled to the door. And damn, did it hurt. Two steps from freedom, he called her name. "I said I'm fine."

Humidity, laced with the scent of salt and pine, hit her face. The sweltering heat had faded to something more comfortable. Sunlight filtered through the canopy of cypress and spruce trees as she climbed behind the wheel. She shoved her keys in the ignition and sank into the hot leather seat.

So much for forty-five minutes to herself. Due to the circus of activity, she'd be lucky to get home in time to head off Mama's transportation van.

Chapter 5

Vet bag in hand, Drake knocked on Zoe's front door. Crickets chirped in the fading dusk and a whippoorwill cooed from a nearby tree while he stood waiting for her to answer. Wisteria from vines along the side of her house wafted on the soft breeze, and it was not nearly as soothing as Zoe's lavender scent.

For the past two hours, he'd showered, paced his house, and did everything in his power to erase the sensation of her taut little body clinging to his. Ever since Cade's wedding a couple months back, he'd been wondering what in the hell was wrong with him where she was concerned. Unable to nail down a reason, he'd fought to numb the strange uneasiness around her and the errant thoughts which kept drifting to a break in the ten commandments of sanity.

And tonight he'd pegged the culprit for the constant itch under his skin. Attraction. It had been so long, he'd forgotten what it felt like. Honestly, he'd thought that particular sensory was permanently damaged.

He was going to hell. Or was already there.

Screw the theory of opposites attract. Throw out the obvious reasons why this was wrong—like the fact he'd known her since diapers, they worked together, she'd never shown any sexual interest in him, and she'd been Heather's best friend—he was still left with the mother of all hell-no's. This was Zoe. Plain and simple. Zoe.

He was man enough to admit he couldn't handle her. With a passing glance, she had the ability to make a guy weep, beg for mercy, eat out of the palm of her hand, lose all thought process, shrivel his goods, and have him believe he wanted all of it. She considered this phenomenon a Tuesday afternoon.

The door opened and there stood the little devil in question. She wore a pair of gray cotton shorts that must've been painted on and showed an interstate of leg, coupled with a loose white tee, which hung over one shoulder. Even the pink hair in a knot on her head made his blood roar like liquid fire.

Going to hell in a handbasket.

He held up the vet bag. "I waited until I figured your mom was asleep." She waved him inside. "She just went down, so try to be quiet."

Yeah, he was such a party animal. Frowning, he crossed the threshold and shut the door. Zoe hobbled through the living room and into the kitchen, favoring her left leg. Her gait was more steady than when she'd left the clinic, so he hoped that meant she was feeling better. Setting the bag aside, he followed her and leaned against the doorjamb between rooms.

Two plates of uneaten food sat on the table. Dishes were piled in the sink. Three cabinets were open for seemingly no reason. A pile of towels was on a kitchen chair as if she'd finished laundry and dumped it there. Not a mess necessarily, but the place was more disorganized than the night before. At least there was no pasta painting the floor.

She opened the fridge and bent over. "Do you want anything to drink?"

His lips parted, but nothing emerged. He trained his eyes to the ceiling to avoid staring at her round, perfect little rearend and the way her shorts were molded to her like second skin. "No, thanks."

When she straightened, her shirt slipped, and his gaze grazed across her shoulder blade and part of her back. A yellowish-green bruise covered the entire expanse and disappeared behind her shirt.

"Jesus, Zoe." He hadn't realized he'd crossed the distance until she spun around and they collided.

Tilting her head in apparent confusion, she blinked up at him. "What?" She needed to get in line. He was confused as shit also.

And have mercy, the breathiness of her voice stirred him. When he didn't respond—couldn't because he was caught up in the bow-shape of her mouth and the bluish, gray-green of her hazel eyes—she cleared her throat, followed by lifting her brows in a nonverbal what-the-hell.

Right. Cupping her shoulders, he spun her around and got a better look at the bruise. It was an older one, judging by the color. Then he got distracted again and locked on to the tattoo on her nape. A sun with a black circle half covering the rays, mimicking an eclipse. She had a few tattoos here and there, and he often wondered about their significance.

Shaking his head, he dipped his finger in the collar and gently tugged her shirt aside. Best he could tell, the discoloration ran across her upper back. He caught the dark purple of a new injury below the old one and clenched his jaw.

At times, and because of her petite stature, Zoe had such a fragile quality to her. She was far from it, but in moments like these, he had to wonder just how breakable she really was, and if he'd somehow missed the point when she'd shattered. Severely independent, she rarely asked for help.

But none of that mattered. He should've seen the signs. She wasn't just hurt on the inside, masking the pain with indifference. She had physical marks as well. As her friend, he should've helped her, regardless of how many times she refused.

An urgent, frayed need to hold her wove around him until he could hardly think of anything else. Her familiar scent, the regal line of her neck, the gentle slope of her shoulders. He took it all in and battled the way her body called to his. Nothing worked.

"May I?" Unknown sensations rattling his chest caused his words to be uttered through gritted teeth. Forcing a swallow, he softened his tone and clarified his question by fingering the hem of her shirt. He raised it a fraction. "May I look?"

Still as stone, she paused and finally nodded. "It's just a bruise, though."

He doubted it. Nevertheless, and knowing he wouldn't like what he'd find, he gently lifted her shirt, making sure to only expose her back. Every upward inch of the garment stole more of his air until there was none left.

Christ Jesus. Her skin was a canvas of color. Old bruises. New. Black, blue, purple, green. Nausea curdled his stomach while anger pounded his temples. He suddenly remembered the paperback Cat had thrown at Zoe the other night, and misery heated his eyes to add to the assault. This was a monster he couldn't slay.

No woman, no matter the cause, deserved to be marred like this. But since this was Zoe in front of him, he nearly fell to his knees. Her smooth skin smelled like heavenly lavender, but looked like a war zone. He swiped his hand down his face, but nothing would erase the image of beautiful Zoe, mottled with bruises.

How long had this been going on? How long had she had to suffer out of guilt and obligation? And love. She loved her mom more than anything. Catherine's state of mind was beyond understanding her actions and surroundings. If Zoe's mom were to have a segment of lucidity, she'd tell Zoe to place her somewhere, to not uphold the promise to keep her at home for the duration.

He cleared his throat. "The book wasn't the first thing she hit you with, was it?"

She bowed her head. "No. She doesn't do it often, though. That's her fallback response to fear—throwing things. I can usually cut her off before it gets that far."

Where else did she have bruises? "Zoe—"

"No. Don't tell me to put her away." She moved aside, but he put his hand on the counter beside her and caged her in.

"She wouldn't want this and you know it." Zoe was Cat's life. She'd die before hurting her. Somewhere in all Zoe's confliction, she had to understand.

Her shoulders trembled—from oncoming tears or a chill, he hadn't a clue—and he lost all sense of reason. He pressed his palm to the delicate curve of her spine and splayed his fingers. Such warm, soft skin. He didn't know why it surprised him, yet it was unexpected just the same. Every atom in his body came alive, hyperaware of her.

She gasped and arched into his touch liked she'd felt the charge, too. Another surge of heat wove from the contact, and he inhaled. Hard. Her irregular breathing shifted them closer, or maybe he'd unconsciously moved, and something awoke inside him he thought long dead.

Desire.

The room spun. Shaking, confused, he dropped his forehead to her shoulder. And that wasn't helping either because his lips were dangerously close to the pulse in her neck. He paused a suspended beat, fully prepared to get his shit together and step back, but her hand settled in his hair. Wove through the strands. Stroked. As comforting as it was arousing.

Damn. What was he doing?

He straightened and hastily tugged her shirt down the rest of the way. "Can you…" He ran his hand over the back of his neck. Cleared his throat. "Can you hop onto the counter? Let me look at your ankle."

More touching. How in the hell was he supposed to deal with...more?

Without a word, she turned, grabbed the counter edge, and hoisted herself onto the countertop. She eyed him with skepticism through impossibly thick lashes.

Wrapping a hand around her calf, he lifted her leg and inspected her foot. She had a trace of swelling in the ankle, but it wasn't discolored. He manipulated the foot, watching her closely. She didn't wince, so he palpitated the area with his thumbs. Again, no signs of pain.

He set her leg down and straightened. "I don't think it's broken, nor sprained. You might've irritated the ligaments. Do you have ibuprofen?"

"In the cabinet by the microwave." She reached into a cookie jar beside her and pulled out a key. "The cupboard's locked."

He took the key and stared at it. He had no clue she'd gotten to the point where she needed to lock up medication to keep her mom safe.

After he rooted through the cabinet and found what he was looking for, he dropped three pills in her hand and gave her a bottle of water. She didn't like it, but he told her to go put her foot up in the living room while he fished a bag of peas from the freezer. He met her in the other room where she was slumped on the couch and had her leg reclined on the coffee table.

He sat beside her foot and set the makeshift icepack on her ankle. "This should keep the swelling down. If it still hurts in the morning, I'm doing an x-ray."

"Whatever you say, Dr. Drake."

He frowned at her dry response. "X-ray tomorrow or ER tonight. You pick."

"I just twisted it. Lay off."

She looked tired. Not the kind of tired eight solid hours would cure either. "Why don't you head to bed? I can lock up after Cotton's exam."

"Can't go to sleep before eleven-thirty. If Mama wakes up between now and then, she sometimes wanders or gets into trouble. I have to head her off. If she hasn't awoken by then, she'll stay asleep."

Guilt clawed at his throat. Not for the first time, he realized he'd been so self-absorbed he hadn't noticed everything she'd been dealing with as of late. Call it big brother syndrome or a white knight complex, but he wanted to...take care of her.

"You'll probably find the cat in my room. I'd get him for you, but this little red engine just can't." Though her tone was light, her implication wasn't. Her rope was frayed and she was burning her candle at both ends.

He thought about what had happened at the clinic earlier. The way he'd tried to explain what having her so close was doing to him. Hell, at the time, he hadn't been able to put a finger on it. Unused to much social interaction, he'd bumbled. And the look on her face was still haunting him hours later. Like he'd hurt, embarrassed, and brushed her off, all in one breath.

At a loss, he said the first thing that came to mind. "It was just a bad day, Zoe. It'll pass."

Her laugh lacked any trace of humor. "Right, Drake." She waved her hand to encompass the room. "Just a bad day."

He may have been unconsciously selfish before, but he would end that now. "You can talk to me, Zoe. I'm here."

"No, Drake. I can *text* you with anything, but as for actual talking? No." The frustration in her voice was only one bar above the one in her expression.

He stared at her. Hard. Long.

Did she really believe that? True, they'd been way more open with each other via text. That had been the draw, really. Not having to look at someone's wounded eyes while spilling his guts. He hadn't been the only one to open a vein either. She'd shared her own truths.

As kids, they'd hung out a lot. Never once had he felt like he'd had to censor himself, even in their teens. In fact, it wasn't until around the time he'd proposed to Heather that Zoe had backed off. They still saw each other, still talked, but not like before. As if she'd chosen to focus more on her friendship with Heather than him.

He hadn't paid attention. Aware now, he knew if he wanted to bridge their gap, he needed to take the first step. Zoe was nothing if not stubborn. Scratching his jaw, he stared at the tattoo of a paintbrush on her inner wrist. She had another of a shooting star on her other wrist.

He let out a ragged exhale. "Those texts saved me from utter annihilation. You saved me, Zoe."

Her wide gaze flew to his. Held. So expressive, her eyes.

"That's the God's honest truth. You reached out to me in the dark and gave me a lifeline." He sighed. "I didn't intend for the texts to be a replacement for me."

Her gaze drifted away and she tapped her fingertips on the cushion beside her. "I've never had a good day," she said so quietly he had to strain to hear. "You said today was just a bad one, but that's wrong. Every day is one more in a succession of bad ones. People use that phrase, *the best day of my life*." Her laugh was nothing more than a puff of air. "I have no idea what that means. I've never experienced it myself."

If she'd doused him in gasoline and set him on fire it would've shocked and hurt him less. He had to clench his fists in order not to reach out and touch her. "Things are rough right now, but—"

"No. You don't know the half of it."

"Then tell me."

She shook her head. Closed her eyes. Laid her head back. A complete dismissal if he ever saw one.

He waited her out, but she offered no more gutting insight. "Zoe."

A slow, measured inhale was the only response. Finally, she rubbed her forehead, eyes still closed, dark lashes shadowing her cheeks. "There's stuffed peppers in the cockpot, if you're hungry."

A smile tugged his lips at her Freudian slip. "I think you mean Crockpot. I shudder to think what you'd slow cook in your version."

"Keep hovering and I'll demonstrate." She yawned and resettled, resting her cheek on her hand on the couch arm. In moments, her deep, even breathing indicated she was asleep.

Shaking his head, he rose and went in search of the cat. Finding him right where Zoe indicated, he entered her bedroom and did an examination, then the vaccine. Cotton took it all in stride, but Drake spent a few minutes sitting on the bed petting him anyway.

Pictures of her friends and Zoe with her mom lined the white dresser. Other than that, there weren't many personal touches to the room. When Zoe had moved back home, she'd given away or sold everything from her old apartment. Drake suspected that had been step one in erasing the woman he'd known.

He walked over to the dresser and eyed the photos. A few were of her mother from when Zoe was a kid. Her and Heather at his wedding. Zoe, Cade, and Flynn last year on the softball diamond. Another of her, Avery, and Gabby at Shooters with Brent photo-bombing.

He picked up the one of himself and Zoe dancing at Cade's wedding a couple months ago. She'd dyed her hair back to her natural light brown for the day and had it pinned up in curls. The lilac-colored dress had been the perfect compliment to her olive skin tone. The photographer had caught her with her head down, a smile teasing her lips, and Drake staring at the top of her head.

Setting the picture back, he picked up another. Him and Zoe with Heather at prom. Cade had been Zoe's date, but he was absent from the photo. Drake took in Heather's emerald dress and loose blonde hair sweeping her shoulders, then moved on to Zoe. Bright red dress, red lipstick to match. She had her hand on her chest and was captured mid-laugh. That was her—the life of the party. Or she used to be.

With an absent pat for Cotton, Drake poked his head in on a sleeping Catherine and noted the clock. Zoe had said eleven-thirty was the magic time, and it was only ten.

Since Zoe was still asleep on the couch, he thought about carrying her to bed, but she'd get pissy about it in the morning. He adjusted her so she wouldn't wake with a stiff neck and covered her with a blanket.

Then, he settled in a recliner until eleven-thirty-five, and headed home.

Chapter 6

Drake saddled up to the counter at Shooters and waited for Emma Jane to finish with a customer. Though the bar wasn't incredibly busy for a Friday night, locals had the bartender on her toes.

Avery had talked him into coming out with them again tonight. Cade's wife was good at that, making him join society. Truth be told, it hadn't been much of a hardship lately. Though he wasn't a people-person, he was getting sick of his own company and staring at his house walls.

Rock blared from a jukebox. Low lighting added to the dive ambiance to intermix with stale perfume, alcohol, and desperation in the air. Pool balls clacked and cheers erupted over a game of darts. Not his favorite scene, but he supposed it beat sitting at home. Besides, hanging out with his brothers and friends usually proved entertaining.

Finally, Emma Jane wiped the counter and made her way over. Sweet smile in place, she tucked a strand of brunette hair behind her ear. "What can I get you, Drake?"

He scrolled through his table's drink order in his head. "Two beers. Whatever's on tap is fine. A whiskey neat and a martini."

She nodded and set about fixing the order. Her gaze scanned the patrons around her, then back to the glass she filled from the tap. "I'm glad you came by." She set the beers on a tray and reached for a bottle of Jack Daniels. "I wanted to give you a heads-up. You're the subject of discussion tonight. Apparently, someone let it slip you're back in the dating pool."

He froze, staring at her. The only people he'd discussed that with were his brothers, and no way had Flynn or Cade repeated the information. Hell, Drake had barely entertained the notion himself, so what the hell?

Emma Jane had been in Flynn's graduating class. If memory served, he and her had hooked up in the past once in awhile. Nothing serious. Her uncle owned the bar and her twin brother, Eric, manned the kitchen. She wasn't flirty by nature and she wasn't the type to start shit for the sake of boredom. She was also a single mother with a little girl at home. Ergo, her reasons for mentioning the rumor probably had good intentions.

Pouring martini mix into a glass, she peered at him. "I don't mean to upset you. I thought you'd want to know."

Disturbed, he nodded. "I appreciate that."

She tilted her head, indicating the room. "You've got about twenty women watching your every move. So far, none seem brave enough to venture over."

He could only pray it stayed that way. For years, Animal Instincts had been inundated with single females making fake appointments just to get in Cade's orbit. Flynn had his share, too, though not as drastic. Now that both were off the market, things had died down. Drake, luckily, had escaped the ridiculousness because he'd always been affiliated with Heather, and then her death.

Christ. Who the hell had started the gossip?

He tossed some bills on the bar, leaving an extra large tip. "Thanks, Emma Jane."

She smiled. "Anytime. And just say the word, I'll try to quash the chatter."

Drake handed out drinks and reclaimed his seat at the table. Still stewing, he flicked his gaze around the bar and, sure enough, several females were checking him out. Uneasiness wove around him, through him. Hell, the last time he'd been on the dating circuit, Bush had still been in office and he'd been worried about SAT scores.

"Hell to the no." Zoe leaned forward, resting her forearms on the table. "I'm not wearing a pink bridesmaid dress."

Gabby pushed blonde locks away from her face. "Oh, come on. Your hair is pink. Why not?"

"I look awful in that color. And thanks for the reminder to change my hair."

Gabby frowned, turning to Flynn for help.

"Do not get me involved in this," Flynn signed. *"Just tell me where and when to show up for the wedding."*

Cade lifted his drink in a toast. "Amen, brother."

Avery shot her husband a warning glance and looked at Zoe. "It won't be so bad."

"It absolutely will." Zoe ran her fingers up and down her lager bottle. "Tell them, Drake. I look hideous in pink, right?"

Why ask him? "You'd look good in anything." Drake swirled the whiskey in his glass.

Silence hung.

He glanced up to find all eyes on him. Damn it. He'd forgotten his verbal filter. First time for everything. He shifted uncomfortably in his seat, not sure what to make of Zoe's stunned stupid expression. "It's true. Besides, it's Gabby's wedding. She gets what she wants."

Her gaze still trained on him, a wrinkle between her brows, Zoe spoke to Gabby. "What about yellow? Avery and I can both wear that color."

"That has my vote, too." Brent cocked an eyebrow, staring Drake down. "Since *Zoe* would look good in anything, yellow works for Avery and all seasons."

Drake scrubbed a hand over his face. "For the record, Gabby and Avery would look good in anything as well." And... This was not helping his cause. He just needed to shut the hell up. Funny, that had never been a problem before.

Someone hooted from across the room. "Hey, Zoe. Come dance with me, you sexy thing." A gaggle of male laughter followed.

Drake glanced up to a group of guys near the pool table. Firefighters, if memory served. Jason from their softball game stood there, but it had been the dark-haired idiot next to him that had shouted to her. Drake couldn't remember his name, or if he liked the guy, which was steering toward the no column. His fingers tightened around his glass.

Zoe laughed and yelled over the noise. "Aw, Wayne. If you buy some rhythm and find some decent music, I'll meet you on the dance floor."

Wayne pressed his hands to his chest as if wounded. "You're breaking my heart."

Drake would be more than amendable to breaking several other of his parts. Alas, Zoe blew the guy a kiss and they went back to their pool game. Drake slammed the rest of his whiskey in silence.

"Anyway." Brent's grin was wicked. "I loaded the jukebox earlier for you, Zoe. Your song should be coming up soon."

"Oh yeah? I could get into that, for the right tune." She looked at Gabby. "You up for some dancing?"

Gabby set her drink aside. "I can't keep up with you, but I'll try."

"There you go, Cade." Zoe winked. "A little girl-on-girl action for you."

Grinning, Cade nodded, then salvaged himself by kissing Avery. "Are you going to hit the floor with them? Make all my fantasies come true?"

Avery tilted her head. "That could be arranged."

Drake pressed his fingers into his eye sockets. "Visual, visual."

Brent's shriek of glee had Drake jumping off his seat in surprise. "Now we're talking. Let's dance, Zoe." Brent grabbed her hand and dragged her to the small dance floor, where a few other couples were already moving.

It took a moment, but Drake pinned the song change as Shaggy's *Angel*. The fast-pulsing Jamaican reggae-ish beat filled the room, and he leaned back in his seat. He got a little caught up in the skinny jeans molded to her legs and the way her loose blue shirt dipped nearly to her ass in the back, exposing a real estate of skin. Ten seconds later, the air in his lungs evaporated.

Lifting a finger, Zoe dragged it across Brent's chest and circled him on the dance floor. When she came back around to his front, Brent grabbed her backside and they moved in a slow, seductive trance as if they'd been lovers for a decade. Her hips popped to the beat and she spun in his arms, raising hers over her head. Then—*Christ, then*—she slid down his body in a crouch and came back up like a snake in heat. From behind, Brent's hands flattened on her stomach. His head dipped close to her neck while they all but…

Hell. Drake forgot how well she could move. It had been awhile since he'd seen Zoe in action, and damn if he never wanted to be a gay man so badly in his life. Brent's sexual preference might be his only saving grace at the moment, considering Drake had a barbaric urge to stomp across the room and haul her away. Fire licked his skin watching her. His heart pounded inside his chest, shifting ribs. If she kept this up, he stood no chance fighting these insane, new feelings clawing at him. As it was, he was barely managing basic thought.

God help him. Of all the women on earth, why did the first stirrings of attraction and desire in years have to be for Zoe Hornsby? Who could he have possibly pissed off to deserve this kind of punishment?

"Ah, there she is." Cade nodded his approval. "There's our *other* Zoe."

Avery's brow furrowed in confusion. "Other Zoe?"

Cade grunted. "The wilder version from our youth. She doesn't let this side of herself come out to play much anymore. Haven't seen her let go in awhile."

Chin in her hand, elbow on the table, Gabby sighed dreamily. "I want to be her when I grow up."

Screw that. Drake wanted a cold shower, a bottle of Jameson, and a padded cell. Not necessarily in that order. He had to adjust himself in his seat as his jeans became problematically too tight. He shot up a silent prayer to every patron saint he could think of to aid him. He'd need internal stitches after tonight, no doubt.

With much effort and deep regret, he tore his gaze from the dance floor. Except that didn't help because the firefighters had stopped their game of

pool to watch Zoe, too. Catcalls rang out as the song came to an end and...
yeah. There was a God.

Flynn shook his head as Zoe and Brent reclaimed their seats. *"I bow
down, Zoe. I think you got Brent to bat for the other team."*

Throwing her head back, she laughed. Deep, throaty, and purely sexual,
the sound nailed Drake right in the solar plexus. "I doubt it." She drank
the last of her ale. "Who's driving me home?"

Brent had picked her up since he lived right down the road and she'd
said it saved room in the parking lot not having two cars. It was still early
yet, and the others were having a good time. Drake's mom was watching
Cat tonight, but Zoe wouldn't want to be out too late.

Drake stood. "I'll take you."

Mistake number four-hundred and seven. Having her scent in his truck
didn't help calm his pulse one iota. Lavender filled the dark cab as he wove
through the quiet streets, his head a riot.

"Something on your mind?"

He glanced at her and back to the road. "I'm working through it."
Nothing a lobotomy wouldn't fix.

She kept her gaze out the passenger window, her voice quiet. "Does it
have anything to do with you being ready to date again?"

Since bashing his head against the steering wheel would only be
counterproductive, he gripped it tightly instead. Something about her
tone indicated him not telling her was a betrayal in her eyes. "I've been
thinking about it. I only just mentioned it to my brothers the other day."

"And, what? The notion jumped out of your head and into the rumor mill?"

"I don't know how word got out." It wasn't as if he wanted the attention.
"I've been trying to figure out how to tell you."

She was silent a tense beat. "You don't need my permission, Drake."

No, but damn if he didn't want her blessing. She'd been the closest
person to Heather besides him, and she was his friend, too. More than
that, she understood how difficult his grief had been because she shared
it, was right there with him. For whatever reason, he'd grown to depend
on her insight, and moving forward without her felt wrong. Going in any
direction without her, for that matter. Adding complication to the mix were
his growing, complex feelings for her.

"What do you think?" He let out the breath he'd been holding.
"I want to know."

"She'd want you to be happy."

He knew that already. Before she died, he and Heather had the
"remarriage" discussion. She'd said, in no uncertain terms, that she'd

wanted him to find someone else when he was ready. At the time, he hadn't wanted to talk about it, but looking back, he was glad she'd made him. Except he didn't think either of them had anticipated Zoe being a person of interest or a candidate.

Which was moot anyway. Zoe had no interest in him that way.

"I know Heather's wishes. What I don't know are yours."

Her swallow was an audible click in the quiet car. "My opinion shouldn't matter."

He ground his jaw. "Don't diminish yourself. You matter." He glanced at her and swore her eyes were wet. Probably a trick of the street lights. He could count on one hand the number of times he'd seen her cry. Still, his chest tightened.

After a heinous pause, she cleared her throat. "You have too big, too noble a heart to not share it with someone. A man like you shouldn't be alone. That's what I want for you, what you deserve."

He might've believed her sincerity if her voice hadn't sounded like broken glass. As he tried to conjure a response to her unerringly kind words, he was reminded again of Zoe's tender side most never got to see.

"I think Heather was the luckiest person on the planet, and whoever you choose to be with will feel the same."

Damn her. "And what about you?" It wasn't as if she'd dated much, if at all, the past few years. If anyone deserved the fairy tale, it was her. She'd sacrificed so much for him, Heather, and her own mother.

"Some people are just born lonely and destined to stay that way." She shook her head and pinched her eyes closed as if she hadn't meant to say that aloud.

Son of a bitch. "Zoe—"

"Drop it, Drake. I'm fine with my life the way it is."

He was about to pull the truck over and do something, anything, to knock—or kiss—some sense into her, but he turned onto her street...and his heart misfired.

Red and blue lights flashed in the dark, reflecting off the houses and signs. Neighbors gathered in the road just outside Zoe's house, where an ambulance and squad car were parked at the curb. The sheriff, Parker, turned from his post on the porch and said something into a two-way radio.

Zoe grabbed the dashboard. "Oh God. No. What's going on?" She fumbled with the seatbelt and was climbing out of the truck before he'd even pulled over. She ran across the driveway and onto the lawn. Drake's mom was standing with her arms crossed.

Drake jumped out and met them. "What happened?"

Mom shook her head, blue eyes pleading, her short bob of dark blonde hair shifting with the motion. "After Cat was asleep, I went into the basement to grab some cleaning products." She turned suddenly to Zoe. "I thought I'd help you out a little, freshen up a bit." Her voice broke. "Your mom must've heard and followed me. She fell down the stairs."

"Oh God." Zoe rushed for the front door, where Parker stopped her short of entering the house.

"She's okay, Zoe." Parker held firm when she tried to get past him and waved off two of his deputies who stepped forward to assist.

Drake climbed the porch and caught a glimpse of an unmoving Catherine on a stretcher in the living room, medics around her.

Zoe wailed and tried again for the house, only to be brought up short by Parker. "Listen to me, Zoe. She's okay. Her vitals are good and she was awake when they got here. She didn't hit her head. They had to sedate her to keep her still, since she was confused. They're thinking a broken leg. She's headed off to the hospital."

"I'm going with her. I'll ride in the ambulance."

EMTs brought Cat out on a stretcher, her face sickly pale. One of the medics cupped Zoe's shoulder. "There's no room in the cab. Follow us to Mercy General, okay?"

As they loaded Cat into the ambulance, Zoe ran for the garage.

Drake cursed and chased after her, catching her by the arm before she could open the hatch. "I'll drive you. You're in no shape."

"I've got this, Drake."

He took the keys out of her trembling hands and met her wide, frantic gaze. "And I've got you. Now get in my damn truck. I'm driving you."

She turned around, giving him whiplash. "Gayle, can you lock the house?"

His mom, looking torn and frenetic herself, nodded. "Sure, honey. Just go. I'll meet you there."

Worry ratcheting his gut, he followed the ambulance toward the interstate. Redwood Ridge had an urgent care, but not a hospital, and Mercy General was in the county to the south about thirty minutes away. Zoe fidgeted in her seat, biting her nails and rocking.

He grabbed her hand and squeezed. "You heard Parker. She's going to be okay."

She violently shook her head. "I never should've gone out tonight."

"This could've happened at any time. It was just an accident."

Her rocking increased. "I know. It's not your mom's fault."

He squeezed her hand again for emphasis. "It's not yours either."

Chapter 7

Zoe paced the ER waiting room, crawling out of her skin. An hour since they'd arrived, and no word. They hadn't let Zoe go back and be with Mama until they'd gotten her assessed and done with x-rays.

This was all her fault. She never should've gone out tonight. Between work and softball, she'd depended on Rosa and Gayle too much. They'd been her mother's closest friends, but they weren't family. Zoe was her daughter. She should've been taking care of her mom, not out having a drink with friends.

Selfish. She'd been damn selfish.

Mama had busted her ass Zoe's whole life, sometimes working two jobs just to scrape by. She'd put her love life and everything else on hold to give Zoe a decent home and food in her belly. She'd attended every science fair and ballet recital and sporting event. She'd bought Zoe her first set of paints and had encouraged her whimsical side.

And where had Zoe been in an emergency? In the bar. She rubbed her forehead while she paced, her stomach aching and her throat tight.

Drake's gaze tracked her every move from the chair he'd sunk into, but she couldn't face him right now. She had enough on her plate without having to think about him. Still, it had hurt so damn much to learn from people at Shooters that he was ready to date again. Four years of grieving had been long enough, in her mind. It wasn't his desire to move on that upset her, but rather how she hadn't registered on his radar enough for him to inform her.

Worse, was the thought of having to watch him date other women. It had been hard enough to stand by while he'd fallen for Heather, and that had been a measly crush on her part back then. She'd gotten over it, over him, in the time since. But then Heather had died. If Zoe were being honest, a naive part of her had hoped one day he'd stop grieving and see...her. Daydreams and fantasies. Guilt and shame. Suddenly, she felt like that heartbroken teenager all over again who'd stupidly made a birthday wish. Her seventeenth had been the best and worst day. Mama had to work a double shift, but she'd left Zoe a ginormous cupcake on the kitchen counter.

That day, Zoe hadn't seen her closest friends yet to get well-wishes. During lunch break at school, she'd been sitting outside on a grassy hill in the quad by herself. Homecoming was coming up, and she'd been dredging up the nerve to ask Drake to go to the dance with her. She'd told Heather she had a thing for someone, but not who. Heather had encouraged her to ask the guy to the dance, and she'd planned to later.

Drake plopped down beside her, and they'd laughed about crap she couldn't remember. He'd given her a locket as a present, shaped like a rose. His form hadn't filled out yet, not like he was now, but he'd been a handsome bastard, even then. Midnight hair cut just above his ears, chocolate eyes, and that damn dimple on his left cheek when he grinned. He'd played baseball, like his brothers, but also ran track, so his body had been tall and lean.

Zoe walked to the window in the waiting room, glancing past the rain-speckled glass to the dark parking lot half full with cars. It must've rained after they'd arrived. She bit her thumbnail, shoving aside memories that kept flooding.

After talking for a bit in the quad, Drake had picked a dandelion. White fluff clung to the stem and trembled in the cool breeze. "Candles are overrated. Wish on this instead. You have better odds of it coming true."

Laughing, she'd taken it from him and made one wish—for him to say yes—before blowing the fluff. It scattered in the wind. Drifting. Wafting. Floating. Like her heart.

"Happy birthday."

"Thank you." She'd opened her mouth, ready to spit out the question super fast, but Heather had knelt beside them, looking frazzled.

"Oh, God. Kevin already has a date to homecoming. I was pinning my hopes on him." Heather pushed her long, wavy blonde locks from her pretty face, her blue eyes focused on Drake. "Do you have a date yet? Maybe we could go together as friends?"

For a fractured beat, Drake had looked at Zoe like he was seeking permission. But then he shook his head and grinned at Heather. "Haven't asked anyone. I'd love to."

After idle chit-chat, the two of them rose and headed toward school, leaving Zoe shell-shocked.

Heather had turned her head and done a double-take. She'd stared at Zoe with confusion before awareness dawned in her eyes. Sending Drake on without her, she squatted beside Zoe. "It's him, isn't it? Drake's the boy you're interested in?" She bit her lip. "Oh, Zoe. I didn't know. I can tell him never mind to the dance."

Even back then, Zoe had known it wouldn't have mattered. She'd never be a match against her best friend. Heather was gorgeous and smart and nice. The most popular girl in school. Everyone loved her, including Zoe. She, however, was just the good time to party with on weekends.

Dangerously close to tears, Zoe shrugged as if it hadn't mattered. "Don't be silly. We were just talking."

And that, sadly, had been that. Zoe had spent the night of her birthday crying in her pillow. She'd gone to the dance with Cade—a freshman to her junior—as friends. A week after homecoming, Drake and Heather had started dating. Six years later, he'd proposed. A year after that, they'd married. And four years ago, they'd buried her on a rainy spring day shrouded in fog.

Zoe hated this hospital. It was where Heather had been diagnosed with ovarian cancer, where Drake's father had been rushed after his heart attack, and where Zoe had gotten the jarring news her mother's memory blips were early onset dementia. She'd never get better. Nothing ever got better.

Eyes burning, Zoe drew a slow breath and focused on the wet pavement outside the window and the way the raindrops reflected under the streetlights. Mama needed her. There was no sense dwelling on the past. Itchy and nervous, she paced again.

Her gaze landed on Gayle, hunched in a chair beside Drake. She'd been like a second mom to Zoe growing up, and guilt had to be eating the woman alive. Guilt was something Zoe knew intimately.

She dropped into a chair on Gayle's other side. "Mama's gotten much worse this past year. I've had to safety-proof the house. What happened tonight is not your fault."

Gayle wiped her cheeks with a balled-up tissue. "I thought she was asleep."

Drake closed his eyes with a weary sigh, rubbing a soothing hand over his mom's back. Zoe was reminded of their conversation in the car on the way here.

"It was an accident." Zoe grabbed Gayle's hand and held it while they waited. "Just an accident," she repeated, slumping in her seat.

A doctor came in ten minutes later. If memory served, it was the same middle-aged man who'd informed them Drake's father had died. Flynn had been the unfortunate son to have found his dad's body at home nine years ago, but the hospital had confirmed he was gone.

"I'm Dr. Crest. Nice to meet you." He held out his hand, and Zoe shook it. "Your mom's back from x-ray. Instead of bringing her to the ER, I had them take her upstairs right away. She had a dislocated left hip, but we reset it. There shouldn't be any long-term damage. However, she's fractured her femur." He tapped his thigh, pointing out the correct bone. "It was a clean break. No surgery is needed. It's in a cast now. With this type of injury, I'm a little concerned about possible clots, so we're going to start a blood thinner as a precaution. We'll keep her here a couple days to monitor her. Due to her mental state, she's going to require at least six weeks, maybe more, in a rehab facility."

Crap. Zoe rubbed her forehead. "Is that necessary? She's never been away from home and, with her confusion, I don't think she'd be cooperative."

Understanding in his eyes, he nodded. "She requires around the clock care while the leg heals. She can't walk on it or stress the fracture. It's going to be painful, no doubt. A facility can monitor pain meds, watch her vitals, and ensure she uses a wheelchair."

Her shoulders slumped. Damn. Taking Mama away from home would probably frighten her even more. She wouldn't recognize anything or anyone.

Dr. Crest patted her arm. "She's going to be okay. We've got her sedated so she can rest. You can go up and see her now. A caseworker will pop by in the morning to discuss placement options."

"Thank you."

Gayle held her hand in the elevator ride to the correct floor, while Drake stared straight ahead, his jaw ticking. If possible, his shoulders seemed more tense than Zoe's.

An hour later, Zoe sat in a chair beside her mom's bed, Gayle on the other side, and Drake in the corner on a loveseat. Mama hadn't woken up, aside from a brief fluttering of her eyelashes, but her vitals were good according to the nurse. She was so still, so quiet, that Zoe found it hard to relax.

"I remember when she found out she was pregnant with you." Gayle breathed a laugh. "I was a couple months shy of delivering Drake. We were so excited to be expecting at the same time. We talked about raising you together, and how you'd be the best of friends, like we were growing up. We even joked about how, if you were a girl, you two would fall in love and get married. Fate, she called it."

Zoe swallowed hard and tentatively glanced over her shoulder at Drake. His unreadable gaze was pinned on her and not one muscle twitched. Half in shadow, he seemed more broody and contemplative than normal. She got the sinking suspicion he was trying to gauge her reaction to his mom's statement.

"Well, anyway." Gayle waved her hand in dismissal. "You didn't follow our crazy plan, did you? But I'm so glad you guys are close, that you stayed friends. You've always been like my own, Zoe-bug."

Unexpected tears threatened at Mama's old nickname for her. It had been years since anyone had used it. "Mama's been saying the name Jimmy a lot. Is that my father?"

Gayle hummed a confirmation. "He was a fisherman passing through town. He left the day after she told him she was pregnant. I promised her I'd never let you dwell on it if you ever asked me about him." Her gaze drifted from Mama to Zoe, her face so like Flynn's and her eyes like Cade's, it was jarring. When she smiled, though, her dimples were all Drake. "You are one-hundred percent your mom. Smart, strong, driven, and strikingly pretty. I think the only thing you inherited from him was your artistic eye. He didn't have half your talent."

Zoe never really wondered much about her father, nor had she felt his absence in her life. Mama had always been enough. Regardless, she was happy to have the information.

Silence stretched and another thirty minutes passed.

She glanced at Drake. "You guys can head home. It's really late. I'm okay here alone."

His fingers tapped a stiff beat on his thigh. "Not a chance."

She was about to argue, but the nurse strode back in. "You've got some visitors in the waiting room asking for you."

Gayle smiled. "I called Flynn and Cade to tell them what happened. Go ahead. I'll sit with Catherine for a bit."

"Are you sure?"

Drake rose from the corner loveseat, scowl in place. "She's sure. Come, Zoe."

They walked out of the room and she looked at him while they passed the nurse's station. "You're bossy when you're tired."

"I'm not tired. I'm worried about you."

She halted and faced him in the middle of the hallway. "I'm not the one in a hospital bed."

His gaze raked over her face as if dissecting her expression. Thing about Drake was, he was a fixer. Always had been. And it appeared he wanted to fix her—a feat that couldn't be conquered, not even by him. He didn't offer any explanations or elaborate on his statement. He just stood there, hands at his sides, staring.

She turned and started walking again. "I'm fine, Drake. I'm made of stronger stuff than most. You know that."

"Even titanium melts with enough heat thrown at it."

What the heck was wrong with him lately? His uncharacteristic behavior was starting to grate her very raw nerves. "Careful, Drake. Your give-a-shit is showing."

"Christ." He grabbed her arm and dragged her into what looked like an empty employee lounge. He pinned her against the wall, hands pressed flat at either side of her head, and his face so close she could count his eyelashes. Dark stubble dusted his wide jaw, adding to his mysterious broody vibe.

Her breath hitched and caught while her body got naughty, naughty ideas. His purely male scent swirled around her and she wanted to sink into him. Heat fanned from her belly out, until she was engulfed in flames. Alpha testosterone waves rolled off him as she struggled to fight the urge to climb him and latch on. Everywhere.

Mouth in a firm line, his gaze darted back and forth between hers. "I have always given a shit, Zoe. That's not something I turn off, even if I could. I care about you more than you will ever know. So yes, I'm worried about you. If you don't like it, I couldn't give a good goddamn."

They stood there, sharing air, her trying not to melt into a puddle at his feet while he panted like he'd run a ten-mile. Then he…dropped his gaze to her mouth. His jaw tightened. His brow furrowed. And any amount of irritation left in his expression died a slow, consuming death. Bewilderment mixed with longing in his eyes the longer he fixated.

She must've had more than the one beer tonight or hit her head and gotten a concussion, because no way in Haiti was Drake O'Grady staring at her like he wanted nothing more than to kiss her. He was obviously struggling against the urge, but yeah. There was a definite interest.

She was poking the bear and knew it, but sometimes a girl just had to tempt danger. "You got upset the last time we were in…what did you call it, close proximity?"

He sucked in a gale force wind, nostrils flaring. His gaze jerked back to hers. "I…" With a slow blink, his throat worked a swallow. "For the past few months, being around you has been unnerving."

He had her pinned to the wall in a hospital and he was unnerved? "What does that mean?"

Offering little more than a slight head shake, he studied her expression as if measuring his words by the milliliter. "There's this ache in my gut and a burning in my chest."

Her lungs threatened to quit. "Maybe it's heartburn."

"It's not heartburn."

"Are you sure? Perhaps some antacids would help."

He closed his eyes as if seeking patience and opened them. "I'm positive. I've been chewing a roll a day for two months. It's not indigestion."

"It sounds like it to me. You know, burning in the chest and—"

"It's not heartburn, Zoe. Would you, for just once, listen to me?" His jaw ticked, and she said to hell with it. Drake off his axis was too tempting. This was all a concussion-induced dream anyway.

"An ulcer, then. We're in the hospital. Why don't you make an appointment—"

"Christ, Zoe." He shoved off the wall and stalked away from her. He laced his fingers and stacked his hands on his head. Back tense, biceps bulging, he took a second to seemingly collect himself before turning around. His arms dropped to his sides. "What I'm experiencing is not an ulcer or indigestion or heartburn." His gaze seared into hers. "And I need to know if I'm the only one in this or if you're feeling it, too."

A drunk dream, for sure. Had to be. A decade ago, she would've given anything to have him stand in front of her and so much as hint he was aware she was a female. That he saw her as more than a friend, or worse, his wife's best friend. But too many obstacles and years and conflict lay between them now. Still, she wanted to give in. Just once, she wanted to feel good.

"You know what? I'm sorry. This has been an unfortunate side effect the last few months, too—my inability to think straight." He headed for the exit. "This isn't the right time or place for this conversation."

Shaking, heart pounding, she slumped against the wall. Shocked into idiocy, she paused to collect her breath and followed him in silence to the waiting room. Cade, Avery, Flynn, Gabby, and Brent stood to greet them.

"How's your mom?" Avery offered a hug.

"She's going to be fine." Zoe recanted what the doctor had said about rehab and everything else.

Gabby stroked Zoe's shoulder. "Can we do anything?"

"No. Thanks, you guys. I'm—"

"Do you still have a key to Zoe's house?" Drake looked at Brent, arms crossed.

Brent's hesitant gaze shifted to Zoe and back to Drake. "Yeah, sure."

"Good." Drake nodded. "Can you swing by there and get a change of clothes for Zoe? Feed the cat, too. Thanks." He looked at Flynn. "Bring my dogs over to your place this weekend please. I'll pick them up on Sunday." He moved on to Cade. "Let the team know Zoe and I won't be playing softball tomorrow. Someone from urgent care can fill in." And last, he spoke to Avery. "Can you reschedule Zoe's Monday clients? Just in case."

Everyone nodded slowly as if they weren't sure they'd heard him correctly. Zoe had to unlock her jaw to close her mouth.

Drake faced her. "You don't have to do everything alone. I'll meet you back in your mom's room." With that, he turned and strode out.

Crickets all but chirped in the silence.

Avery cleared her throat. "Well, that was, uh…"

"Jarring," Cade finished for her. "I think I'm frightened. He just took charge, yeah? Correct me if I'm wrong, but did my big brother just get…involved?"

Drake had been like this after Heather had been diagnosed terminal. He'd gone into robot mode and, with an air of dictator, set a plan in place, then turned back into his caring, compassionate self when things had gotten squared away.

Shaking her head, Zoe thanked her friends and saw them off, preparing to sit vigil at Mama's bedside. She ran into Gayle on her way out, and thanked her as well.

The deep rumble of Drake's voice stopped Zoe just inside the doorway of her mom's room. He was sitting on the bed at Mama's hip, holding her hand. She was awake, but barely, if her heavy lids were any indication.

"Jimmy?"

Closing her eyes, Zoe fought exhaustion and the twist in her stomach.

"It's me." Drake grinned.

Mama tried to sit up. "Where am I?"

"The hospital. Everything's fine." Drake eased her back to the pillow with a hand on her shoulder. "You took a fall and broke your leg. They want you to rest."

"Is the baby okay?"

"Yes, she's fine." Drake never missed a beat, and Zoe could've kissed him for that alone. Arguing reality or correcting her mom didn't work. She was too far gone. Mama had always been intuitive, which had made it harder for Zoe to play along with the old memories haunting Mama's mind.

"Thank goodness. It's a girl?"

He cleared his throat. "Yes."

"I think Zoe is the right name. What do you think?" Mama's eyes widened. "Are you sure she's all right?" She clutched her stomach and eyed the I.V. in her hand, confusion marring her brow.

"Shh." He squeezed her hand. "Zoe is just fine. And you know what? I'm feeling a little psychic. Want to know her future?"

Mama's laugh was sleepy, her lids droopy. "Tell me."

He shifted as if he were settling in, earning another sleepy laugh. "When she grows up, she's going to be stubborn and strong-willed like her mom. In the best way, of course."

She smiled, her eyes slipping closed.

"She's a stunner with her gypsy heritage. Quite gorgeous, also like her mom. The stop traffic kind. Petite, but mighty, she's no pushover. She wields colored pencils and a sketchbook like a master, but she's a genius with a paintbrush. Her smart mouth is quite frustrating, but she's loyal to a fault."

Zoe slapped a hand over her mouth to keep a sob from escaping. Hot tears burned her cheeks. Damn him and his beautiful, stupid, gallant heart.

Mama must've fallen asleep because Drake started to rise. She made a quiet sound of protest and he sat back down. "Jimmy, is that you? Where am I?" The medication was kicking in again. Her words were slurred.

"It's me, and you're safe."

Chapter 8

Drake opened his eyes, yawned, and rolled his head to loosen a stiff neck. He made a mental note to never sleep upright again. Two of his four appendages were numb and turning his head to the left proved painful. Sunlight filtered in through the blinds, creating a pattern on the hospital tile floor. The smell of antiseptic filled his nose and the beep of a monitor jerked his attention to the bed. A quick glance at Cat showed she was zonked out. The poor woman had awoken several times in the night asking either for her brother, Ed, or Zoe's father. Each instance, he'd calmed her, which had made for little down time.

He went to stretch on the very uncomfortable vinyl loveseat in the room, and realized he had weight in his lap. Zoe's pink hair was spread over his thigh, her hand wedged between the top of his leg and the side of her head. Long dark lashes fanned her cheeks as she breathed evenly. Her body was contorted into a tighter version of fetal, but she appeared comfortable enough as she slept. *On him.*

Last he remembered, he'd been fighting not to close his eyes while she'd curled up next to him, using the opposite couch arm from him as a pillow. Apparently, she'd sought a new position. Again—*him.*

Emotions assaulted him, bombarding him from every direction. Too many to name or nail down. One slithered to the top of the heap and stuck. Affection.

Zoe didn't have an off switch, so seeing her at rest was akin to taking a wrecking ball to the breast bone. His hand was settled on her hip, but he moved it to carefully brush a strand of hair away from her chin and got a whiff of lavender for his effort. She looked peaceful, for once not radiating tension or with her usual hard edges. Have mercy, she was lovely in either state, though.

She was the complete opposite of Heather. In all the time he'd been with his wife, he couldn't remember them ever fighting. From day one, the relationship had been easy. Sometimes, too easy. They were vastly similar in personalities, interests, and demeanor. Like an extension of himself. Effortless. Even their love-making had been somewhat predictable, yet rewarding. There had been no heart pounding or frustration or mind screwing going on. In or out of the bedroom.

Zoe, on the other hand, was like bashing his head repeatedly against a brick wall and coming back for more. Willingly. Heather hadn't minded accepting help. Zoe took any offer as a direct insult to her capability. He and Heather had been able to sit in amiable peace or finish each other's sentences. With Zoe, he never had any clue what would spout from her lips next. Heather had been a balm. Zoe was a challenge.

They'd all been close friends once. He shouldn't compare them. But Heather was the lone relationship with which he could evaluate his current predicament, the only instance from hence he could judge. Like night and day, the situations. And for a guy who always had things under control, who preferred his emotions with a reality check, this shift between him and Zoe was killing him. Wrong in all the right ways.

Avery had been accredited by Cade many times for bringing Drake out of his grief bubble, for encouraging him to face life again. She'd reminded him he was still breathing. And though that was true, it was Zoe who'd started his heart beating once more when, for years, it hadn't operated at full capacity.

He'd almost kissed her last night. In a damn hospital, with her mom injured, and without knowing one iota if she had feelings in return… He'd almost kissed her. That pouty little mouth and unguarded look in her eyes had slayed him. Death might actually be preferable.

She drove him batshit, but he simply, achingly wanted her.

She stirred, turning her head until her face was dangerously close to his fly. Her touch, the slight weight of her against him, was enough of an undercurrent without putting her that close to his goods. He lifted his hands in surrender as the breath trapped in his lungs. Her lashes fluttered and she froze. Her gaze jerked to his and she sat upright fast enough to make him dizzy.

She glanced at her mom and back to him. "Next time, you should buy me a drink first before we sleep together."

Smartass. "I did buy you a drink last night. And have I ever mentioned how much I adore the sound you make when you're silent?"

Eyes narrowing, she ran her hands through her disordered hair. Her lids were heavy with sluggish perplexity and her features relaxed. Almost innocent. Her walls were down. A powerful, urgent desire to see her in bed first thing in the morning hit him. Call it curiosity, desire, or anything else, but he wanted nothing more right this second than to watch her slowly wake next to him. And not in a hospital. This was the Zoe no one else ever got to see.

A knock on the open door had both of them jerking their heads in that direction. A plump woman in her late forties with her graying hair in a tight bun stood in the doorway, a clipboard in hand.

"I'm Thelma Smith, the hospital social worker. Is this a good time?"

"Sure." Zoe stretched, her shirt rising to reveal a patch of midriff, which Drake absolutely didn't look at. Long. "Just a warning, I'm not caffeinated."

Though that was all the warning he needed, Thelma laughed herself into a snort. "You're a funny one."

Drake opened his mouth to protest Zoe wasn't, in fact, being funny, but the woman pulled up a chair. She glanced at a folder in her hand, gaze skimming.

After a beat, she looked at Zoe. "Do you and your husband have any place in mind specifically for your mom's rehab assignment?"

Zoe laughed, rubbing her eyes. She glanced at Drake and laughed harder. "Ma'am, I can say with certainty that, if we were married, one of us would be in that bed in a cast, not my mom."

Thelma paled. "Oh, I, uh…"

Drake clenched his teeth and sighed. "She was joking."

"Not really." Zoe slanted him a side-glance.

He closed his eyes and ground her name in warning. When he looked at the social worker, her round gaze darted back and forth between them. "We're friends, and neither of us has ever tried to physically hurt the other." Last thing they needed was a case file on them and the police knocking on their door. Abuse was nothing to joke about, no matter how much his hands itched to strangle her twenty-three out of twenty-four hours a day.

Slowly, Thelma laughed nervously. Awareness sparked in her eyes. "Oh." She giggled. "I see."

Zoe rubbed her forehead. "That makes one of us." She squared her shoulders. "Can you get Mama placed at Pine Crest nursing home in Redwood Ridge? She worked there as a nursing aid for thirty years. I think that might be the next best thing to home. She may recognize her surroundings there."

"I can definitely try. I believe they have a few beds open and they've been cooperative with us before."

As Thelma consulted her clipboard, Drake rose and glanced at Zoe. "I'm going down to the cafeteria to fetch you some coffee and a bagel, which you *will* eat." He hadn't seen her eat anything in he couldn't recall how long.

Up came Zoe's hand along with her eyebrows. "See what I mean? He's so bossy."

Forcing a deep breath, he shoved his hands in his pockets lest he use them unfavorably on her in front of a witness. "I'll buy you an extra large latte with a double shot and promise to leave for a couple hours to go home and shower if you agree to eat something."

She tilted her head, lips pursed. "Deal."

Nodding, he strode out before she could change her mind. Which she tended to do on a thirty-minute cycle. In the cafeteria, he grabbed two coffees, a bagel, and a banana, then brought them to her upstairs. She was still talking with the social worker, so he handed her the food in silence, holding her caffeine hostage until she took a bite. Convinced she'd eat, he set her coffee down and headed home to shower off the night. Hopefully, a measure of stress would wash down the drain, too.

Avery and Hailey were sitting on his porch steps when he pulled in the driveway. They rose to meet him as he climbed out of the truck. Humidity clung to his skin as he breathed in pine and saltwater. He vaguely wondered why his dogs weren't barking, then remembered he'd asked Flynn to take them.

"Hey, I called Zoe to check up on her mom and she said you were heading home."

"Just grabbing a shower. Is everything all right?" He could count on one hand the number of times Cade's wife and daughter had popped over for a surprise visit.

"Oh yes. I just wanted to show you something." She held up a DVD case.

Breathing a sigh of relief, he squatted in front of his niece, who looked so much like her mom with thick brown waves and chubby cheeks that it brought an instant smile to his face. "Hey, Hailey. Whatcha playing?"

She squealed and flapped the hand not holding her iPad in a sign of excitement. She was a nonverbal autistic, but the kid was damn easy to read. With Cade, Hailey cuddled and displayed uncharacteristic signs of affection. Around Flynn, she'd grunt and try to talk, sympathizing with a part of his brother who understood her lack of communication.

Drake felt like she had more of a connection to his brothers than she did him. Until a couple months ago when he'd realized that, in his presence, she'd try new things. It had started out small such as her eating peas where she'd always refused, then moved on to climbing a tree in his backyard one afternoon while he'd babysat. From there, she'd engaged in TV shows she'd never watched and displayed an active role in brushing his dogs.

Hailey tapped her device and passed it to him. Taking it from her, he glanced at the screen and laughed. Rusty as it sounded, it released the knot of tension in his chest. The kid had some kind of app with a virtual goldfish. According to the sidebar, it allowed her to feed it, change its water, and decorate the tank. Drake had a pretty large freshwater aquarium in his living room, and she'd stared at it many times.

Emotion clogged his throat at her small form of attempting to relate to him. "Would you like to feed my fish?"

She squealed and flapped both hands, bouncing on her toes.

"You got it. Come on inside." Once through the door, he passed Avery the iPad. "So, what's that?" He nodded at the case in her other hand.

"My wedding video."

"Okay," he said slowly. "Gabby made us watch that ten times when you and Cade got back from your honeymoon, remember?"

"This disc has the Drake highlights."

Her smile was sweetly understanding. Like a smack upside the head, it dawned on him what it was about her that drew him the moment she'd moved here. From the first second they'd had a conversation all those months ago, he'd been comfortable with her, had allowed himself to take her cues and venture out of his rut. Avery bore strikingly similar mannerisms and traits to Heather. Though there was no romantic chemistry, a tug of family had subconsciously tethered him.

Then he realized what she'd said. "Why does your wedding to my brother have highlights of me?"

Brows furrowed, she drew a slight inhale. "Can I show you?"

Suddenly nervous, he nodded. First, he assisted Hailey in feeding the fish and, after she was settled on the floor with her device, he gestured to the couch for Avery to sit.

She loaded the DVD into his player and settled next to him, remote in hand. Wasting no time, she hit Play.

A scene of the ceremony popped on his TV, one he'd seen quite a few times. Zoe walked down the aisle toward the altar, and his skin heated as he watched. Her natural chestnut brown hair, light makeup on her flawless face, petite frame wrapped in a lavender gown… All of it amped his heart rate for the millionth time.

The camera switched to him and his brothers on the altar, waiting. Drake's gaze was trained to Cade on the screen when Avery hit Pause.

"That right there was the first time you knew something was different with regards to Zoe. Am I right?"

Slowly, he slid his gaze to his sister-in-law. Unable to speak, or take the gentle coaxing in her eyes, he glanced back to the flat screen. This time, he took in his own image. And damn. He'd looked like a gentle breeze could've blown him over. It hadn't been wind that had metaphorically knocked him down, though. It had been Zoe. And he had a sinking suspicion he wasn't getting back up.

Avery started the disc again and the scene changed to his speech at the reception. After a second, the camera moved to pan the crowd, where Zoe stood next to Gabby. Zoe passed her a tissue, gaze never leaving the DJ platform where Drake was toasting his brother and new wife. Nothing he hadn't seen before, either, but he leaned forward, taking a closer look.

For a fleeting blip in time, she'd left her expression open. And what he found drained all the blood from his head. Longing. Hope. Adoring affection. Then, she glanced down, closed her eyes, and shook her head.

Avery paused the DVD. "That's not the first time she's looked at you like that."

Drake closed his eyes, not wanting or able to wrap his mind around her implications. He scrubbed his hands over his face. Doubt mixed with awareness and meshed into holy shit. He wasn't alone in this train wreck. But he'd stood right there in front of her in the hospital last night and had flat out asked her. She'd said nothing. How long had this been going on from her end? Because he felt more than a little blindsided.

The movie started again, this time of the wedding party's dance. Though the camera focus was Cade and Avery, Drake sought out him and Zoe off to the side. Her gaze appeared directed at his chest and his was on the top of her head. An expression of pure torture colliding with confused desire radiated in both their expressions. He remembered not knowing where to set his hands and the crazy way his stomach somersaulted while they'd danced. It hadn't stopped since.

Avery stopped the disc and turned to face him. "You've been acting a tad off lately. Last night, you rammed my suspicion home." She studied him quietly. "Is it the thought of moving on that's upsetting you?"

The room spun, and he cleared his throat. "No, it's the who."

Heather was gone and she wasn't coming back. He'd loved her with everything he had in him, had for more than half his life and would until the day he died, but he was ready to find love again. Maybe not in the same way. There were several kinds and types of love, and none of them were any more significant or trivial in their affliction. But, yeah. He wanted that connection to someone again.

"Is the hesitation because Zoe was Heather's friend?"

His gaze flew to Avery's. "Partly, yes."

Avery nodded, a slight wrinkle between her brows. "I didn't have the pleasure of knowing her. She sounds like she was a lovely woman. I don't think anyone who loved you as much as she obviously did would want you to deny your feelings for someone, no matter who that person is."

The crazy fact remained, Avery was right. He would never know with certainty how Heather would feel about him and Zoe being together. Yet they were the two people Heather had loved more than anything in her short life. A good segment of the guilt he'd been harboring could be laid at that doorstep. Reason was beginning to shove that aside.

No one had known Heather better than him. She hadn't been the envious or judgmental type. Like him, she had been an old soul whose actions were governed by her heart. In fact, on her deathbed, she'd begged Drake to take care of Zoe after she was gone.

"Have you told Zoe how you feel?" Avery set the remote aside and took his hand instead.

He laced their fingers, staring at their joined hands. "I've tried." Not very hard since he'd just recently realized why he'd been in a constant state of cardiac arrest. "I'm not sure how I feel, to be honest, but there is something there." He shook his head. "We're too different, her and I."

"So are me and Cade, yet we work. Besides, you've been friends thirty years. Something kept you connected all that time."

He smiled at his all wise sister-in-law. *"Touché."*

Squeezing his fingers, she let go. "Back when Cade and I first started out, you were the one to talk to him and get his head on straight."

"I also threatened him within an inch of his life if he so much as thought about hurting you."

Her grin lit her eyes. "You also encouraged him to go for it. And when Flynn's feelings for Gabby changed, who was the guy who'd showed him love was right in front of him all along?"

Cade was one lucky jackass, that was for sure. "What's your point, Avery?"

Her gaze softened with a tender smile. "You should take your own advice. And since no one is aware of your predicament, I'm here to play the role of Drake." She scowled, mimicking him in tone and expression. "Let yourself be happy. You deserve it."

Amusement curved his lips. "That was a terrible impression of me."

She rolled her eyes. "I'll work on it." Rising, she called for Hailey. "In the meantime, talk to Zoe. Keep the video. It's yours."

He waited until she got to the door before he said her name. "Zoe and I might kill each other. Did you ever think of that?"

"It crossed my mind."

After Avery and Hailey left, he paced his living room, trying to figure out what the hell to do. If Zoe had feelings for him, he had to figure out what had been holding her back. They would never get anywhere speculating. Hell, half the time they were engaged in conversation he was confused. Toss this into the pile and he'd need a straightjacket.

Once Catherine was settled into rehab and things died down, he'd have a chat with Zoe. Even if he had to hog tie her to accomplish it.

Until then, he'd shower and head back to the hospital.

Chapter 9

Near the end of her workday, Zoe straddled Fraser into submission on a grooming table while she clipped the last of the Jack Russell Terrier's nails. He squirmed and yelped like she was torturing him medieval style, and she blew a strand of purple hair out of her eyes. At least he wasn't a biter. "You're okay, baby. This doesn't hurt, does it?"

With Mama settled into rehab, Zoe had found time to dye the pink out of her hair and switch to purple. Normally, she didn't go that long between color changes, but things had been busy lately. Two nights alone at Mama's house, and Zoe hadn't known what to do with herself. She was thinking about repainting just to keep busy. The place could use a spruce.

Finished with the nail trim, she climbed off the table and praised the dog, even though he'd behaved like a chickenshit. Nothing she wasn't used to, though. She gave him a treat and snapped on his leash, then headed for the waiting room, thinking about what she'd do tonight. Maybe she'd finally head to the craft store and buy some acrylic tubes and canvases. It had been so long since she'd had time to paint her supplies were dried out. Then again, a bottle of wine and a bath sounded more relaxing.

Guilt shifted her stomach. She shouldn't be doing anything fun or relaxing. Mama was held up with a broken leg and not allowed to come home, all because Zoe had gone out with her friends. Logically, she knew it was just an accident and could've happened regardless of whether she'd been home or not. But still. She didn't deserve the measure of relief that she finally had some time to herself. What kind of person did that make her?

Once she made it down the hall, Zoe found Brent and Avery behind the reception desk, deep in conversation with the Battleaxes. Her client's owner, Jennifer Karis, had Drake pinned in a far corner by the printer, playing cozy-up-to-the-vet and batting her eyelashes like a distressed southern belle. Cade, Flynn, and Drake must have finished with patients because the waiting room was empty.

Jennifer flipped her bottle-blonde locks over her shoulder. "I brought you cookies. I made them myself." She skimmed her fingernail across Drake's chest.

Oh, please.

Drake, his expression somewhere between a scowl and panic, cleared his throat. "Thank you."

Why was no one helping Drake escape the woman's clutches? Poor guy probably had no clue how to disarm flirtation and still use his chivalry card. It was a given that females would flock to Drake now that word was out he was dating again, plus his brothers were unavailable now. Perhaps the Battleaxes were distracting Avery and Brent on purpose. Zoe wouldn't put it past them.

Squawk. "Hell's bells."

Zoe glanced at the clinic bird and rolled her eyes at the idiot blonde. "You got that right, Gossip. Jennifer, grow some self respect. Move away from the vet and I won't tell your boyfriend about this. And buy a pair of shorts that cover your ass."

She handed the leash to the woman, earning a sigh of relief from Drake. He rubbed his forehead and stepped closer to Avery's chair, snatching a chart.

Jennifer issued a sound of disgust and a very unladylike huff. "How rude. I was just making small talk. If this is how you treat us, I won't bring Fraser to you anymore."

"Promise?" Zoe shrugged after the woman stormed out. "Something I said?"

Brent raised his brows.

"Whatever. Once she figures out she'll have to cut her own dog's nails and bathe him, she'll be back." The dog, Zoe could handle. The owner, not so much.

"Christ, she was relentless." Drake nodded at her, a silent *thank you* in his eyes.

"Zoe." Avery flashed a praise-Jesus smile. "Look who came by to see you." She gestured at Drake's two aunts and mother, Avery's wide-eyed expression hinting Zoe should run while there was still ample opportunity.

Damn. She'd been hoping they were here to hit up Avery for something event-related, since she headed the committee. The Battleaxes only came by for two reasons—to rope someone into doing something or to play matchmaker.

Zoe eyed the plates of goodies on the desk, no doubt brought in by female clients because it was Drake's non-surgery day. Meaning, he'd done regular clinic and women had booked fake appointments. Her shoulders tensed as she stared down the meddling women, and she suddenly understood where the rumor about Drake being back on the dating circuit had originated.

Marie, the eldest aunt and Redwood Ridge's mayor, stepped forward. "Zoe, dear, we wanted to discuss next week's Fourth of July parade with you." She smoothed her dark brown bob as if it were awry and straightened the lapels of her blue power suit. "You walk for your grooming business every year behind the Animal Instincts float. We were wondering if it would be okay if you were positioned behind the fire trucks instead. You know, dogs and firemen go hand-in-hand."

Nuh-uh. The Battleaxes didn't ask permission. They just acted. Which meant that was not why they were here.

"That's fine." Then a thought crossed her mind. Zoe picked five dogs to showcase in the parade every year. They wore banners for the business. She looked at Brent. "Mama always does the parade with me. If the rehab place lets me take her out, could you push her wheelchair? I need a guy around in case she gets too confused. Plus, I can't hold leashes at the same time." Mama did better with men than women, and she loved Brent.

"Well," Marie said slowly. "Brent's helping me with something else, so he's unavailable. Drake could do it, though. I'm sure he wouldn't mind walking in the parade."

"Oh God," Avery whispered, dropping her forehead in her hands.

Zoe's back stiffened and the hairs on her neck rose with Spidey-sense. Yes, he *would* mind. He didn't like crowds, never mind being the center of attention. He was just starting to get out of the house again, finally rejoining society.

Drake glanced up from a chart, his distracted gaze darting around the group. "Count me in. Cat's used to me. I can handle it."

Zoe blinked in shock. She looked at Avery, whose expression was firmly in the what-planet-am-I-on column under the subheading of say-what.

And, with finality, it hit Zoe just what the hell was going on. She'd suspected, but this confirmed it. Her gut sank and her heart stopped. Since Brent's gaze was everywhere except meeting Zoe's, and he'd aided the Battleaxes in matchmaking before, she zeroed in on her diversion.

"You know, Brent's still single. Perhaps you ladies can find a guy for him."

Hand on his chest, eyes bugged, he wheezed an exaggerated gasp. "Firecracker, I thought we were besties."

Pfft. He shouldn't have gone into cahoots with the Battleaxes then. "Miles at the rec center is single."

Rosa narrowed her eyes in thought, then nodded. "He's a handsome devil. There's potential there."

Hands on his hips, Brent stomped his foot like a petulant child. "Miles is not gay, and I'm not looking to be set up."

"He is too gay," Avery and Zoe said at the same time.

Avery laughed. "I would know. Hailey's with him every day after school. Your gaydar must be broken."

He pursed his lips, eyes glazing. "Interesting. I shall investigate this matter." Snapping out of his dazed daydream, he shook his head. "Anyway, we were discussing Zoe."

"Yes, we were." Marie clapped her hands. "Drake will walk in the parade with you, dear. You two should get together tonight to discuss the details. Maybe over dinner."

No. God. *No, no, no.* This was an all-time low, even for them. Zoe's throat tightened and her eyes burned. Her face heated to scalding.

Avery quietly cleared her throat and nervously faced Drake. "I think you should go do charts in your office."

He frowned. "Why?"

"Trust me." Her pointed stare should've been answer enough.

"That's ridiculous." Rosa waved off the comment. "We're only suggesting—"

"Enough!" Zoe took a deep breath and a slow blink to calm down before she went postal. "I know what you're doing, what you're up to, and this is going too far." Hands shaking, she pointed to Drake. "Hasn't he been through enough? Haven't I?" Her voice cracked, damn it. She looked at Gayle's guilt-laden face. "If you care about me at all, you'll stop this charade now."

Drake's confused expression shifted from Zoe to Avery and back again. "I'm not following."

Tears threatening, Zoe turned on her heel and strode around the desk.

"Hey," he murmured. Gently, he grabbed her arm, concern wrinkling his brow.

Mortified, she shrugged him off, went down the hall, and slammed her grooming door closed.

She placed her palms on her desk and leaned into them, unable to catch her breath. Dropping her chin, she focused on air exchange. She would not, absolutely would not, cry at work. Especially not over the Battleaxes and their shenanigans. Hopefully, she'd cut them off at the pass and they'd move on to torture someone else.

The door opened and closed behind her. The footsteps were too quiet to be Drake's.

Avery put her arm around Zoe's shoulders. "Are you okay?"

Zoe plopped in her desk chair. "No. They have no right messing with him like that."

Nodding, Avery pulled a folding chair over and sat. "Nor you. They mean well, though."

"I really don't care how good their intentions are. Some things are too tenuous to mess with. And of all people, why me? They're freaking nuts, the whole lot of them."

Avery simply stared at her, not saying anything for the longest time. With care, her kind gaze took in Zoe's expression for so long she squirmed in her seat. "Why not you? Don't you deserve someone, too?"

Slumping, Zoe sighed. "Not you, too. Come on."

"I'm serious." When Zoe said nothing, Avery shook her head, her too-clever gaze all knowing. "How long have you had a thing for him?"

"Since I was sixteen." Crap. She shouldn't have admitted that.

Avery's lips parted in shock. "Oh, Zoe. For that long?"

Closing her eyes, she staved the mortification and breathed through the tightness in her chest. She'd never told anyone about this, but perhaps it was time. What she'd been doing to cope wasn't working.

Biting her thumbnail, she stared at her desk. "When we were seventeen, I was going to ask him to a dance, but Heather got to him first. Before you freak out—no, she didn't know about my feelings. He never would've picked me anyway, so there was no sense in mentioning it. Heather would've reneged on principle alone. She deserved him. I backed off." She rubbed her forehead. "I got over it, over him. Then, about a year after she died, my feelings started coming back."

A wrinkle formed between Avery's brows. "There's so much wrong with that statement I don't know where to start. You never struck me as someone with confidence issues."

Well, Zoe could put up a heck of a front when she had to. Truly, the only time she'd ever done the pity thing had been where Drake was concerned. Even then, she'd pretended it didn't matter.

"Nevertheless, you're both free now, Zoe. Why not go for it?"

"Are you insane? Besides my mother and friends, Heather was the person I loved most in this world. We were more like sisters. I would never betray her that way."

"But what if it's not a betrayal?" Avery pressed her lips together. "After everything I've heard about her, Heather wouldn't stand in your way." When Zoe started to argue, Avery shook her head. "She's gone, and if she had known how you felt, do you think she would've asked him out all those years ago? No. And, wherever she is now, she wouldn't fault you for moving on and seeking happiness."

With a half laugh, Zoe stared at her friend and let her words sink in. "It's uncanny. You're a lot like her, actually. She would've loved you."

Avery smiled. "Cade said that once, too, back when we first started dating." She straightened in her seat. "And if that's true, then you know I'm right."

Throwing her head back, Zoe chuckled dryly and stared at the ceiling. "Points for you." She sighed. "There's other obstacles, as well. It's a lost cause, Avery. Thank you, though. You should head home."

Avery checked her watch. "Brent said he'd lock up. I've got to pick up Hailey."

"Go. I think I'm going to stay and put the supply order away." The house was too quiet without Mama, and Zoe had already visited her at lunch. Too much and her mom got over-stimulated and antsy. The Pine Crest staff had suggested once a day visits.

"Um…" Avery's hesitant gaze met hers with a weak smile. "Are you sure? I can do it tomorrow."

Realization clicked, and Zoe grinned. Avery, as their office manager, was an organizational Nazi who had a strict method and order to things. "I promise to check off items on your inventory list and stock them according to your labeled shelf system."

"You're making fun of me."

"Totally. Get your anal-retentive ass out of here or I'll switch your color-coding around."

Avery's eyes narrowed. "You wouldn't."

"Try me."

"Fine." Avery rose and gave her a one-armed hug. "I meant what I said, though. Think about it. And, also… The Battleaxes haven't exactly been wrong about these things. Besides Cade and I, or Gabby and Flynn, they've set up several other couples in town."

Curses. "I'm already mentally switching out your red biohazard labels for the green sterile medical equipment. Oh, and the yellow office supplies for—"

"Okay, okay." Avery rushed for the door. "No need to give me nightmares."

Zoe sat for a few moments in silence before heading toward reception and Avery's desk. Better to stay busy than idle. Brent had, in fact, locked up, and the only lights on were the security ones. Gossip's cage was covered and the clinic animals were in the boarding room. A quick glance down the hall showed all the doctor office doors were closed.

Nothing for Zoe to do but inventory. She stacked the delivery boxes waiting by Avery's desk and dragged them to the storage closet in three loads. Setting a box in front of the supply room door so it wouldn't close, she flicked on the light. Approximately ten-by-ten, the room was wall-to-wall, floor-to-ceiling shelves. Good thing she wasn't claustrophobic.

An hour later, she was on the second to last load. It was too late to hit the craft store, but tomorrow was another day. Chances were, she'd lost her artistic ability after not using it, anyway. She'd have to do several trial runs of a painting to re-hone her craft. Grabbing a bottle of peroxide, she rose on her tiptoes on the stepstool and stretched to set it on the top shelf.

"Need help?"

Screaming at the deep male voice, she whirled around, lost her balance, and pitched toward the floor.

Drake's arm wrapped around her waist before she could fall. He hauled her against his wall of chest as her heart pounded from the near fatal scare. The scent of warm male pressed against her face and, without thinking, she fisted his black scrub shirt and caught her breath.

Fight or flight reflex kicked in and she eased away, patting her chest. "Thanks for the heart attack. I thought everyone had gone home."

One corner of his mouth lifted in what could be mistaken for a smile. The other side quirked and…nope. False alarm. He frowned. "You shouldn't be in the clinic by yourself. Anything could happen and you'd be alone."

"Look, doc. We're locked tight and the security alarm is on. I'm perfectly capable—"

Oh, crap. In his other arm was the box she'd used to pry the door open. *No, no, no.* Her gaze flew to the only exit. Which was closed. With a growl, she tilted her face heavenward. Someone up there really hated her.

"What's your problem?"

She strode around him and turned the knob. Nope. "Please, *please* tell me Cade or Gabby or Brent or Avery or an armed robber are still here somewhere." She'd include Flynn in that mix, but he wouldn't hear her frantic pounding if she tried that route. Whimpering, she pressed her forehead and palms to the door.

"Everyone went home. I finished dictation in my office and was heading out when I saw the closet light."

Moaning, she spun around and slid to the floor in a heap. "Karma really is a bitch." This was what she got for lusting after her best friend's man, even if said friend was dead and said man in question had been giving Zoe swoony eyes first.

"What's with the dramatics?"

She eyed him balefully. "The automatic locking mechanism has been acting wonky. Avery has someone coming in to fix it next week."

He stilled. "Meaning what?"

"Meaning, we can't unlock it from the inside." She pointed to the box in his hand. "Ergo, why I had the door propped open."

His dark brown eyes narrowed on the cardboard as if it were the box's fault, then the door as if he could laser it open by sheer will. "I'll text one of my brothers." He unceremoniously dropped the box and pulled his phone from his pocket.

"Good luck with that. There's no cell reception in here."

Chest rising and falling in rapid succession, he paced the room, holding the phone near every nook and cranny trying to get a signal. She watched, shoulders deflated, mood in the crapper. Giving up, he pocketed the cell and glanced at the only window in the room. Twelve feet off the ground, it hugged the ceiling and was roughly the size of a shoebox. Not even she could climb out that narrow an opening.

"Hell." He pinched the bridge of his nose.

"Exactly. That's *exactly* where we are."

Chapter 10

"You better hope I don't have to pee later."

Lacing his fingers, Drake stacked them on his head. "I said I was sorry." In the supply closet, Zoe sat propped against the door, him directly across from her on the far wall in what he considered a Mexican sit-off. Except there were no weapons and it wasn't high noon. And it was getting very hot in here.

"I blame Avery for not telling you about the faulty lock in the first place." She banged the back of her head lightly against the door. Again. "I have all night to think of ways to repay her. And by that, I mean evil, evil things."

It wasn't as if he was ecstatic to be locked in a small room with her either. Especially not while wearing his black surgical scrubs and smelling like dog fur. She wasn't much better off in her yellow scrubs, still damp from shampooing her last client. Yeah, he'd wanted to have a good, long talk with her, but not while they were caged in with no escape for hours.

He stretched his legs out in front of him, the soles of his shoes brushing hers.

"I hope there's not an emergency at Mama's rehab." She checked the phone in her lap as if she'd miraculously get a signal by staring at it.

His chest pinched. "They have others as an emergency contact if they can't reach you, right?"

"Yep. *You.*" She frowned. "And your mom, plus Brent and Gabby just in case. Hopefully, everything's okay."

"I'm sure it will be." Still, he felt like a jackass. "At least you didn't have plans or anything." Had he said jackass? He meant asshole.

"I had a threesome planned with me, Netflix, and my cat, but thanks for the reminder."

This was what he got for trying to lighten the mood. She flustered the crap out of him on a good day. And this had not been a good day. Sixty percent of his clients had been non-emergencies. A plethora of females whose animals were "feeling off" or "acting unusual." And he hadn't found a damn thing wrong with one of them. He'd never gotten so many offers of dinner in all his life. He didn't know how Cade had diverted when he'd been single.

Drake scrubbed his hands over his face. "I apologize for screwing up your date, in that case."

She snorted. "Date." The word dripped with disdain. "My last date was with Cade at your Aunt Marie's re-election party, and it doesn't count being a plus one as friends."

What? "That was three years ago."

She lifted her hand with wide eyes as if to say, *no kidding.*

He frowned. Zoe had always been the life of the party and had never lacked male company. He knew her mom's care took up a chunk of her time, but had she seriously stopped all social activities? And if Cade had been her most recent date, when had she last had a real one?

"I used to think you and Cade would wind up together."

Her you-done-gone-crazy look only irritated him more.

"You guys hung out a lot and shared similar interests. You were each other's fall back crutch for events, too. It made sense to me."

Her foot twitched. "I never slept with your brother. Either of them."

He knew that, and the thought of her possibly being with Cade or Flynn caused his blood to boil. Which was stupid because both had found their soul mates, were happy. His fingers clenched while he fought to devise a change in topic. Errant thoughts landed him on what had happened at the front desk at closing time.

"I guess we should talk about the parade."

Closing her eyes, she shook her head, looking so weary his throat ached. "I've got five dogs I'm walking who'll wear my Doggie Style grooming logo on a banner. If Pine Crest lets me take Mama, I just need you to push her wheelchair and keep her calm. There. We talked about it."

He hadn't a clue what had gotten her hackles up again until he recalled how upset she'd been when his aunts and mother had been here. Hell, she'd all but been in tears and had stormed off. His gut twisted even as confusion over the incident shoved around in his skull. Zoe, at times, could go all over the emotional scale, but crying wasn't like her.

"And look at that. We didn't even need to do dinner to have the conversation."

Glancing at her again, he took in her closed expression and became even more confused. Why would his family's suggestion to discuss the parade over dinner put her walls up? "We could get together one night, anyway." When Heather had been alive, they'd shared meals with Zoe at least once a week.

Dropping her chin, she sighed. "I hate it when I plan a conversation in my head and the other person doesn't follow the script."

Script? Hell, he didn't even have a solitary page of the CliffsNotes. "Zoe—"

"Think about it, Drake. I know you've been out of the real world for a while, but even you must recognize why Cade named them The Battleaxes. They meddle, they sucker people into doing what they want, they bend townsfolk to their will, and they play Cupid."

Wait. The parade, dinner...had all been a ruse to set him up with Zoe? His heart did some kind of stutter beat. Images of her reaction from earlier when they'd brought up the subject pushed to mind. She'd gotten defensive with the ladies—pissed off one second, wounded and hurt the next. Then her eyes had filled. She'd said something, too, and he tried to remember. *Hasn't he been through enough? Haven't I?*

Oxygen seeped from his lungs. He rubbed his jaw, trying to process. Her expression hadn't been so different from the one he'd caught on Avery's wedding video. Had she been trying to protect him? From her?

"Better breathe, Drake. There's not a defibrillator in here."

He searched her hazel eyes and found no answers, other than, once again, he wanted her. He didn't know what to be more upset about—the fact his family chose her and wanted them together or that Zoe was doing everything in her power to stop them from succeeding. He'd seen it on her face in the video. She felt something, too. Exactly what, he hadn't a clue. And Christ, it needed to be discussed. But this entire scenario was akin to walking across hot coals shoeless.

He cleared his throat. "The idea of them trying to set us up disturbed you."

She stared at him. Long. Hard. "Besides all the obvious reasons why it would be a horrendous idea, you and I would be a one-way ticket to frustration-town."

If that wasn't the worst non-answer he'd ever heard, he didn't know what was. "And what do you plan to do about their attempts?"

She shrugged. "Ignore them. Hard as I can."

Call him crazy, but he suspected that would work about as well as pretending there wasn't something already flickering between them. He knew why he was having a bitch of a time with the shift, but he didn't know her reasons. Wasn't sure he wanted to because she was right. About all of it. Together, they were a bad idea.

And yet he wanted her. More and more by the damn second.

She pulled out her ponytail and ran her fingers through the purple strands. A shade darker than lavender, like her scent. Loose waves fell to her shoulders. He was just starting to get used to the pink and she'd dyed it again. For too long, she'd been doing this—one outrageous color after another. The only reprieve had been Cade's wedding when she'd returned it to her natural hue.

"Why do you color your hair?"

Avoiding his gaze, she ducked her head. "Why does it matter to you?"

Because she mattered to him, along with everything she did, said, or thought. He may not understand her actions, but he knew her. There was something behind this particular quirk and, for two years, he'd been wanting to ask.

Pulling his legs up, he rested his forearms on his knees. "Humor me."

Rubbing her forehead, she looked away, her gaze indicating she was no longer in the room. At times, her appearance could be so expressive it hurt. Her pouty little mouth, her eyes too big for her face. He couldn't read her now, and just as he thought she wouldn't answer, her quiet voice drifted toward him.

"A couple years ago, I was in the kitchen making dinner. Mama was at the table, and when I set her plate down, she looked at me like she had no idea who I was. She'd had memory lapses before, frequent ones, but that was the first time she didn't recognize…me."

Her teeth sunk into lower lip, and he wanted—needed—to hold her. But her mannerisms and body language indicated that was the last thing she required right now. Seemed the only thing holding her together was sheer will and bravado. Hell if he'd crumble that for the sake of his own desires.

She let out a near silent breath, her gaze on his chest. "I realized she wasn't the only one who didn't recognize me. I hadn't painted in too long, gone out with friends, or dated. All I ever did was go to work and come home to her. I'd given up my apartment, my identity, my life in order to take care of her. There was no choice. She's my mom. I love her."

As if it didn't matter, she shrugged. "So I went to the drug store and bought blue dye. Seemed fitting at the time. I figured if Mama didn't recognize me, no one should. And whenever I look in the mirror and don't get surprised by my reflection, I know it's time to change colors again." If possible, her gaze grew even more distant. "I still can't eat meatloaf without thinking about that night."

Christ in Heaven.

In his own grief, he'd sometimes forgotten he wasn't the only one who'd lost Heather. She and Zoe had been joined at the hip since they were two years old and playing in the sandbox. Zoe had been there when Heather had taken her last breaths, had been given the heart-wrenching job of reading her eulogy. Only a year had separated Heather's cancer diagnosis from Catherine's dementia. Zoe hadn't just lost her best friend, was not only slowly losing her mother. She'd had any sense of individuality stripped, too.

Closing his eyes, he battled through the compressing sensation in his chest and the band blocking his airway. She'd taken care of everyone else, including him. But who'd taken care of her?

The sound of her clothes rustling as she shifted filled the quiet. "You know what they say. When a door closes, a window—" She surged to her feet. "Give me your cell phone."

He was going to require a neck brace with all this whiplash. "Why?"

He lumbered to a stand and dug in his pocket, passing her his cell.

Thumbs flittering, she opened a group chat with Cade and Flynn. "Okay, give me a boost." She pointed to the window. "I can hold the cell outside and try to send a text."

Clever. Wished she'd thought of it before she'd filleted his innards.

Squatting, he tapped his shoulders for her to climb on. Once she was situated, he held her calves to keep her steady and rose to full height. She was a petite thing, making the task not much of a challenge. He tilted his head, watching her progress. She unlatched the pane and tugged on the small frame. It slid forward to open a fraction.

Her small hands worked their way outside, her thumbs scrolling. "Got a signal. Only two bars, though."

Two bars were enough. He waited, trying to keep still so she wouldn't fall. "Ha. Sent." She brought her arms back inside, relocked the window, set his phone on a nearby shelf, and cupped his cheeks, thrusting his head back so he looked at her upside down. "Help is coming."

Then she…kissed him. Inverted, like in Spiderman film fashion. A quick smack that she probably hadn't intended to be sexual. But he had to plant his palm against the wall to stay upright, and she didn't pull away afterward. She held his face in her hands, a wrinkle between her brows, lips parted as they all but shared air. Pink infused her cheeks and her eyes dilated while her gaze took a long perusal of him.

Every organ in his body shut down, all except his heart, which was jack-hammering to stroke capacity. Finally, she whispered his name, and he lost it.

Reaching back, he wrapped his arm around her waist, eased her down, and pinned her to his chest until her feet barely dangled off the ground and they were aligned. He held her jaw with his other hand, stroking the petal soft skin of her throat with his thumb. Her warm breath caressed his cheek, as uneven as his own.

Through heavy lids, she stared at him with those collapse-his-lungs hazel eyes. He didn't know if it was a trick of the light or her aroused state, but her irises had more green flecks than brown or gray. Her lashes fluttered and her gaze dipped to his mouth.

Up until right now, he could've given any number of excuses for what he'd seen on the video or the expressions he'd infrequently caught when she'd thought he wasn't looking. But no. There was no doubt. Not with her heart thumping against his chest and the pulse going hyperactive in her neck. Certainly not with that oh-no/hell-yes combo she had going in her eyes.

Okay. Moment of truth. Kiss her and blow sanity out of the water, or set her back on her feet and...blow sanity out of the water.

Resting his forehead against hers, he brushed their noses, and whispered a plea. "Zoe, honey." He swore he could feel every red blood cell swimming through his veins. He'd asked her once before, and he'd only do it one more time. "I'm not alone in this, am I?"

Her fingers clutched the back of his shirt. Eyes wide, she offered a barely perceptible shake of her head.

"You'd be in feral cat mode, shredding me with your claws if you didn't want this, too, right?"

Trembling, she nodded.

Option one for the win. He closed the meager distance, kissing the corner of her mouth. It wasn't as if he'd forgotten how, but it had been such a damn long time since he'd done this that he needed slow or he'd implode. Even then, he'd spent ten years with the same woman.

But having Zoe against him wasn't familiar and it certainly wasn't benign. Working his way across her mouth, he increased the pressure by a margin and kissed the other corner. Her lips parted with a gasp and her lids fell closed. He let his own lids drift shut and kissed her lower lip, then the upper, earning a needy whimper from her.

Breaths soughing, fire licking his skin, he tilted his head and went deeper. An open-mouth assault without tongue, but with twice the heat of anything he could recall. She moved against him, matching his ministrations with tender care of her own as if she knew how hard he was struggling not to plunder.

With a quiet moan, she eased away a fraction. "Drake." Her voice was a needy whisper, but he had no idea if she was asking for more or demanding something else.

His muscles shook with restraint, so he carefully set her back on her feet. "I can't seem to catch my breath." Hell if he cared either.

Her laugh skated across his neck. "I—"

Footsteps sounded outside the door. A click of a key in the lock followed. Suddenly, he didn't want to be rescued.

However, his brothers didn't need to catch him and Zoe making out like teenagers in a closet. Hands on her shoulders, he stepped away and grabbed his phone off the shelf. She erected more distance as if ashamed of what they'd done. Eyes wild, she crossed her arms and stared at the ground.

The door opened and Flynn filled the entry. *"Your S.O.S. interrupted something. Just sayin'."*

Judging by his bedhead and rumpled pajamas, Drake could guess. "Sorry."

"Thank you, thank you!" Zoe hugged Flynn hard enough to have his brother stumble back a step.

He smiled once she pulled away. *"No worries."* He glanced at Drake, eyebrows raised.

Drake shook his head in a silent I-don't-want-to-talk-about-it and followed them out of the closet. He told Flynn to take off and waited in the hallway for Zoe to grab her purse from the grooming room. A few minutes later, she brushed right past him and kept going toward reception at a clipped pace.

She was freaking out, which made him freak out harder.

Trying to think fast, he activated and unlocked his cell. *In the spirit of moving on, do you want to come over and help me paint tomorrow night?* He held his breath.

She froze, her stiff spine to him and her facing the door to freedom. Slowly, she unpocketed her cell and stared at the screen, unmoving. Seconds passed.

He thumbed another text. *I can make meatloaf for dinner. Perhaps it'll give you better memories if someone else cooks.*

Her phone chimed and, as she read what he'd sent, her hands shook. Rubbing her forehead, she made a sound of duress and pushed through the door, disappearing into the night.

Two hours later, as he was still wound tighter than a German clock and settling into bed, her response came. *Yes.*

Chapter 11

Zoe was going to lose it. Completely, utterly, in grand fashion, lose it.
She paced the living room in Mama's house, biting her thumbnail and trying to decide if she should back out of tonight's painting party with Drake or show. She'd finished work early and had headed home with the notion she'd visit Mama in rehab, shower, and go to Drake's. She was closing in on two hours until she was supposed to be there and she had done little more than wear the rug down to threads.

To think, Fridays were supposed to be the best day of the week. With his added invite to make dinner, she had no clue if this was supposed to be a date.

With a passing thought, she was tempted to call Avery, but Zoe didn't need any more witnesses to her epic breakdown. She was acting like an indecisive vapid female, but damn it. This was Drake.

And he'd kissed her last night. An I-can't-feel-my-knees, where-did-gravity-go kind of kiss. God, she was still dizzy. He hadn't claimed her with scorching heat or devoured her whole. No. He'd gradually, at his own crawling pace, took her mouth with tender endearment as if seducing her to the idea of being with him.

Drake was a meticulous guy. He always took his time and thought things through. She'd nearly died waiting for him to amp the tempo. But, oh no. He'd had control at all times. Her brain had pooled to goo and her heart hadn't caught regular rhythm since, but had he cried mercy?

Nope.

In all her years, with as many lovers as she'd had, not a one had kissed her like that. As if she...mattered, was worth tasting or taking the time to explore.

If this were any other man, she'd jump head first. Yet this wasn't just any guy. The complications were still evident once the dust had settled. Their joined history with Heather was only a smidgen of the issue. After her discussion with Avery the other day, Zoe figured she could get past that, in time. Avery hadn't been wrong in the things she'd said. Drake didn't just care about people. He loved with every fiber of his being and every cell of his body. Once he made the leap, there was no going back. It was why he'd taken four years to get over Heather and why they'd been together so long. Love wasn't just an emotion for him. It was a way of life.

And he wanted a wife, a forever. Kids and dogs and picket fences. Once upon a time, she'd wanted that, too. Zoe may still be an epic romantic at heart—and she'd maim anyone who agreed—but fairy tales were for other people. She wasn't the girl who got swept off her feet. She was the prelude lover or the one left in the dust.

Could she change the town moniker of "the good time"? Sure. But that didn't mean she should. She could never have children. Or shouldn't. Period. And Drake deserved a family, deserved to get everything he wanted.

If she thought, for one second, he wouldn't get attached, she would gladly step up and help him transition back into the dating scene. She'd never get over it and she'd be gutted once things ended, but having the man she'd always wanted and measured every other guy against, even for just a short while, would be worth it. At least she'd know that, for a short blip in time, Drake had wanted her, too.

Another stupid fantasy to add to the list and grind into a fine powder. Drake didn't do casual, which meant she had to—probably, maybe—set him straight tonight.

Whatever. Shaking her head, she went into the bathroom and showered off the clinic. Donning a pair of ripped jeans and an old white tee she'd used in the past for painting, she headed out.

The staff were just finishing supper clean-up as Zoe strode into Pine Crest. Before heading to Mama's room, Zoe made a beeline for the nurse's station to check in.

Frances, a woman who used to work with Mama when she'd been on staff, glanced up from a chart. "Zoe, great to see you. How are things?"

She leaned over the counter and hugged the sixty-year-old woman who reminded Zoe of Mrs. Doubtfire. "Not bad. How is she doing?"

Tucking a pen into her salt-and-pepper bun, Frances nodded. "Cat's been quite the helper. Most of the time, she thinks she still works here, so we play along. She scoots around in her wheelchair passing out Jell-O and collecting water cups. It keeps her busy."

Wow. Mama had been here a week, and for the first half of that, she'd been restricted to bed to elevate her leg. "Is she taking the pain meds?

How's she eating?"

"Cat's got a great appetite. She's not taking the medication as much. We've been sticking to over-the-counter during the day and the narc at night. She's been cooperative about resting mid-day for an hour in her room."

Before the fall, when Zoe had to work, Mama attended adult daycare and had been mostly pleasant, too. Though Mama didn't recognize her, she was pretty tame on weekends for Zoe. It was the period after three or four in the afternoons when her sundowning started that the mean came out. "Has she, you know, thrown things or anything?"

Frances pressed a hand to her chest. "Heavens, no. She's more confused at night, of course, but the medication and routine help."

Slowly, Zoe nodded, not sure how she should take that news. On one hand, she was relieved Mama was doing so well. It meant she could come home on schedule if she was cooperative. But, on the other hand, Zoe couldn't help but think the care she'd been giving her mom wasn't enough. It had been a constant struggle to get her to eat, take her pills, and get ready for bed. Zoe had distraction down to a science, but it didn't always help.

Issuing her thanks to Frances, Zoe popped into Mama's room, but the aid was giving her a bed bath and Zoe didn't want to upset the balance, so she headed out.

The sticky heat and humidity began to fade as dusk approached. She drove with the windows down, sea salt fading from the air the farther she got from town and closer to Drake's. Letting the scent of cedar, spruce, and peat moss calm her nerves, she wove through the winding private drive past Gayle, Cade, and Flynn's houses.

Pulling into Drake's driveway, she cut the engine and stared at the house. All three O'Grady boys had built their homes from the ground up and all resembled log cabins. Drake's had a wrap-around porch, pine rocking chairs, and forest green shutters framing the large windows. His front yard was all natural with mature birch, foxtail pine, and cypress trees. A neat row of evergreen bushes lined the porch.

Zoe didn't think she'd ever view this house as anything other than Drake and Heather's dream. It had four bedrooms, two full baths, and a half bath on the main floor. Ginormous living room in an open floor plan leading to an equally ginormous kitchen. They'd planned to fill it to the hilt with family, but that hadn't happened.

He'd done little things outside to distinguish the place from what it resembled before Heather died. New porch furniture. No flower pots or wind chimes. Bushes instead of wildflower beds. Though she couldn't see it from her position, out back near the thin trickle of a riverbed, he'd torn down the gazebo and erected a stone deck, complete with a built-in grill area. The patio furniture was also new.

Sighing, Zoe exited the car, climbed the porch stairs, and rang the bell. She had a key and she'd all but lived here during Heather's end stage, but Zoe didn't know how to behave in this new chapter with her and Drake. The last time she'd been here was two years ago when he'd asked her, via text, to clear out Heather's personal effects.

Damn. She should just go home.

The front door opened and Drake stood there, one arm braced on the frame. His midnight hair was damp from a shower and dark stubble shadowed his wide jaw. A green T-shirt molded to his sculpted, lean body and did wonders to enhance the slight bulge of a bicep. Loose gray sweats hung on his hips and...screw all. His feet were bare. So hot.

He scratched the back of his neck, his gaze giving her outfit a slow perusal. "Hi."

Curse that deep voice of his.

"Hi." She blinked in the silence. "May I come in?"

Shaking his head as if to clear it, he stepped back. "Yeah, sorry."

She eased around him into the living room and stopped short. The mahogany floors, scarred ceiling beams, stone fireplace, walnut kitchen cabinets, gray slate countertops, and stainless steel appliances were the same, but nothing else. Gone were the pictures on the wall, the furniture, and...everything else. Even the ugly pig cookie jar Heather had adored was missing from its place on the island. The only thing that remained was his sixty-gallon fish tank in the corner.

"Drake, I think you should call Parker. You've been robbed."

With a heavy sigh, he shut the door. "If you ever go five minutes without sarcasm, I might expire on the spot."

Said the pot to the kettle.

"You're really serious about redecorating." She glanced at the staircase and wondered if the re-haul included the second floor.

Looking suddenly uncomfortable, he crossed his arms and lowered his chin. "I bought two cans each of three different paint colors. I kinda got lost after that and maybe went too far." Closing his eyes, he rolled his head to stretch his neck. "You and Gabby helped Cade and Flynn decorate when they were finished building their houses. Heather did ours, and I'm a guy, so...yeah..."

As he gazed around, his eyebrows pinched. Shame settled in her belly. He'd asked for her help and she was acting like a bitch. This was a huge step he was taking, and she knew from experience it wasn't an easy one.

For whatever reason, he'd sought her out when he'd realized he was ready.

"Hey." She waited until he looked at her. "I'm sorry. What rooms are getting painted?"

His Adam's apple bobbed with a swallow. He stared at her a long beat and then away as if the action had hurt. "The living room, which bleeds into the kitchen, my bedroom, and…"

"And the guestroom?" she offered gently. That's where Heather had passed away. Drake had wanted her comfortable upstairs, but the mechanical bed hadn't fit in their bedroom with all the furniture, thus the guestroom had been converted.

"Yeah." His rough tone nearly tore her in two.

"What colors do you have?" She glanced at the six cans he'd set on the floor by the island. The entire house had beige walls. The old furniture and art had added the splash of color instead.

Clearing his throat, he walked into the kitchen. She followed and took the paint swatches he offered. Dark burgundy, something between a gray and blue, and forest green. Nice choices.

"Any idea what you want and where?"

After he shook his head, she studied the swatches. Heather had hated the color green, making it a good choice to use in the guestroom to eradicate all bad memories of her time there. Blue would be more soothing for a bedroom and burgundy against his stone fireplace would really do wonders for the eye. She told him as much, and he nodded.

"What about furniture?"

Grabbing an iPad off the counter, he swiped the screen. After a few taps, he moved next to her, showing her a dark ivory corduroy sectional. "It comes with a chair, too. They're being delivered tomorrow with a new mattress for my bed." He scrolled over and pointed to a scarred pine coffee and end table set that would match the ceiling beams.

"They'll look awesome."

"You think?"

"Yep. I wouldn't lie to you. Well, not about redecorating anyway." And he didn't appear to need her help. Her assurance or her company, maybe, but not help.

A fond smile curved his lips. Setting the device aside, he glanced behind him. "Dinner should be ready in thirty minutes."

At her shock in seeing the empty rooms, she hadn't noticed the scent of roasting meat. He also had two saucepans going on the stovetop. Heather had been a terrible cook, leaving Drake to do most of the meals. "It smells great." Except… "Where are we going to eat?" He'd gotten rid of the kitchen table, too.

"Figured we go out on the patio. A new kitchen set is coming tomorrow." The sound of pitter-patter scratched the floor and Drake's two dogs came running down from upstairs. Cyprus, the gray and white Pitbull, made it to her first. He'd been a rescue from a dog fighting ring Flynn and Gabby had accidentally stumbled upon during a home visit. Poor guy had been in pretty bad shape, but had taken well to people. Moses, the German Shepherd, aptly followed and did his usual welcome by dropping at her feet and rolling over.

Laughing, she squatted and gave the dogs some love. "Who's the best furballs on the planet? You two. Yes, you are."

Moses barked and Cyprus gave her face a tongue bath.

Tension turned Drake's shoulders rigid.

Her hands paused over the dogs. "What's wrong?"

"Nothing. I'm still a bit nervous about Cyprus, is all. It's only been a few months since I brought him home, and with his violent background, I've been watching him close."

"Has he shown signs of aggression?"

His gaze darted between her and the dogs. "No."

She understood his concerns, and they were legit, but Cyprus was just a big baby, happy for some love. "You won't eat me. Will you, boy?"

He pawed her arm.

"See? He's okay." She scratched his ears, one of them mangled from his dog fighting days. His tongue lolled from his mouth, his ears were up, and his stump wagged. No signs of distress. "I won't be too tasty, anyway. Right, boy?"

He nudged her arm, and she laughed, rising to her feet.

Drake sighed. "Please just take it easy with him for a bit." He glanced around. "Do you want to see the upstairs while we wait?"

Since he needed to loosen up, she made a point to check her watch. "Wow. Fifteen minutes in the door and you're inviting me upstairs. That might be a record for me."

A cross between pissed off and stunned stupid spread across his face until realization gradually dawned in his eyes. At her slow grin, his threatened to follow. The dimple on his left cheek made a rare appearance. "I never know what to say to you."

"Really?" She tilted her head, unsure whether that was a compliment or not. "Thirty-one years as friends in the same small town and you haven't figured it out?"

"The day anyone figures you out, Zoe, will be a cold day in hell."

Her grin widened. "You say the sweetest things."

He grunted, pointing to the stairs. "Shall we?"

With the dogs following, they walked past his home gym and the empty bedroom Drake and Heather had planned to make a nursery, then stopped outside the guestroom. There was a full-size bed, nightstand, and tall dresser, purchased after Heather died. The I.V. stands, oxygen tanks, and hospital bed were gone, but Zoe could understand why he'd want to paint. Her throat closed just remembering Heather's last moments in here.

Pivoting on his heel, he strode into the master bedroom. She trailed after and took in the space. The last time she'd been in here was to clear out Heather's clothes. Everything else was the same. Pictures from their wedding, their life together, dotted the dresser and walls.

He shoved his hands in his pockets. "I haven't been able to…get rid of the stuff in here." Gazing at the photos, his jaw ticked. "I know I should, but…" Closing his eyes, he drew a breath and opened them.

Tears burned her eyes, and she had to swallow twice before speaking. "You don't have to eradicate her from your life, nor should you. Anyone you choose to date would understand that, and if they don't, they're not right for you." And Zoe would kill them dead. "I suggest picking a couple pictures you want to keep and putting them downstairs on the mantle instead. The rest can go into storage or to Heather's parents." That way Heather was still around, had a place, but not a primary focus everywhere he turned.

When he said nothing, she touched his arm. "Hey, there's no rush to do this, Drake. If you're not okay—"

His laugh was dry. "I kissed you last night, and you're telling me to…" He turned and faced her, lips pressed in a thin line. "I kissed you last night, and you're the same old Zoe, encouraging me at my own pace. Why, honey? Why, when everyone else is pushing and prying and never leaving me alone, do you always know exactly what I need?"

She snapped her mouth shut. Her mind ping-ponged back and forth between the term of endearment he'd *never* used for her before and the blunt way he'd essentially told her *she* was what he needed.

Sucking a harsh inhale, nostrils flared, he crossed his arms. "I'm ready to do this. Really, I am. Doesn't make it any easier, though." Hesitantly, he glanced at her. "I have new linens and curtains for after we paint."

"Okay, well—"

"I kissed you last night."

God, this infuriating man. "You said that already." Many times.

"You have yet to comment on it."

Stomping her foot and screaming at the top of her lungs wouldn't send the right message, but it might make her feel better. "What are you looking for? A blog post? A tweet?"

"Zoe." The vulnerability in his eyes made it damn near impossible to keep her defense in place. "How about acknowledgement it happened?"

As if her lips would ever forget. "It happened. We were both there. Honestly, I'm trying to wrap my head around it. Are you happy now?"

He opened his mouth as if to speak and quickly shut it again. After a long, intense stare down, he finally sighed. "Happy is not the term I'd use."

Did that mean he hadn't liked kissing her? That...sucked. Because she'd more than enjoyed it. It had left her with more questions than answers, plus a boatload of guilt, but she'd sure enjoyed it. "What term would you use then?"

Up went his brows in a clear you-asked-for-it. "Frustrated. Aroused. Confused. Tense. Unnerved. Turned on. Take your pick."

Holy, holy cow. "Ditto," she whispered. And since someone had to use their mind for common sense purposes, she looked away and refocused on the task at hand. "I have a plan."

His eyes narrowed to slits. "Does it require the need for bail money?"

"Sadly, no." She pursed her lips. "Though I do always aim to behave in a manner that would render it impossible for me to run for county office. Alas, my current idea doesn't entail anything illegal."

"I hesitate to ask, but go ahead. Tell me."

Such a comedian. "Why don't you and I paint the living room tonight? We don't have softball tomorrow because of Fourth of July this coming week. I will visit Mama in the morning and come over here after. You can then handle the guestroom and I'll do your bedroom."

Every muscle in his body went rigid. His questioning gaze seared into hers. "You want to redecorate my bedroom? By yourself? Why?"

Because this was where the most intimate moments with Heather had been. If he was part of the revamping process, he might not be able to fully move on from the memories created in this space. Since that was his ultimate goal, Zoe's way worked best. "Having you walk into a new room and seeing it with fresh eyes will give you what you need most. Change."

Shoulders sagging, affection in his eyes, he stepped forward. "Zoe—"

The oven timer beeped. Thank God.

Grinning, she walked around him. "Feed me, slave driver."

Chapter 12

A patio table and a citronella candle flickering between them, Drake scanned the dark yard in an attempt not to stare at Zoe. A humid breeze relieved the sticky heat and the trickle from the nearby riverbed mingled with the chirp of crickets. Birch and sequoia leaves crackled, their branches creating shadows within the shadows.

She'd been at his house for an hour, and already his nerves were frayed. It had started with her *may I come in* request. As if she hadn't already burrowed under his skin. How much farther could she go? Then the chaos continued straight through redecorating discussions and into dinner. Outside. On his patio. Under the stars. Hell, there were even fireflies winking in the distance.

Her outfit hadn't helped. Jeans that had more holes than denim and a skin-tight white T-shirt which left nothing to the imagination. And yeah, he was starting to imagine all sorts of things. It wasn't simply her clothes or the way she wore them that had his pulse thrumming.

He'd seen her in something similar, though it had been too long. Her painting gear, as she'd named it. Memories of her wielding a brush over canvas floated around in his head and stuck. Christ, she had such talent. He hadn't seen her work in years, other than manning her caricature booth at town events. Which was not her expertise, nor were the cartoon murals she'd done on the clinic walls.

Zoe's niche was naturist scenes, but with a twist. A play on surrealism, she claimed. She'd paint a field of grass and then throw in something crazy—such as an ant tea party. Or a brick wall teeming with vines and a ghost sitting on top. His favorite to date had been a summer pond with tiny people crouched on the lily pads instead of frogs.

"You can still cook well, Drake. This is really good."

His gaze shifted to hers, and he smiled. She'd eaten all the meatloaf, scalloped potatoes, and green beans. "Thanks. It's been awhile. Kind of stupid cooking for just one. You know, Mom taught all three of us how to use the kitchen."

Zoe nodded, dropping her chin in her palm. The candlelight changed her hazel eyes to more of a mossy green. A hum from her throat had his gaze dipping to the long, smooth column of her neck. "She wanted well-rounded boys. Nothing wrong with that. Though the cooking part didn't really stick with Cade."

Laughing, he rubbed his jaw. "No, I don't suppose it did."

Her chest expanded with a deep breath, and down came her walls. He watched as, little by little, her expression opened to reveal the affection he'd always known was underneath. The heart of her she proved with actions, but rarely spoke aloud. He didn't know what caused it, but he'd kill to keep her this way.

Nudging his plate aside, he sat back. "What's with the faintly amused smile?"

"Nothing." She shrugged, her gaze studying him, smile never slipping. "Haven't heard you laugh much lately. I missed the sound."

"Right back at you." Twofold.

"Well," she drawled, rising to her feet. "Now that you put me in a food coma, let's start painting."

She reached for their dishes and he stopped her with a hand on her forearm. Stacking the plates, he bumped his chin toward the sliding door. Following her inside, he set the dishes in the sink, put away the leftovers, and joined her in the living room.

Hands on her hips, she glanced around. "Do you have new pictures in mind?"

He'd taken down the photos on the mantle as well as the art Heather had chosen for the walls. That was about as far as he got. "Not really. Figured I'd go through photo albums." Heather had a few of Zoe's older pieces up in the hallway, but they were too small for this room. "Do you still have that lily pad painting?"

She blinked at him.

"What?"

Abruptly, she bent and retrieved a roll of blue border tape from the bag by the paint cans. "I'm just surprised you remember it. That was, like, eight years ago."

What was with her sudden backbone? "It's my favorite."

Adjusting her ponytail, she stared at him. "I have it in storage. It's yours if you want it. Probably would look better in the guestroom upstairs, though. The color scheme matches."

Slowly, he nodded, not understanding her defensive posture or the way she looked like he'd hauled off and slugged her. "Does it bother you to give it away?"

"Nope."

"Then it upsets you I want to hang it?"

"Nope."

He frowned, needing an inch from her and getting zilch. "Remember when I said I never know what to say to you? This is one of those times. Give me some direction because I obviously did something wrong." She wasn't exactly pissed off, per se, but her rigid shoulders and utter avoidance of meeting his gaze at least gave him an inkling to her mood.

Unwrapping cellophane from the tape roll, she walked to the garbage and tossed out the clear wrap. Head bowed, she returned, brows worried in thought. "You've never shown interest in my paintings before. You don't have to offer to display one for the sake of being nice. I was only asking about the walls because—"

"Zoe."

"No, I'm serious. You—"

"Zoe. I mean this as kindly as possible, but shut up." He walked toward her until they stood toe to toe, then dipped his face to look in her eyes. "My mother has two of your pieces hanging in her living room. Cade has three, Flynn and Gabby one each, at least. I have a couple upstairs in the hall."

"Yes, but Heather wanted them." Her tentative tone had his eyes narrowing.

"As did I, Zoe. You used to show Heather all your work the second the canvas dried. Your talent blows me away. The detail, the imagination. So why the hell wouldn't I want to display them, too?"

Eyes round, she stared at him. Not one muscle shifted, nor did she seem to be breathing.

And hell. Her eyes got a little misty. Not enough to well or for tears to form, but he'd obviously touched a sore spot. Hand to God, how had she not known her art left him speechless? Maybe he hadn't been supportive enough, or perhaps he'd just not known what to say, but damn if he wouldn't make himself clear.

She swallowed with what looked like effort and turned away.

He stuck his fingers in the back pockets of her jeans and hauled her against him. She let out a barely perceptible gasp and white-knuckled the tape, pressing the roll to her chest. He'd never had her at his mercy, never thought it was possible. Yet she sank against him as if unable or unwilling to shift away. Desire coiled low in his gut, but he had a point to make first.

Resting his chin on her shoulder, he brushed his nose against the soft skin under her ear. He breathed in her lavender scent and closed his eyes. "I'm not requesting your art because I feel obligated or because we're friends or out of a sense of being polite. I want to look around my house and see pieces of you here right along with my family, with Heather. You've been a part of my life since birth, Zoe. You're important to me."

"Damn you, Drake." The broken, whispered curse showed just how affected she was by him, even if her body weren't sending him signals.

Hell if he had any idea where to go from here, but at least he knew now they were in the same book and not just two volumes sharing shelf space.

"I often find myself damning you, as well."

Her breathy laugh puffed like smoke. "I'd like to point out that you're touching my ass again."

Unable to help it, he chuckled and rested his chin on top of her head. "I willingly admit to it this time." Centimeter by centimeter, he slowly withdrew his fingers from her back pockets, enjoying the slight curve of her and how her breath caught with the intimate touch. "If we want to get this room done tonight, we should get started."

He'd much rather explore the sizzling chemistry, but a breather was in order and his furniture was coming tomorrow. Time to think wasn't a half bad plan either. It felt like they'd gone from zero to holy shit in under a week.

Three hours later, they had two coats of burgundy paint on the walls and most of the mess cleaned up. He'd caught her glancing at him several times and snuck his own peeks when she'd been occupied. Pretty hard not to with the way she moved in those jeans. Fluid grace and tempting as sin. Like right now as she washed her hands at his kitchen sink, her back to him and hips swaying. Cute and seductive in the same breath.

He'd set his iPod to random with Ed Sheeran's *Photograph* song currently playing. The lyrics about love healing and hurting and being the only thing the singer knew were hauntingly similar to Drake's own mindset. And reminded him not to let Gabby load her sappy songs anymore.

Whistling for the dogs, he let them outside. When he came back in, Zoe was on the second to top rung of the stepladder, peeling border tape off the ceiling beam joists. Her arms were stretched over her head, her white tee riding up to expose a patch of midriff.

He walked through the kitchen toward the living room. "You should've waited for me. You're a little short for that task."

"I prefer vertically challenged, and I think I've got all of it."

He grabbed the base of the ladder just in case as she twisted to pull off the last strip. Her shirt rose higher, and his gaze landed on her taut stomach above the low-rise of her jeans. Circled around her belly button was a tattoo ring of tiny purplish-blue flowers. As the breath trapped in his lungs, he lifted his hand and pressed it over the ink.

She teetered and plopped her rearend on the top of the ladder. The tape fell from her fingers to the floor like ribbon.

He should've asked if it was okay, should've not startled her while in a precarious position. But his heart pounded and his airway was blocked. Without thinking, he grabbed her hips and shifted her down two rungs until she stood in front of him, her belly at eye level. Gently, he lifted her shirt and traced the flowers with his fingertips. Her stomach quivered and concaved at his touch.

He cleared his throat. "When did you get this tattoo?"

She looked down at him, her expression swiveling between turned on and nervous rabbit. "A few years ago." She paused. "They're—"

"Forget-me-nots. They were Heather's favorite flower."

"Yes." She bit her lip, trembling under his fingertips as he stroked. Her chest rose and fell in rapid succession. "Drake?"

Christ, the way she said his name. Breathy, needy, and with traces of apprehension he was certain he'd never heard in her tone before. Well, not until recently, anyhow. He had a sudden urge to genuflect every time she uttered it.

Tearing his gaze from hers, he refocused on the ink. This was one of her many tattoos, and each one seemed to have its own motive. He just couldn't pin down what or why or if there was a pattern. Cause and effect played around in his consciousness, but no definitive answers were forthcoming, only suspicion. It was time he asked.

He lifted his gaze to hers while splaying his fingers over her soft skin. A charge zinged from the contact and radiated up his arm. "Why did you get this tattoo in particular?"

She stared at him like she was trying to decide if she should respond or as if she were choosing her words with extreme care. "It was a way to keep her with me. A reminder to forget *her* not."

Slayed him. Every time, she slayed him. He closed his eyes for a beat to collect himself before sliding his hands around her waist and easing her down another rung until they were eye-to-eye. Drake visited Heather's grave once a week, and every Sunday for the past four years, a fresh-cut bouquet of forget-me-nots were set in the in-ground vase by her headstone. Didn't matter the season, they were always there like clockwork. He'd figured it had been Zoe all along, but the confirmation had his sinuses prickling.

Zoe, with her heart too big for her chest and eyes too big for her face, had used her body as a canvas to tell stories. Map memories.

He stroked her ribs with his thumbs, then lifted her hand and kissed her inner wrist. "I understand what the paintbrush tattoo implies." Her art, of course, but he didn't get the symbol on her other wrist. Lifting it, he kissed that spot, too. "What does the shooting star mean?"

Again with the should-I-answer expression. "It's a meteor, actually. The star was more aesthetically pleasing to look at."

Meteor? A memory fizzled as his gaze wandered.

Once, somewhere around senior year of college, he and Heather were supposed to double-date with Zoe. Except her partner had blown her off and Heather had gotten the flu. Drake and Zoe had wound up at Redwood Ridge Park with a cheap bottle of wine and watched the meteor shower. They'd gotten drunk and he'd laughed his ass off listening to her make fun of the other gazers during the once in a lifetime cosmic event.

Wait. She'd tattooed a memory of him? Or was she referring to something else, making him the most self-centered jackass this side of the Klamath?

She bit her lip. "That was a pretty great night. My date abandoned me, but it wasn't a total wash. We had fun." She bowed her head. "You asked me to go ring shopping with you as we were heading home."

That's right. He had. They'd gone the next day and, thanks to Zoe, he'd found the perfect engagement ring for Heather.

Filling his lungs with much needed oxygen, he wrapped his fingers around the back of her neck. He teased her nape where the sun and black circle were inked, earning a shiver. "And what does the sun tattoo mean?"

Closing her eyes, she shook her head. A second passed and she opened them, her gaze heavenward. "When I was a girl, my mom and I watched the solar eclipse. I was maybe eight years old, and when it was over, she said, *I love you so much, my love blocked out the sun*." She laughed, distant and sad. "I was young enough to believe she was telling the truth, that she'd caused the eclipse. Still, it was Mama's creative way of showing she loved me."

Strike him now. Zoe hadn't just collected pieces of her past. She'd inked her favorite good memories, and he was one of them. Yet, there weren't that many, considering. Four, to be exact. Unless… "Do you have any other tattoos?"

Her wistful smile fell and she glanced over his shoulder in utter avoidance. "Just one. It's…um. Not easily viewed." She tapped the front area near her pelvic bone by her hip.

Wanting to peel her clothes off to see for himself, he cupped her jaw instead. "What is it a picture of?" He found himself needing to know so badly his head ached. Not only out of curiosity, but to get an inside glimpse of her. Thirty-one years old, and she had only five great memories worth making permanent?

"That's on a need to know basis."

He almost laughed. Or cried. "Fine. I'll find a way to get you to tell me." Or show him. Have mercy, yes. He paused, staring at her, wondering who'd taken over his body and turned him into a flirt.

Her eyebrows rose in challenge. "Oh, really? Methinkst the paint fumes have gone to your head."

Something had, but it wasn't fumes. He thought about keeping his trap shut on the matter, but he wanted her to know. "*You've* gotten in my head." And his chest. And under his skin. And…well, everywhere, to be honest. Crazy thing, he wasn't minding so much.

There went the pulse in her neck. "Like an aneurism?"

Exactly. Impossible to remove and ready to blow at any given time.

He stepped onto the bottom rung, pinning her to the ladder and thrusting them so close the holy ghost couldn't wedge space in between. Gripping the tread above her head, he brought his lips within hovering distance.

She fisted the front of his shirt and let out an uneven breath. Lids heavy, pupils dilated to oh-my-God, she glanced at his mouth. "You don't play fair."

"I'm not playing at all."

Gingerly, he kissed a corner of her mouth like he'd done their first time, then moved to the other corner and did the same. He grazed his lips across hers, feeling her out, savoring, but she had other ideas.

With a fistful of his hair, she tilted her head and licked the seam of his mouth, begging him to open in compliance. As if he had a choice. And the second his lips parted, things went from hot to scorching to singed with one stroke of her tongue. She moaned, or he groaned. Too difficult to tell, really, because both their chests rumbled and the pounding rush of blood roaring in his ears made any sound obsolete.

He'd all but forgotten the intimacy of kissing. How it could make or break a budding romance. Tell a story. Demonstrate what one person felt for another when words weren't manageable. And Zoe wasn't just combustible energy and passion. She was tender heartbreak. Repairer of rifts. A satiating balm. The erratic beat of a wounded heart. The very caretaker for his soul. All in one tight little bundle of restrained misery masked as content.

His little Zoe was starving for so many things, and he desired nothing more than to give them. Needing to touch her, he unfurled his fingers from the ladder and slid his hand under the back of her shirt, his mouth never leaving hers. He caressed the curve of her spine and kissed his way over her jaw to her neck. Lavender and warm woman assaulted his sensory into overload.

Cupping her perfect jean-clad rearend, he hauled her closer. She wrapped one leg around his, placing the throbbing erection behind his sweats in alignment with her heat. Slamming his eyes shut, he opened his mouth wide against the tendon in her neck. Her head fell back, offering him better access, and he fought for middle ground.

They had to slow down. Somehow.

He must've paused because she lifted her head and looked at him, her lids at half-mast. Her mouth was swollen from their kiss, and something close to pride shoved around in his chest.

"Tell me about the tattoo." Hell. He was supposed to be taking a common sense break, but his mouth hadn't gotten the memo.

"No." A wicked, wicked grin started in her eyes, formed on her lips, and he waved a white flag.

"I give." He sighed and kissed her forehead. Stepping off the ladder, he took her hand and helped her down.

Chapter 13

Large crate secured in both hands, Zoe rang Drake's doorbell with her elbow and blew the hair out of her eyes. After she'd visited Mama this morning, Zoe had run to the store to pick up a few things based off her conversation with Drake last night. A bead of sweat, courtesy of the warm day, trailed down her back while she waited.

The door swung open and he stood there in a loose pair of black nylon shorts and a red tee. He surveyed her load and lifted his brows. "What's that?"

"It's called heavy. Give me a hand."

Without a word, he took the crate as if it weighed nothing and held the door for her with his foot. Once inside, he set the package down.

The dogs came running in, tails wagging. Plopping to the floor to show them some love, she cooed and scratched their ears. "Who's the biggest, sweetest furbabies? Yes, you are."

Drake crossed his arms. "Do you talk like this around infants, too? It's disturbing."

"I've talked to animals the same way all my life. Identical to how I converse with men—slowly and with as few syllables as possible." She hugged the dogs, getting kisses in return. "Isn't that right?"

"I'll try not to take offense," he drolled.

"Your choice." Rising, she brushed the tufts of dog hair from her clothes and glanced around. She nodded her approval. "I like it."

The furniture had been delivered, and the dark beige of the sectional and chair went well with the burgundy walls and stone fireplace. The tables matched the beams. The kitchen table looked like a polished black angular design that seated eight. All he needed were some pictures.

"Yeah?" He took in the room, then looked at her with a warm smile. "Totally different, isn't it?"

"That's what you were after." She brushed the hair off her cheek. "If you look in my car, there's a surprise for you."

His expression turned skeptical. "The kind that will bite or poison me?"

"I can do those things, but I'm right here. I think you're safe."

"Right." He disappeared outside and came back holding the eleven-by-ten framed canvas of her lily pad painting. Kicking the door shut, he eyed the print, a smile curving his lips. "Forgot how cool this actually was." Glancing up, his grin widened and the dimple emerged. "It's awesome, Zoe."

Heat infused her cheeks, but she nodded. "Thank you."

Setting the painting aside, he nudged the crate with his foot. "Is this for upstairs?"

"Yep."

"Going to tell me what it is?"

"Nope. But you can carry it up to your room for me." She batted her eyelashes and grinned with feigned innocence.

"That look is more disturbing than the baby-speak." With a grunt, he hefted the crate once more and ascended the stairs.

She followed and did a double-take as he set the load on his bed. He'd painted his bedroom. Everything else was exactly the same, but he'd done the walls and ceiling in the dark gray-blue tone he'd picked.

"I couldn't sleep."

She turned to face him, disappointed he'd started without her. "This was supposed to be my deal."

"I know, but it didn't sit right having you do the whole room." He cleared his throat and gave her a tentative side-glance. "Are you mad?"

"Are you still standing?"

"Good point." He rubbed his neck. "The guestroom is done, too."

He gave insomnia a new name. "Did you sleep at all?"

"Couple hours." He jerked his chin toward the door. "Do you want to see the other room?"

"Sure."

She followed him down the hall and stopped over the threshold. She'd been right. It looked like a completely different room and bore no resemblance to the awful hospice situation that had plagued it before. The army-ish green was a color Heather never would've chosen and went with the leaf design quilt on the full-size bed. Still, more could be done. But she'd tackle that when he left.

"Okay, downstairs with you." At his blank expression, she waved her hand in dismissal. "I've got stuff to do. You leave."

"What more is there to do?"

She pushed him toward the exit. "Out. And don't come upstairs unless I tell you it's okay."

In the hall, he planted his feet. "Zoe." He sighed and tucked a piece of hair behind her ear. He fingered the purple strands, gaze trained on the motion. "I hate to say this, and I'll probably regret it, but I like it when you're bossy."

Oh, she could do so much with that little tidbit. "You don't say."

Amusement in his eyes, he pressed his lips together in an obvious attempt to fight a grin. "Already regretting it."

She hummed. "More on that later."

With a nod, his smile slipped. "Fine." He kissed her forehead, completely surprising her with the softness of the act, and went downstairs.

Heading back to Drake's bedroom, she locked the door behind her and surveyed the situation. The room was easily twenty-by-twenty with a walk-in closet and adjoining bath on one end and a patio door to a balcony on the other. He'd certainly saved her a lot of work, but the place still had too many traces of the old space.

She emptied the contents of the crate onto his bed and collected the photos from the dresser, setting them in the now empty tote. From there, she grunted and growled her way through moving the ginormous king-size bed to the opposite wall, and then did the same with the dresser. Brushing her hands together, she nodded. Much better.

After taking down the old curtains and putting up the new ones he'd bought, she set out the white birch candles she'd found at the store and arranged them on the dresser. Much, much better.

Last night, she'd thought about bringing him another of her paintings to hang on the wall, but decided a mural would totally transform the room. Nothing crazy or monstrous, just a few white birch trees to match the candles. Besides, those trees were her specialty and she could whip them out pretty fast.

With a pencil, she sketched out one on either side of the dresser, making sure the leaves went up onto the ceiling, and then did another to the right of the patio door in the corner. Mixing paint, she got lost in the act of creating, losing herself in the bend and flow of the brush, the scent of acrylic, and the merge of color.

She had no idea how long she'd been at it, but after she finished, Drake's laugh caught her attention. She walked to the balcony door and gazed down at his yard.

The dogs were running around, chasing each other and a ball. Drake had taken off his shirt, and a light sheen of sweat glistened his olive skin. Sinewy muscle shifted as he moved in his easy athletic grace. God, the man was a sight. Six pack abs, ropey forearms, slight bulge of bicep, thick thighs, narrow waist.

It was the genuine smile on his face that had her attention most of all. He'd been like that when he was younger. Not as daredevil as Cade or carefree as Flynn, but Drake had an allure all his own. Quiet confidence, avid compassion, dry humor. And a killer grin. Her chest cavity expanded just seeing it again, like an old friend who'd been away.

Moses, his German Shepherd, was six years old and had been Drake's trusty companion through some dark times. He loved that dog and took it nearly everywhere with him. Cyprus, the Pitbull rescue, was only about two and had twice as much energy. They seemed to get along great. They listened to Drake's commands as he teased them with the ball.

There. Yes, *there*. Drake laughed again, this time throwing his head back. She sighed in utter contentment. His black hair had navy hints in the sun and a slight wave toward the ends. She'd loved the soft thickness of it in her hands as they'd kissed. How she'd missed this side of him.

With regret, she moved away from the balcony and tossed out the leftover paint. She brought the tote into the hallway and stopped outside the guestroom. On instinct, she rearranged the furniture in this room, too, then hung the painting to finish things off. Happy with her work and that he'd gotten the change he'd needed, Zoe headed downstairs and washed her hands.

On the island counter were a couple of photo albums and the old mismatched frames from the living room mantle. It looked like he'd already picked out what pictures he'd wanted, so she set them in the frames for him. Cade and Avery kissing at their wedding. Flynn and Gabby sharing a chair in her living room—her mid-laugh, him nuzzling her neck. A great shot of his parents on their front porch. Avery's daughter, Hailey, holding her yellow lab puppy, Seraph. The three boys together by the riverbed when Drake was roughly ten years old.

And...Zoe. A close-up picture of her with a paintbrush in her mouth, a plethora of colorful splatter on her face, eyes wide in mischief. Heather had taken it at Zoe's old apartment the year she and Drake had gotten engaged. Heather had stopped by to hang out, and Zoe had been finishing a painting.

Zoe swallowed past the lump in her throat, missing her friend so bad she thought she'd crack in two. She'd gotten over Heather's death, had moved past it, but sometimes a punch of longing would hit out of nowhere and it was just like the day she'd died all over again. Sighing, she looked for a picture of Heather, but the only one he'd set out was of her and Zoe eating a popsicle in Mama's backyard when they were kids.

Moving into the living room, she dug through the crate and found a picture of the whole gang, minus Avery, outside the clinic, taken the year before Heather died. Avery hadn't moved to town yet. Zoe had told Drake not to erase Heather from the house completely, and this was a non-couple photo, plus it had Brent in it.

Zoe arranged the photos on the mantle, put away the albums, and then stood in front of the fireplace looking at his memories.

The back door opened and closed. Dog nails skittering across the floor followed. Cyprus and Moses nudged her leg, and she absently petted them. Drake had put his shirt back on. A crime, that.

He glanced at her and then the photos. "That's my favorite picture of you. Cade calls that your shit's-gonna-hit-the-fan face."

She laughed. "I remember when Heather took that. She kept bugging me to finish painting so we could watch *Practical Magic*. Again."

Blowing out a sigh, he glanced around. "I can throw burgers on the grill for dinner."

Guess he wanted her to stay. "You cooked last night. I can find something to whip together. Why don't you look upstairs while I hunt in your fridge?"

He shoved his hands in his pockets. "Don't you think you've done enough work?"

"Said the man who stayed up all night painting." She crossed her arms. "Why couldn't you sleep, anyway?" He'd had bouts of restlessness after Heather died, but he'd been better lately. According to him, he'd get at least six hours a night.

Expression stoic, he stared at her. His gaze drifted over her hair, her face, and finally met hers. "I couldn't stop thinking about you."

The air seeped from her lungs. "Oh." Was it hot in here? Yes, it was. Or perhaps he hadn't meant that as a good thing. Were they moving too fast? They'd only kissed a couple times, but last night involved hands and tongue and... It was definitely hot in here. She shouldn't be doing this with him anyway. She'd helped him with the house, it was time to back away. "I should go home. The stuff I removed from your room is in that crate. You can take it to Heather's folks or store it. Up to you—"

"I kept thinking about how you felt pressed against me and the wild way you made my heart pound. Honestly, Zoe, I didn't think the organ worked anymore. Then I kissed you and now I can't shut off the switch you flipped."

Heaven help her. She spun on her heel and made haste for the kitchen. "I'll get dinner. You check out the upstairs."

His quiet laugh disappeared as he climbed the staircase.

She stuck her head in the freezer to cool down, then searched his fridge. He had the makings for quesadillas, so she started dicing chicken and grilling it in a skillet. She spread shredded cheddar and chicken inside tortillas, browned them evenly on both sides, and kept going until she had a decent stack, then cut them into wedges. Finished, she set out salsa, sour cream, and paper plates.

Except Drake hadn't come back downstairs. It had been about thirty minutes since she'd started cooking. It didn't take that long to glance at two rooms.

She eyed the dogs sitting obediently at her feet. "Think he took a nap?" Concern gelling in her stomach, she headed upstairs. Maybe he was rearranging things or something. Perhaps taking a shower.

But when she got to his bedroom, he was doing neither of those things. Instead, he stood smack in the center of the room between his bed and the dresser, not one muscle moving. Hands at his sides, head cocked, he remained still as stone with his back to her as if completely unaware of where or even who he was.

Worry ratcheted to an ulcerative pain. "Drake?" Guilt shoved around in her chest and clamped her airway. He hated the change. She'd broken him. She was supposed to be helping, and she'd done the opposite.

Slowly, he turned to face her. Panting shallow breaths, he shook his head. His forehead creased, his jaw opened, and... His eyes were red-rimmed. Shiny. *With tears.* Looking shell-shocked, his gaze pleaded with her for something. Anything.

"Shit," she breathed. "Hey, it's okay. We'll change it all back. I promise. Easy as—"

With a violent shake of his head, he made a sound like a trapped animal and ate the distance between them in three steps. Hauling her against him, he hugged her hard enough to empty her lungs and lift her feet clean off the floor.

"Zoe..." He cupped the back of her head and buried his face in her neck. The arm around her back cinched. "Christ, thank you. It doesn't even look like the same room. The guestroom, too." His breath hitched, ruffling her hair. "Thank you."

Unsure what to do, she rested her cheek against his temple and wove her hands through his hair. He shook for the briefest of moments, and she knew he was fighting more tears. She stayed silent, rubbing his back and massaging his scalp and letting him collect himself. Meanwhile, her soul bled out and she was pretty sure she'd fallen face-first for him the rest of the way.

He kissed her cheek, her temple, her forehead, where he rested his own against hers. "I'm supposed to be the one taking care of you."

She eased away to look in his now dry eyes. "What does that mean?"

"When she died, Heather made me promise to take care of you." His smile ripped a hole in her heart with the napalm of tenderness. "I used to think you were too independent for that, but I was wrong. You were too busy taking care of me for me to notice I'd neglected my promise."

Sweet Lord. Closing her eyes, she fought to resurrect the strength he thought she owned.

Heather had made Zoe promise that very thing about Drake the day before she'd passed away. To take care of him. And in her typical best friend fashion, it had been Heather's way of telling Zoe, telling Drake, that she was okay with them being together. As friends or as more, she'd subtly given her blessing to two people who had been nowhere near ready to hear it. The knowledge didn't erase all the other why-nots to get involved with him, but it eased Zoe's guilt to a degree.

Opening her eyes, she smiled. "Friends take care of each other. There's no score sheet here."

He cupped her cheek, ran the pad of his thumb across her bottom lip. Then he kissed her. Soft, sweet, and with total abandon. He explored her mouth until there was no cavern unchartered and no breath left to collect herself. And then he did it again.

"Drake," she murmured when he pulled back. They needed a garden hose to cool down. "First, you're crushing my boobs, which are one of my best features. And two, the chicken quesadillas are probably cold."

With a quiet laugh, he set her down. "I agree on your first point and let's remedy the second. I have this little thing called a microwave."

Chapter 14

I want to date you.

Biting her thumbnail, Zoe sat on her bed, freshly showered, and stared at her phone. Drake had texted five minutes before, and she was still trying to formulate a response. Tonight, once again, he'd proven their first kiss hadn't been a fluke. Or their second or third. She'd meant to put a stop to what was happening between them or, at the very least, be honest with him about expectations.

But damn. He made her weak. So, so very weak.

Screw it. She thumbed her response and hit Send. *I don't date.*

The icon indicated he was typing. She looked at Cotton next to her on the bed. "He's going to talk me into it. Just watch. You need to help me be strong."

Cotton rolled over and purred in response.

Ever? Why not? I've seen you out with other men.

She smacked a hand to her forehead. *Out, yes. Date, no. Dating leads to relationships. I don't have time.* It was a cop-out answer, but rooted in truth.

What's wrong with a relationship? If it's right, you can make time.

Damn him. No guy, no matter the circumstances, would be right. Five years ago, if there had been no Heather, this would be a non-issue. But things were different now. Relationships meant marriage conversations and wedding bells and baby showers. Things she couldn't have. Especially with Drake.

Her lack of response must've prompted him to keep trying. *Go out with me.*

Pressing her lips together, she rubbed the knot in her chest. This was exactly what she didn't want. She'd rather gnaw off her right arm than hurt him. *Please, don't push this. Let's just keep things where they are for now.* Another cop-out. She sucked.

Talk to me, Zoe. I want a reason.

She screeched in frustration. "Men are stupid, barbaric creatures." Cotton looked at her through slanted, unamused eyes. "Except you, dear cat." Zoe sighed. None of her motives would be something Drake would understand. I can't.

Since when does Zoe Hornsby have that word in her vocabulary? "Oh, he's good." Nice try. The typing icon whirled. *I. Want. To. Date. You.* He was killing her. *Look, I'm serious. I care about you and you're the last person I want to hurt. But I can't. I'm just the good time. Take it or leave it.* That had been her justification in allowing things to go as far as they had. That she'd make it clear to him she was the good-enough-for-now girl. The rebound.

She sat for ten minutes, but no more texts came. She'd either royally pissed him off or she'd done the inexcusable and hurt him. Sick to her stomach, she rubbed her forehead and fought tears. She thought she could help him move on and get a little slice of Heaven for herself via memories to take with her when it ended. But maybe she should just avoid all contact with him until he found a woman who could give him what she couldn't.

God, fate just loved to heckle in her face. Tease her with the guy she'd always wanted and then issue a time limit. Taunt her with old dreams and wishes, then remind her it couldn't be forever. Giving in to the pain, she flopped on the bed. Chest tight, she cried in her pillow like she'd done at seventeen. Pathetic.

As she was about to turn out the light, a pounding came from the front door. She and her cat exchanged a look, then Zoe rose, wiped her eyes, and padded down the hall. Standing in her dark living room, she eyed the door. Redwood Ridge didn't have much crime, but she wasn't about to play games with the odds.

More pounding rattled the door. "I have a key, Zoe, and I'll use it. Let me in."

Drake. Holy hell. What now?

After a silent few moments, she backed up, deciding to ignore him. Maybe he'd think she was asleep and he'd go home.

"I can hear you breathing."

Or not. She crossed her arms. "Go away, Drake."

"Have it your way, honey."

A jingle of the lock and her door swung open. Six feet of pissed off male strode in and kicked the door shut. The shadows in the dark room made him even more ominous as he ate the distance between them. He backed her to the wall and flattened both hands on either side of her head. Dipping his face close to hers, he seethed. Like a caged beast at his limit.

She could count on one hand the number of times she'd seen Alpha Drake out in the open.

"The good time. The good time?" he said so calmly she shivered. "Explain that absurd term. Now."

Both turned on and a little frightened, she stared at him. His chocolate eyes drilled her into place and demanded answers. "It's pretty self-explanatory." His chin dipped, gaze still on hers. Long lashes lowered in a blink and then he was right back to dissecting her expression. "Why would you demean yourself with that phrase? Worse, why would you assume that's all I want from you?"

"Because I know you don't want only fun."

A sudden inhale, and he straightened. "You've been crying."

"Have not."

"Your eyes are red and your lashes are still wet."

"Allergies." She crossed her arms.

He scrubbed his hands over his face and shook his head. "We've never lied to each other. In fact, we've been nothing but brutally honest. You know each and every dark place and horrible thought that's ever been in my head. You've seen me at my absolute worst." He set his hands on his hips, shoulders sagging. "What is going on? Is this about Heather? Your mom?"

"You know what? Yes." Shoving off the wall, she wove around him. "You watched the love of your life die right in front of you after months of slowly fading. Mama is all I have and she's only going to get worse. After everything you've been through, you don't need my baggage. You need to find a woman who can offer the happiness you deserve."

Brows pinched, jaw slack, he shook his head. "First, I didn't just lose my wife. You lost your best friend. And I'd do it all over again because I loved her that much. So would you. It sucked and it was painful, but it was worth it to have her as long as we did." He stepped closer. "Second, your mom is not all you have. She gave up a lot for you and you're doing the same for her, but you are not alone. She is not baggage, mine or yours." He closed the remaining distance and towered over her. His jaw ticked. "And third, I don't want someone else. I want you."

Mary Mother, she couldn't do this. As if she hadn't learned her lesson, she had to go and fall for him again. The last remaining true noble gentleman in existence. And just like the first go around, she couldn't have him this time either.

Frustrated, she spun and paced the living room, keeping the couch between them. She didn't know how to get through to him other than telling the absolute truth. The problem with doing that was Drake would get around it. He'd sacrifice his own needs and desires if he fell for her or thought there was a relationship to build upon. She crossed her arms, facing the window to the quiet street.

He pinched the bridge of his nose. "I don't know where this is going between us, Zoe, if anywhere at all. But you're cutting us off at the pass before we have the chance to find out."

Frozen, she stared off into space. "There's no future." Not for her, not for Mama, and not for Drake if he didn't accept what she was saying.

"You're scared." The shocked tone of his voice had her jerking her gaze to him. "That's it right there. You're scared."

"I'm not afraid of anything." Which wasn't true. She was afraid of everything.

"I used to think that, too. What happened to you?" He ran his fingers across his mouth, down his jaw to his throat. "You used to be a romantic, Zoe. Not the sunshine and rainbows kind like Gabby. The true literary kind who believed in destiny and soul mates. It was apparent in every painting you created. It still is in the way you give a piece of yourself to those you love. What happened to kill that…that hope inside you?"

A dull ache behind her eyes began to grow. The one in her chest she'd had for five years was expanding. "Life happened. I woke up and realized happily ever afters were bullshit created by Hollywood and greeting card companies."

"You don't seriously believe that."

He was right. She didn't. Though it was true on her account, she knew love wasn't bullshit for other people. Her every action all her life had been born from love. Just like the one she was attempting to do now, if he'd only let her.

"Tell that to Cade and Avery, to Flynn and Gabby." He paused, and she knew what he was going to say next. She tried to brace herself and failed. "Go to Heather's grave and tell her that, or look me in the eye and say it to me."

Closing her eyes, she held her breath and wished he'd just go away. She should've had the courage to lie to him back when he'd asked if he was alone in his attraction.

"Look at me." He sighed. "Zoe, honey, look at me."

Turning, she complied. She had two weaknesses, and numero uno was smack in front of her. For more reasons than she could count, she wished Mama was in her right mind so she could talk it out with her. Back then, Zoe had been biding her time to tell her mom about her feelings for Drake. She'd wanted her mom's approval before going forward. But, like most things, she'd believed she could do it tomorrow. But tomorrow came and went, he'd wound up with someone else, and there were no more tomorrows left. His understanding, all too-caring gaze swept over her face. "Be honest with me about this one important thing. Before the hope died, what did you want most in a relationship? What qualities or little nuances were you seeking from a partner?"

Having no idea where he was going with this, she rubbed her forehead. For the sake of honesty, she'd judged all couples on Drake and Heather. Habit, she supposed. To give him a true answer, she'd have to combine what she'd witnessed from them with longing of her own. What was the harm in telling him? It would change nothing.

She bit her lip. "I guess it didn't matter what he looked like, but handsome wouldn't hurt. He'd have to have a deep appreciation for sarcasm and a good sense of humor. Family would have to be everything to him. More organized than me, but not anal." She thought about her dreams before life stole them, and shrugged. "Marriage and kids. No picket fence. Instead, sloppy picnics and snowball fights and enough passion to sustain an energy crisis."

He was concentrating so hard she nearly fumbled. Expression tight, he nodded. "Go on."

With a sigh, she raised her hand and let it drop. "He wouldn't mind cuddling on the couch when I'm sick or afraid to hold my hand in public. Having a guy who knows I'm the only thing in his orbit, like waking up and his first thought is to reach for me or kiss me good morning. He'd appreciate my need to be alone when I paint, but he'd quietly watch me from a doorway because he likes looking at me."

Hell, it had been so long since she'd thought about these things that melancholy settled in her bones. "He'd never forget my birthday and would know I'd want a gift not store-bought. Kiss my forehead to diffuse my temper or laugh when I'm on a tirade." She worried her brows, a single longing deep in her subconscious floating to mind. "He'd...write me poetry."

Drake stilled, his gaze penetrating. "Poetry?"

"Don't look at me like that. Most of the greatest poets were men. Yeats, Browning, Hemingway." She lifted her brows. "You wrote poetry for Heather."

His jaw worked a grind. "She told you that?"

"She told me everything. Don't be embarrassed."

"I'm not. It's just such a...private thing." He rubbed his neck. "I haven't done it in years. Wrote a few after she died. I don't even think my brothers know I used to dabble."

Facing the window once more, she swallowed. "They were good, your poems." She could feel his gaze on her, but she was too tired and too gutted to look at him.

He cleared his throat. "The guys you've been with, did any of them do those things on your list?" When she didn't answer, he rubbed his chest. "None of them? Not one item?"

Nope. Why bother when she wasn't the girl they'd bring home to meet the family or the one who'd last longer than fling status? It would've been nice, though, if just once she'd had her hand held in public. So simple an act.

Whatever. She rolled her eyes.

"Fine." He nodded. "That's what you'll get."

"What?" She whirled on him, but he was heading toward the door.

He paused with his hand on the knob. "I'll give you what they didn't."

Clenching her fists, she huffed. "Drake, you're not listening to me."

"You got that right." His brows rose in challenge with a determined set to his jaw. "Here's the thing, Zoe. As far back as my memory goes, you're there. Making me madder than a hatter or laughing my fool ass off, you're there. Picking up my pieces or leaving me to stew, you're there. At some point, I'll need to separate our friendship from this chemistry, but understand me."

He strode toward her and held her chin, tipping it up so she would look at him. "When we're together, when I'm kissing you, touching you… I'm not feeling friendly. And we are going to explore that because you feel it, too. Ergo, I don't give a good goddamn what your excuses are or how hard you push. We owe it to ourselves to see if this is heading anywhere."

Bringing his lips within millimeters of hers, he narrowed his eyes. Tension and desire rolled off him in waves. "Think about this, while we're at it. You're the first woman in four years who's reminded me I'm a man, that I have needs. Remember that little fact when you want to spout about what I deserve."

Before she could blink, he crushed his mouth to hers in a searing, soul-shredding kiss that left her staggering when he pulled away. Once she got her bearings, he was at the door again.

"Have a good night, honey."

Chapter 15

Drake stood off to the side of Cat's wheelchair at the end of the parade route and waited for Zoe to finish talking to the owners of the dogs she'd walked. Each breed had their own little vest with her Doggie Style grooming logo, and had strutted through the festivities like they knew they were the highlight.

His nomination went to Zoe on that account. She wore a sleeveless purple sundress shades lighter than her hair with a hem that hit her mid-thigh. It showed more skin than he could ignore and gave him thoughts that drifted way past impure with this many people around. She had her hair up in a high ponytail, exposing a regal neck he wanted to kiss and nip until she made those breathy sounds she had the other night.

Biting back a groan, he focused elsewhere. With the parade over, townsfolk were vacating the main strip and heading toward the nearby park. Sunlight beat down on the local storefronts and reflected off signs, but it wasn't so hot he couldn't breathe. A nice breeze wafted from the Pacific just on the other side of the grounds. Grilled hotdogs and popcorn scented the air and reminded him he hadn't eaten breakfast. Happy, excited kids ran around with cotton candy and temporary tattoos in true summer fashion.

Speaking of tattoos… Zoe's was driving him insane with curiosity. The one she refused to tell him about and was placed in area number fifty-two of spots he'd like to kiss, just below the patch of skin behind her knee and above the dip in her lower back. Watching her move in that dress, though, was shooting the sweet spot over her collarbone higher up the list.

Damn. He looked at Cat instead. She had her casted leg propped on the foot pedal and a grin on her face. She'd tossed out Tootsie Rolls to the children while he'd pushed her wheelchair in the parade. Seemed like she was having fun. His Aunt Rosa was supposed to be meeting them soon to take Cat back to rehab.

He noted her water bottle was empty. "Are you thirsty? I can hunt up some lemonade."

Cat shook her head, her attention on a group of kids tossing water balloons. Her wistful smile indicated she was enjoying herself. "My little girl loves those things." She pointed to the kids.

He stopped breathing and then snapped out of it. Quickly, he waved to get Zoe's attention. The past year, Cat's memory had lapsed back to a time before Zoe was born. If Cat was remembering Zoe, for however short a time, she'd want to hear it.

Nodding her good-byes, she made her way over. "Hey, Mama. Are you enjoying the nice weather?"

Cat's smile fell and confusion crossed her features. "Yes. What was your name again?"

She knelt in front of her mom's chair. "Zoe. I walked with you in the parade."

"Oh, right." Nodding, she glanced away.

Straightening, Zoe turned to Drake. "Was there something wrong?"

Though his gut sank at the moment past, he forced a smile. "Nothing at all. Thought maybe we could walk around for a bit." He jerked his thumb toward the park.

Before they could get far, Jason jogged over, still wearing his Redwood Ridge firefighter shirt from the parade. He wrapped an arm around Zoe's shoulders. "Loving the outfit, Zoe. You know how to dress to make a guy drool. Want to have a wet T-shirt contest?"

While Drake ground his molars to dust, Zoe laughed. "Naw. With your abs, you'd win."

"Might be a tie." He dropped his arm, but was still too close for Drake's comfort. "Are you going to be at the fireworks tonight?"

"I don't know," she said distractedly. Judging by her confused expression, she'd caught Drake's narrowed gaze. Or the steam coming out of his ears as he was sure there was some. "Maybe."

Jason's grin widened. "I was going to let you play with my glow stick."

Attention properly diverted, she slapped a hand over her face and laughed. "Well, I'll have to take that into consideration. Now, if you'd said sword, it would've been a no-brainer. I'll find you if I hang around."

"Please do." He gave her a one-armed hug and stepped away. "I gotta head out. I'll catch you later, perhaps. Drake, good to see you."

Drake nodded and waited until Jason was out of hearing distance before turning to Zoe. "Does he always flirt with you like that?"

Zoe snorted. "Yes." But her tone indicated it was a ridiculous question. "Started somewhere around third grade. It's like breathing." She tilted her head, suspicion in her eyes. "Jason and I never hooked up, for the record. Never will. We like each other too much." She lifted a finger as if having an afterthought. "Oh, and if Parker comes by and we make sexual jokes about handcuffs, just remember I never dated him either."

Unsure what to say, Drake stared at her while he tried to regulate his blood pressure. Jealousy had never much played a factor in his life, but here he was, standing on a crowded street, ready to kill two of Redwood Ridge's finest.

"You're going to burst a blood vessel. What's going on with you?"

He shoved his hands in his pockets. "I'm not sure I have the words to convey the problem."

Her ah-ha expression indicated she knew precisely his issue. "Try. Open your mouth and let words tumble out."

With a gaze heavenward, he exhaled. "Homicidal thoughts filtered through my mind when he was around you."

She burst out laughing, then quickly tried to cover the act by placing her fingers over her lips. "And why is that?"

Smartass woman. She was either unaware how embarrassing this was for him or she didn't care. He fisted his hands in his pockets. "Because I should be the one flirting with you. And I don't know how."

"I see." With a solemn nod, she sobered. "There's nothing to be jealous about. And anyone can flirt." When he said nothing, she glanced around as if searching for something in particular. "Cade! Come here."

Drake's youngest brother made his way over and exchanged quick pleasantries with Cat. "What's up?"

Zoe crossed her arms. "Flirt with me."

"Uh…" He rubbed his neck. "If this is a ploy to amuse Avery, she's not with me. She took Hailey to find popcorn."

With an eye roll, she waved her hand. "No. I'm proving a point to your brother here. Flirt with me."

"Huh. Okay. Give me a sec, yeah?" He tapped his chin. "I noticed your business name is Doggie Style. I could teach you some other positions." He frowned. "I feel a little dirty saying that to you."

"Bwa ha ha. Not bad. Give me another."

Drake ran his tongue over his teeth.

Hands on his hips, Cade pursed his lips in thought. "Since it's the Fourth of July, why don't we go make some fireworks?"

Zoe's grin only infuriated Drake more. "That was almost as good as

Jason's glow stick comment."

"Damn." Cade smacked his forehead. "Glow stick. Why didn't I think of that?"

"It's okay. You're out of practice." Zoe rubbed her hands together. "Now, do you want to sleep with me after that?"

Cade flinched. "Christ, no."

Zoe curtsied and patted his chest. "Good boy. You were very helpful. Run along now."

Shaking his head, Cade laughed. "Always did love your crazy side, Zoe." After a quick fist bump, he took off.

"See? Easy as that." Her grin nearly dislodged Drake's irritation. Nearly being the operative word. "Oh, come on. Give it a try."

"No."

"Why?"

Determined to shut her up and stop this stupid display, he wrapped an arm around her waist and drew her flush against him. "I'd rather show you what I want to do than talk about it."

Hazel eyes wide in surprise, she parted her lips to, no doubt, protest. He put his mouth there instead.

He sank into her kiss, drugging and as strong as the tide's undercurrent. No matter how sharp her tongue or her wit, her mouth was so damn soft. A delicious little contradiction.

Since they were at a crowded venue, he lifted his head. "How was that as far as flirtations go?"

Her lids slowly lifted. "Not bad."

With a smile against her lips, he brushed his nose with hers. "For the record, I don't care who you flirt with or who does it back, as long as I'm the only one you're kissing."

Someone cleared their throat, and Zoe jumped.

He let her go as she spun to face his Aunt Rosa, who stood next to Cat's wheelchair with a knowing smirk.

"Hello."

"Crap." Zoe smoothed her ponytail. "You didn't see anything, Rosa."

"I absolutely didn't see you kissing Drake. On the street. Right after the parade…" She typed something on her phone, sunlight glimmering so brightly off her unnatural red hair Drake had to squint. "Attaching picture and…there." She looked up. "Totally correct. I saw nothing."

Zoe turned a scary shade of crimson. "I'm going to kill you."

If he had a nickel for every time he heard her say that… Except this time, it was directed at Rosa. "What's wrong?"

"What's wrong?" Zoe's voice hit banshee level. "What's wrong? Your aunt just posted about us. No doubt on Twitter and, if I know her, she probably created a Pinterest board."

Aunt Rosa tsked. "We created the Drake/Zoe board two weeks ago."

Zoe growled. "I told you to leave this alone."

"What's Pinterest?"

Palms to her forehead, she paced away from him and back again. "This is not happening."

Looking unaffected by Zoe's apparent meltdown, Aunt Rosa grinned innocently. Too innocently. "You two run along. I'll take Catherine around for a bit and then back to Pine Crest."

"Am I working today?" Cat pouted. "That stinks."

"Take it down, Rosa. Whatever you posted, just take it down. You're like a geriatric small town version of *Gossip Girl*, and I'm fed up."

As if preparing for a bank heist, Aunt Rosa gripped the handlebars of Cat's wheelchair, spun in the opposite direction, and walked at an extremely brisk pace toward the park.

Zoe stared after them like she was debating the pros and cons of manslaughter.

"Okay." Drake grabbed her hand. "Let's get you a hotdog."

She dug in her heels, tugging back. "What are you doing?"

He tightened his grasp. "I'm holding your hand in public."

At once, she quit fighting and deflated on the spot. "Drake," she said through a weary sigh. "No. It's bad enough your aunt just put who knows what all over the internet. Everyone will see."

"Thus the public part." She stared at him through such tortured eyes his backbone went up. "Since when do you care what people think?"

Closing her lids in a long blink, she bit her lip. "It's not my reputation I'm worried about."

He had a sinking suspicion this tirade went back to the "good time" comment she'd made the other night. And she looked utterly, utterly wrecked. Keeping her hand in his, he stepped in front of her. "Hold my hand and walk to the park *with me*. Get a hotdog *with me*. Watch the fireworks tonight *with me*. Are you sensing the pattern? I chose you. I said I'm not giving up on us until we explore the potential."

"And I told you there is no potential."

Bang head here. "I also believe I said I wasn't listening." Giving her no choice, he headed toward the park.

The rest of the day, she was unusually quiet. She kept her head down and only engaged in social pleasantries when there was no choice. He barely got her to eat one hotdog, no matter how many offers he dispersed for popcorn, cotton candy, or roasted corn. She acted so out of character his gut burned. By the time dusk came and went, he needed a Valium. Townsfolk were setting out blankets for the fireworks and he spotted the area his brothers had staked out. Stopping by a tree, he faced her. "Let me grab us something to drink and we can meet up with the others."

She nodded.

Frustrated, he stood in line at a booth ten people deep and crossed his arms to wait. Muttered conversations chattered around him, but he tuned them out until he surprisingly heard his name. Two women he didn't recognize a few turns ahead of him in line were whispering not so quietly.

"...and with Zoe Hornsby. Can you believe it?"

"I know. She's going to break that poor guy's heart, and he's had his share of grief. To think, she calls herself his friend."

"I wouldn't worry about it. Girls like her don't last long. She's nothing more than a rebound."

"And when that happens, I'll show him what his next wife really looks like."

He ground his jaw as they giggled. Having grown up in Redwood Ridge all his life, he was accustomed to gossip, especially considering his meddling aunts and mother. But what those women in front of him said had been outright cruel.

Far as he knew, everyone loved Zoe. The guys wanted to date her and the women wanted to be her. At least, that's the impression he'd always gotten. He suddenly understood Zoe's detached mood. Was that how she viewed things with him? Like she was the rebound? He didn't believe in that nonsense or the rules of dating. People either liked each other or didn't. There was a spark or there wasn't.

Turning, he looked over his shoulder. Zoe was in the same spot he'd left her, by the tree, arms crossed and avoiding everyone. An unbearable ache spread behind his ribs and took root. She was no one's rebound, good time, or doormat. But did she know that?

He paid for two bottles of water and made his way back to her. Brent and a guy Drake recognized from youth functions was talking to Zoe. She was smiling, at least.

Drake handed her a water. "Everything okay?"

"Sure." Her smile was as genuine as her artificial hair color. "Drake, this is Miles. He works at the rec center."

Drake shook the guy's hand, briefly taking in his short brown wiry hair and Milano skin. His eyes were a focal point of aquamarine. "Good to see you again. Avery said Hailey adores you."

Miles grinned. "The feeling is mutual."

"Brent and Miles are on a date." She wiggled her eyebrows.

Miles' affectionate gaze shifted to Brent. "Our third, actually."

Zoe sighed dreamily and hugged Brent. "I'm so happy for you." She looked at Miles. "Hurt him and I'll maim you ten ways from Sunday."

"Point taken."

Brent cocked his hip. "The others are waiting. You ready?"

They settled on a blanket next to Cade, Avery, Flynn, and Gabby. Zoe tried giving Drake a marginal berth. He leaned over, wrapped an arm around her waist, and hoisted her to deposit her between his legs. She sat stiffly, unmoving.

Drake glanced at Avery. "Where's Hailey?"

"The fireworks are too loud for her." Avery tucked a strand of wavy brown hair behind her ear. "My mom took her home."

"Uh oh." Gabby frowned at her phone. "Um, Zoe..." She passed her the cell, and Drake looked over Zoe's shoulder to the screen.

It was a Twitter app on Redwood Ridge's feed. There was a picture of him and Zoe kissing from earlier. The tweet read: *Our favorite vet is back in action and showing a certain groomer some Animal Attraction.* He mentally rolled his eyes at the play on the clinic name.

Zoe clicked the @ responses, and anger pounded his temples. Most were supportive, but a few were just catty. Again with the rebound comment or bets on how long they'd last.

Before he could say anything, she backed out to the main screen, her hand shaking, and clicked on a red P. The town's profile popped up and he discovered what Pinterest was, which looked like a bunch of photo files to him. She tapped one that said Drake/Zoe. There were a few pictures of them from Cade's wedding, the same one from Twitter, and another when they were perhaps three years old, hanging off a tire swing.

Without a word, she handed the phone back to Gabby and rose to her feet. The entire group's eyes were on her. As if unsure what to do, she rubbed her arm, glanced around, and stepped off the blanket.

She got three feet before his brain connected rational thought to words. "Where are you going?"

She paused, but didn't turn around. "Home. I'll see you at work."

Hell no. He shot to his feet. "I'll take you."

"No, you won't. I'll walk." She kept right on going.

Cade grabbed Drake's arm before he could get anywhere. "Let her go."

Never. He'd never—

Shocked immobile by that first errant thought, he closed his eyes. Guess that was his answer right there. He'd been wondering if their friendship had accounted for his connection to her and if the physical punch was just lust complicating the mix. But no. For him, there was more going on than just simple attraction. And she'd been trying to tap the brakes from day one. Plus, she'd taken off like a bat out of hell first chance she got.

Furious, confused, he glanced at Cade. Calm understanding looked back at him. After a quick scan of the others, Drake found the same. Apologetic, sympathetic, and pleading all around. His anger dissolved, leaving him with an ache between his eyes, a pounding in his chest, and a hollow hole in his gut.

Carefully, he sat back down just as the fireworks began. Booms exploded, thrusting color against the black backdrop of night and winking stars.

Too many emotions and thoughts collided around for him to get a grip on any one in particular. He itched to go after her, ram it through her thick, stubborn skull that he didn't view their relationship as some of the town did. Pick apart her brain until he figured out her underlying issue.

Knee bouncing, he suffered through the show, not having seen any of it.

Chapter 16

Wrist-deep in a bowel resection surgery on an Alaskan Husky who'd eaten gravel, Drake checked the vitals monitor. Stable. Excellent. He could close up and get the hell out of work on time.

"You doing okay, hot stuff?"

Drake glanced up at Brent over his surgical mask. "I'm fine, and don't call me hot stuff. Ever hear of sexual harassment?"

"Yes." Eye roll. "I've been waiting to experience it for five years now. And you're my boss, not the other way around. Sexual harassment doesn't apply here."

Unable to help it, Drake grinned. First time in two days. Two long damn days since Zoe had stormed off during the fireworks. She'd come into the clinic after he'd arrived and had left before he'd gotten out of the OR. He'd thought about texting or dropping by her place, but she seemed to need time. He was giving it to her. Begrudgingly.

Drake frowned at his task. "Suction."

"That's what *he* said." Brent put the suction hose inside the dog's cavity. He laughed. "You're feistier than usual."

"Must be my hot new boyfriend." Brent paused. "You're laughing and smiling more in the past two weeks than I've seen you do in four years."

"Good for you. Miles seems like a nice guy."

Miles was a soft-spoken man and Brent didn't shut up long enough to breathe, but they fit well together, best Drake could tell. He and Zoe were polar opposites as well. Barring this wall she tried to erect around herself with regards to dating, they clicked, too.

Which was interesting. Drake had been hesitant to start something with Zoe because of the friendship, the fact they worked together, and Heather. If he rooted around for deeper issues, he'd also lay insecurity at his own feet. She had mounds more experience than he did with this kind of thing. He'd been with Heather since high school. He never thought he could handle Zoe.

But he'd been wrong. Turned out, she seemed to be the one unable to trust her feelings. He was planning on having a talk with his brothers tonight and then gauging Zoe's mood at their softball game tomorrow. From there, he'd figure out what to do.

Regardless, something had to be done. He wasn't sleeping, barely eating, and Brent was starting to become an amusing form of entertainment. Not good.

He finished closing the dog, charted a couple notes, and scrubbed out, leaving post-op care in Brent's capable hands.

Making his way toward the reception desk, Drake frowned at the raised voices. Zoe's, to be exact. He rounded the corner and found Avery behind her desk, his aunts and mother near the door, and Zoe pacing in between. The waiting room was empty, indicating Flynn and Cade had finished with patients.

Drake eyed the tense faces. "Is there a problem?"

Zoe whirled on him. "They," she pointed to the Battleaxes, "have you and I booked at a veterinary conference in Portland next weekend. Did you know anything about this?"

He thought back and vaguely remembered Aunt Rosa mentioning something about it near Christmas last year when she'd still been their office manager. "Rings a bell."

Avery tapped away at her keyboard. "Yours and Zoe's schedule is blocked off for Friday through Monday. The log date says December third." More clicking. "And it's already paid for. No refunds."

Zoe rubbed her forehead. "Of course. And all that means is they've had this matchmaking scheme in place that long."

"You give us too much credit. Consider it a vacation." Aunt Marie shrugged. "Neither of you have taken much time off in I can't tell you how long."

"I wouldn't put the JFK assassination against you three. And this would be a work-related trip, not a vacation. I don't have time to get away. Mama needs me around. What if there's an emergency?"

Aunt Rosa glanced up from her phone. "She's safe at Pine Crest. We all can take shifts stopping by to visit. Besides, Portland is only four hours away."

Drake eased behind Zoe and set his hands on her tense shoulders. "They have a point." Lightly, he kneaded her muscles to diffuse the ticking bomb. He'd have to check the convention calendar, but maybe they could blow off a couple things and get out in the city. "You do need some time off. So do I."

With an expunging sigh, she dropped her chin. "Fine. But if we get there and only one hotel room is booked, you three will have to look over your shoulders the rest of your lives."

Drake grinned. All her attitude had drained and she relaxed under his ministrations. He worked his thumbs up her neck and wished the clinic would vacate. He'd love nothing more than to keep loosening her up until she grew pliant enough to reason with. Alas, there were witnesses so, with a final squeeze, he let go.

Zoe snatched her purse off the counter. "I need tequila. Lots of tequila." She strode out the door.

Avery tapped a pencil on the desk. "Cade and Flynn said they'd meet you at your house. I'll close up."

Nodding, Drake grabbed his keys from his office and exited the back way to avoid any more people. He'd asked his brothers earlier if they wanted to have pizza tonight, and he was beginning to regret even that much.

Cade and Flynn were waiting on his porch when Drake pulled in the driveway. All the dogs were playing in the yard. Cade held a pizza box from Le Italy and Flynn had a six pack.

Drake climbed out of his truck. "You read my mind." He unlocked the front door and followed them inside. The dogs scampered in all directions. Since both brothers stopped dead and glanced around, Drake shrugged. "Did a little redecorating." He cleared his throat. "Zoe helped."

Flynn nodded and passed the beer to Drake so he could sign. *"It looks nice. Zoe and Gabby helped with my house. Cade's, too."*

"I know. I was there." His gaze shifted between the two of them, standing around looking like lost idiots. "Should we eat on the back deck?"

"Yeah. Sounds good."

"Works for me."

Shaking his head, Drake trailed after them. They shot the shit about football and work stuff while they took on the whole pizza, then settled back in their seats in uncomfortable silence.

Cade and Flynn exchanged several looks that Drake interpreted as you-do-it, no-you-do-it before Cade eventually rubbed his neck. "So, uh. You and Zoe."

Lacing his fingers, Drake stacked them on his head and laughed until his side ached. "You two are chickenshits. Yes, me and Zoe."

Cade frowned. "Well, excuse the hell out of us. This is kinda new territory. You dating. And…Zoe. Didn't see that coming."

"Hit me like a freight train, too."

Flynn stared at him so long Drake grew uncomfortable. *"At the risk of sounding like a sap, you look really happy. I missed you. So much. Missed seeing you like this."*

Hell. Drake swallowed hard.

"Are things all right between you? She took off rather fast during the fireworks, yeah?"

He shook his head, dropping his hands to his lap. "She keeps spouting stupid crap about ruining my reputation by being with me and how she's just a good time. It's pissing me off and makes no sense."

Cade set his beer aside. "Her and I were a lot alike, at least before her mom got sick and Avery came along. We both got labeled with monikers—her as the party girl and me the playboy. She was never promiscuous, though."

"I know that." He did. But she had other defensive blocks in place besides what he'd mentioned.

"No doubt, she's concerned about the town thinking she's a rebound, and a bad choice, too."

Drake clenched his fists. She would never be a bad decision, and if people knew her half as well as he did, it would be a nonissue. He'd managed to get out of bed the first year after Heather died because he had Zoe. Breathed. Ate. Etcetera. And if one more person threw the word rebound at him, he wouldn't be responsible for his actions.

Taking a cleansing breath of humid mountain air, he glanced at the horizon. The riverbed. The forest. The shadows of the Klamath. The darkening skyline. He wished he was looking at Zoe instead.

"It's not surprising she'd want to protect you. She cares about you. Always has."

He didn't need anyone telling him. "Yet she won't date me."

Cade frowned. "Why? Because of Heather?"

"I thought so at first, but I don't think that's it. Or all of it."

Flynn took a swig of beer and set it down. *"Have you tried talking to her?"*

"Having a conversation about this topic with her is like pulling teeth from an un-anesthetized rabid dog." Nine times out of ten, Drake would take the canine. Pulling his hair out might be more productive. "The only thing I could get out of her was guilt about baggage regarding her mom. Said I'd already watched Heather get sick."

The color drained from Cade's face and he went deadly still. His gaze wandered off, his forehead wrinkling.

"What?"

Cade closed his eyes and rubbed his neck. After a moment, his concerned gaze trained on Drake. "Early onset dementia can be hereditary, yeah? I don't know if you can test for it, nor do I know the odds."

Drake's heart relocated ribs with a pounding, erratic beat. His lungs all but collapsed. Flynn, pale also, pulled his phone out of his pocket, his thumbs going to work rapidly over the screen. Her behavior made total sense now. The walls. The determination to do everything herself. Her trying to keep him an arm's length away. Leaning forward, he dropped his elbows on his thighs and pressed his palms to his eye sockets. Christ Jesus, he wanted to weep. Or scream.

Shit. Just...shit.

"She wouldn't want you to go through that again." Cade's quiet voice drifted across the gentle breeze, and the careful control in his tone indicated his fear was as amped as Drake's. "Knowing her, she'd die before putting you through the pain of losing someone like you did with Heather. And if she does get what her mom has, it would be much worse. Not months of hospice with an end in sight, but years of her mind whittling away before her body gives out."

Unable to sit, Drake rose, clutching his stomach. He paced the length of the deck and back again. Not her. Damn it, not her. That quick wit and fiery temper and beautiful heart and insane talent and... His throat closed. Not her.

Flynn groaned. "According to this, she's got a fifty-fifty shot at getting it if she inherited the mutation gene."

Drake had to listen extra close due to Flynn's odd speaking dialect. And that news didn't sound good at all no matter who said it. The pizza he'd eaten threatened to come back up.

"Early onset tends to be familial and only makes up five percent of cases." Flynn glanced up from the phone. "Has she been tested?"

Drake cursed a wicked streak and fisted his hair. "I don't know." But he was going to find out. He swiped his keys off the table. "Let my dogs out and lock up."

The drive to her house took twenty years instead of minutes. Her car was in the garage and her living room lights were on, but she didn't answer the doorbell or his frantic pounding. Using his key, he let himself in and locked the door behind him.

He called her name, but she didn't respond. After checking the entire house and not finding her, he fought to breathe through the onslaught of panic and stopped in the middle of her tiny kitchen. There was a half-eaten sandwich on the table and... The basement door was ajar.

Taking the stairs two at a time, he rounded the corner and halted in his tracks.

With her back to him and wearing nothing but a white tank top that fell to her knees, she stood in front of an easel. Her purple hair was up in a messy knot. There was a paintbrush in her mouth and one in her hand, which was gliding over the canvas in smooth, deft strokes.

The air punched from his lungs and he deflated. All the tension, all the frenetic worry, disappeared. She was painting again. Under blinding fluorescent lights, in a wood-paneled basement, surrounded by decades old furniture and art supplies, Zoe was painting again.

A rocky shoreline took up the right side of the canvas with foaming waves rolling in on the left. On a small section of beach at the bottom were two crabs. Sword fighting. A grin split his face and he leaned against the wall, arms crossed.

Seemingly unaware of his presence, she moved with fluid grace, her head slightly tilted. Her feet were bare on the green shag carpet, and he followed the path up her long, toned legs to her tiny waist, regal neck, and stopped on her partial profile. Such beautiful olive skin. She had a light dusting of freckles on her shoulders and, though he couldn't see them just now, on her nose, too.

Emotion tightened his airway and he knew he was already half in love with her. It wasn't a big leap by his estimation. He'd loved her for years, so the shift seemed natural. Try as he might to fight it, or her attempting ten times harder to do the same, it wouldn't matter. He had a feeling they'd wind up right here. With him utterly, desperately sunk.

She swirled the brushes in a glass of thinner and wiped her hands with a paint-speckled towel. With a glance over her shoulder, her brows lifted. "Checking off another item on the list you dragged out of me? Watching me paint? You already held my hand in public. You should've stopped there." Her voice was oddly flat, her features relaxed by comparison. It figured she'd known he'd been here all along.

"I used to watch you all the time from that couch." He jerked his chin at the ugly plaid sofa. If memory served, it was uncomfortable as hell, but he'd sat for hours, completely enraptured.

"That was a long time ago." She walked closer and flipped off the light, leaving only the staircase illuminated behind him. She went to move past him, but he wrapped his arm around her waist and held her in front of him.

"And there is no stopping when it comes to you. Not the list or anything else."

Closing her eyes, she let out an inaudible exhale. "I need to clean up. I smell like paint and thinner."

"You smell like lavender and it invades my sleep."

Her gaze lifted to his. A little confused and a lot hopeful. Huge hazel eyes framed by thick lashes. They plagued him while he was asleep or awake. He used his free hand to cup her jaw, run his thumb across her lip. A pouty little mouth he wanted to kiss all the time. So he did. Lowering his head, he brushed her lips with his. Gentle. Coaxing. Her breath fanned his cheek a split second before she plundered. He wanted to draw out the kiss, take his time, but she didn't allow it. She never allowed it. With determination and gusto, she went at him. Heat caused sparks which morphed into white hot flames.

Too soon, she lifted her head, her gaze studying him, her breaths uneven. Then she kissed him again. Or killed him. Same difference.

Just as he was about to up the ante and pin her to the closest hard surface, she suddenly pulled away. His arms slapped to his sides with the abrupt momentum change. She walked around him and climbed the stairs as if nothing had happened. Not one word.

Taking a second to collect himself, he sighed and followed. Since she was scrubbing her hands and forearms at the kitchen sink, he sank into a chair and waited. And waited. She was silently putting her walls back up, and he was reminded of why he'd come over.

"Have you been tested?"

She paused, then rinsed the suds with stiff movements.

"Answer me. The genetic mutation gene. Have you been tested?"

Shutting off the faucet, she reached for a towel and slowly dried her hands. Her profile offered no insight, nor did she deign to speak to him.

He cleared his throat. "That's why you won't date me or talk about the future or so much as even try." So help him, he was going to lose it if she didn't say something. It was an asshole thing to do, but he played upon her weakness. Him. "Don't do this to me. I'm freaking out, Zoe. I need you to talk to me. I need—"

"No." She placed her hands on the counter and leaned into them, closing her eyes. "No, I haven't taken the test. I was too scared or maybe I just didn't want to know for sure." She rubbed her forehead. "When we got Mama's diagnosis, I put my affairs in order, too. There's an updated will and Brent's set up as my power of attorney for healthcare."

Relief mixed with confusion and irritation. "Why Brent?" Not that he wasn't one of Zoe's closest friends and a stand-up guy. But why not Gabby or one of Drake's brothers? They'd known her all her life. Hell, why not…? He clenched his jaw. "Why not me?"

She whirled on him, anguish and anger shining in her eyes. "I will not put you in that position. Not again. If it comes down to it and I show symptoms, Brent will make sound decisions for me based on facts first and emotion second. You…" Her breath hitched. "You wouldn't do that. You're incapable. You'd play the white knight, the martyr, because that's who you are, Drake. And no one, especially you, is sacrificing anything for me."

Leveled, he stared at her. And he knew, just knew, he'd been blind. This wasn't merely about shielding their family and friends from one possible terrible outcome. It wasn't simply about their history or what future lay in wait. All along, this entire past five years had been about her protecting him in particular.

He thought back to what he'd witnessed on his brother's wedding video. Months ago. Before he'd kissed her or had known he was ready to move past the grief, she'd had...longing in her eyes.

Zoe straightened from the counter, her head down. "Please lock up on your way out." And with that, she left the room like it was the end.

Chapter 17

Leaving Drake in the kitchen, Zoe walked down the hall and stopped in the middle of her bedroom. She should've known he'd figure out her reasons for not wanting to get involved. Between grieving over Heather and work, he'd not had the wherewithal the past few years to connect the dots.

God, and the look on his face when she'd told him she'd set up Brent as her POA. Like she'd daggered his chest. Did he seriously not understand she'd done that for him? So, if it came down to it, *he* wouldn't have to make excruciating decisions? Watch her forget, day after day, who her friends and family were as her mind rotted? Because, of everyone in her life, the blow would hit Drake the hardest.

In typical Drake fashion, he was trying to do the right thing. Except there was no right thing here. He had to stop, realize the truth, and move forward. Without her. He'd had his wife, the love of his life, taken away from him. And with Heather's death, his dreams of kids and family had been ripped away, too.

Zoe would not be another burden, no matter how much he cared about her. One day, he'd thank her.

Sighing, she glanced down at herself. Had she known he'd pop by, she might've worn more than an old tank top. Though it covered most of her and fell to her knees, it wasn't much by way of dress. Grabbing the hem, she went to remove it.

"Wait." Drake's footsteps padded into the room and stopped behind her. The deep timbre of that one word echoed off the walls. He moved in front of her, and before she could let go of the shirt, he covered her hands with his over the garment. "Please leave it on."

She glanced away instead of at his chocolate eyes, which held too much depth. Devotion. Years of fond and painful memories. "I thought you'd left."

With a humble twist of his lips, he shook his head. "Not going to happen." His gaze searched hers. "I like the way you look in this." His fingers clenched. "Only this. Subtle sexiness."

"Please stop." She closed her eyes and hated the needy pleading in her tone. "I've never asked you for much, but I'm asking now. Please just walk away before we get more tangled than we already are."

"No offense, honey, but I'd rather be tangled." He backed them to the bed and sat down, drawing her to stand between his knees. Hands on her hips, he looked up at her. "I'm staying. Tonight, tomorrow, for however long it takes. I'm staying."

"We're not having sex."

Humor lit his eyes, curved his lips. "My intention, just to be clear, is not sex. Though we will get to that point sometime soon. That's a promise. Tonight, I'm just sleeping with you. As in, eyes closed, drool on the pillow."

"I don't drool."

"Snoring, then." He quickly shook his head. "I'll find out soon enough if you snore, so just be quiet."

His grin slipped as his thumbs stroked her waist. Watching her closely, he slid his hands over her hips, down her thighs. When he reached the hem of her shirt, his fingers dipped underneath, and back up he went, taking the material with him. Her nipples pebbled behind the soft cotton and her nerves fired, pinging lightning in every direction. Her breath caught as he splayed his fingers over her legs, the tips just brushing her panties. His dark eyes dilated, and she shivered, unable to fight the pull anymore.

"Show me, Zoe." One finger stroked her hip bone, drew seductive little circles. "Show me what ink you put here." Though barely a whisper, his deep voice seemed to fill every crevice of the room and wind around her.

Debating, she bit her lip. Never in a hundred years had she anticipated Drake ever seeing the tattoo. Chances were, he wouldn't understand the significance or even remember the day in question. Plus, she was too weak to tell him no. Swallowing, she nodded.

Never taking his gaze from hers, he raised her shirt and held it under her breasts. Leaning forward, he kissed her belly over the tattoo ring of forget-me-nots, and the tender gesture made her eyes burn.

Then, his lashes lowered. Holding the shirt with one hand, he teased the band of her panties with the other. She sent a silent thank you to the heavens she'd worn her cute yellow hip-hugger lace set this morning. Carefully, as if she'd break, he eased the elastic from the bottom and moved the material aside. As he stared, his brows pinched in thought. She could all but see him scrolling through memories, trying to locate this one.

She didn't need to glance down. She'd designed it herself. A long-stemmed dandelion with white fluff on top. A few pieces were inked to make it look like they'd been blown off, drifting in the wind. The longer he stared, the more her heart puttered.

His Adam's apple bobbed with a swallow and, judging by his tight expression, the task had been difficult. His chest stopped moving as his lips parted. "Is this…" He cleared his throat and offered a barely perceptible shake of his head. "Is this from your seventeenth birthday?"

Crap. Her lungs emptied. He remembered.

When she didn't—*couldn't*—respond, his gaze finally lifted to hers. Shock and unmasked optimism stared back at her.

"You remember that? It was so long ago."

His laugh was little more than a puff of air. "I'd brought a candle to school, figuring I'd buy you a cookie or brownie from the cafeteria to put it in. But when I saw you in the quad, surrounded by all the dandelions, I tossed the candle. I remember a lot of things about that day."

Of course, he did. It had been the first time Heather had asked him out.

His finger traced the tattoo, irreverently gentle. "You always made such a big deal about birthdays. Claimed the wish was the most important part. I thought blowing dandelion seeds would give you unlimited wishes."

Damn. The sentimentality in him sometimes could decimate. She'd seen it first hand over and over with Heather, with his family. But Zoe never expected any traces for her. Then or now.

A quick grin flashed and then disappeared. "You turned down every guy who'd asked you to homecoming."

Crap. She had to put a stop to him right this second. Taking a step back, she lowered her shirt and crossed her arms. Unable to look at him, she stared at his hands, held out in front of him as if in surrender.

"Why didn't you say yes to any of those boys when they'd asked?"

She couldn't breathe. "I went with Cade."

"After I agreed to go with Heather." He dropped his hands to his thighs, fingers clenched. His jawed ticked as his gaze searched hers.

"Stop." She closed her eyes. "Just stop."

"Why choose that day, that memory, to tattoo?"

Damn him. She bit her tongue and stared at the wall, determined to be more stubborn than him. She had almost no pride left. Couldn't he freaking see that?

"Why, Zoe? Of all—"

"Because it was the best and worst day of my life!" Huffing, she fisted her hand over her chest. As he stared at her, gaze dialed to hell-no and jaw slack in shock, she said screw it. "You were the only person besides Mama who remembered my birthday that year, and she had to work a double shift. That kind gesture will stay with me forever."

Crap. No. She would not cry. Her chest hitched. Yes, apparently she would. Hot, outlandish tears blurred her vision and trickled onto her cheeks. He stared at her as if torn between wanting to hold her or run. He should take door number two because she wasn't done. He'd opened the can of worms. Now he could go fishing.

She bit her thumbnail. "For months, I had been trying to find a way to tell you, and when you handed me a dozen wishes, I got my courage. They all scattered to the wind with my hope you'd say yes. But I never got to ask you to the dance."

"No," he breathed. An I-want-do-die expression twisted his features as his gaze drifted off. He could join the club. She didn't have enough fingers and toes to count the number of times she'd wanted to crawl in a hole.

"Unbeknownst of my feelings, my best friend made the leap and got there first. And that's all, folks."

"Ah, hell, Zoe." His voice was so kind she wanted to scream. "I had no idea. You…" He ran a shaking hand over his mouth, down his jaw.

"Are you happy now?" A sob tore at her chest. "You've solved the great mystery of me. You know all my tattoos and meanings. Bet you regret asking, don't you?"

He flinched and reached for her, but she stepped farther away. "I'm sorry. I obviously hurt you and—"

"Apologies aren't needed, Drake. If it had gone down the way I wanted, you never would've wound up with Heather. That's the way it was supposed to be. She was the right person for you." She wiped her tears, mortification heating her face. "It was a silly crush. I got over it. I got over you then and I'll do it again."

"Please don't." He launched to his feet, strode toward her, and held her face in his hands. Desperation, remorse, and alarm radiated in his eyes. "You're right. The timing wasn't right for us then, and I wouldn't take back my time with her. I'm only sorry you got hurt in the process." He swallowed, gaze darting back and forth between her eyes. "But Christ. Don't get over me. I have this awful, wonderful feeling there's no getting over you."

Damn him. And be still her pathetic heart. "Drake, we can't—"

"Take the test." He gave her a little shake and rested his forehead against hers. "Take the test and we'll deal with whatever the results say. At least we'll know."

There he went using "we" again. "If it comes back positive—"

"If that happens, we'll figure it out together. Whether we make it as a couple or remain friends, *we* will figure it out." He inhaled deeply, closing his eyes. After a moment, he pulled her to him, cradling the back of her head. "Stop fighting me, Zoe. For once, do things my way."

She wrapped her arms around his waist and pressed her cheek to his chest. Now that he knew everything, he'd never let her get away with any attempt to protect him. She'd known that all along and it was why she'd spent the past five years avoiding this scenario. The only person more hard-headed than her was him.

She'd have the blood test taken. For him and for herself. If it was negative, she'd let things progress with Drake naturally and see if they had a shot at happy. If it was positive, she'd end the relationship right then and there. No matter how insistently he pushed, she'd push harder. In time, they'd stay friends, and Brent could handle the inevitable healthcare decisions. Drake would move on.

But right now, in the cocoon of his arms, she felt safe for the first time in years, if ever. It was selfish and wrong to lean on him. He'd had enough suffering thrown at him. Yet the optimistic side of her she'd tried to keep dormant clawed its way to the surface. She'd wanted this, wanted him, for so very long. She'd take this smidgen of joy for however long it lasted.

And because it was Drake, she told him the one thing she'd never been able to admit, even to herself. "I'm scared." Not just for the hazy picture of the future, but being with him, too. Luck had never been on her side.

His arms cinched and his chest expanded with an inhale. "Me, too." He rested his chin on top of her head. "You realize this might be sign one of an apocalypse. You admitting you're afraid. Us together, agreeing on something. We should board up the windows. Gather supplies…"

Burying her face in the soft cotton of his shirt, she laughed. She stayed still a minute longer and then eased away. "I need to change. I'll be back in a second."

He nodded. "Any objection to me taking off my shirt?" He rubbed his neck. "I don't typically sleep in clothes."

She set her hands on her hips. "Is this a ploy for sex? I told you no sex tonight."

"Never mind—"

"Because you have looked in a mirror, correct? All those abs and ridges are bound to change my mind."

Brow furrowed, he opened and closed his mouth. "I can't decide if that's a compliment about my body or an insult you'd think I'd trick you into something."

Poor, poor man. She laughed. "Relax. I'm joking. Well, not about the abs part. Regardless, I don't care what you do or do not sleep in." She grabbed a set of PJs from the dresser. "I'll be right back."

Exhausted, she headed into the bathroom, brushed her teeth, and changed. When she returned, he was on the bed, back against the headboard, with Cotton in his lap purring. He still wore his shirt and nylon shorts, but he'd turned off the overhead light and had switched on a lamp.

He glanced at her and his hand paused over the cat. Slowly, his gaze skimmed the length of her and back again. "Now who's not fighting fair?"

She looked down at herself. Okay, her pajamas were a little revealing. Baby blue with a cupcake pattern, the tank top was tight and showed a patch of belly, while the shorts were matching boy-cut briefs.

Shrugging, she tossed her painting shirt in the hamper. "Want me to change?"

"No." The coarse, low tone of his voice sent shivers up her spine.

"I could make all kinds of pussy jokes right now."

He looked at the cat in his lap and grinned. Carefully, he set Cotton on the floor and crossed his arms, gaze a little uncertain. "At the risk of having my man card revoked, I'll admit you're a little intimidating, Zoe."

"Just a little?" She pouted and decided something on the spot.

If they were going to try this relationship thing, she may as well embrace whatever came with the territory. She was tired of fighting the pull. She didn't think he was entirely ready for intimacy, and it was too soon for sex, but they could…make out.

From the foot of the bed, she crawled on all fours over to him. Through lids growing heavier and heavier, he watched her progress. By the time she straddled his hips, his breaths were soughing between parted lips.

"I take it back. You're extremely intimidating." An internal battle waged over his expression, then he set his hands on her bare thighs and squeezed. "You said just sleep."

"But you're not ready for bed." At his questioning glance, she fingered the hem of his tee. "You're still wearing your shirt."

He paused, then reached behind his neck to remove it.

"Let me."

She slipped her hands under the shirt and pressed her palms to the ripples of his abs. His arms dropped to the mattress beside them and he *whooshed* an exhale. Keeping her gaze on his, she moved her hands higher over his washboard stomach to his pecs, where she grazed her thumbs across the flat discs of his nipples. The back of his skull hit the headboard. Enjoying his reaction and the warm, hard male beneath her touch, she traced his nipples again with feather-light fingertips. They beaded as his chest rapidly rose and fell.

Sliding her hands around his back, she urged him to sit up, and when he complied, she tugged the shirt over his head. His hot, dark gaze landed on hers at the same moment his hands reclaimed her thighs. They stared at each other a suspended beat, and the longer it went on, the harder it became to breathe.

Finally, his gaze drifted over her hair, her face, her lips…as if he were memorizing her features. His fingers toyed with her shorts, then grazed her hips. Watching her closely, he dipped under her tank top and traced her ribs, then shifted around to flatten his hands low on her back.

His touch was more like a caress and unlike the way she'd ever been held before. Like he was learning her body and savoring rather than trying to instill desire. Her breasts grew heavy and her core damp, despite the gentle ministrations. Proving he wasn't unaffected, his erection grew the longer he held her and pressed against her heat, sending her pulse into overdrive.

Judging by his stillness, he was either unsure of where to go from there or was waiting for her to set the pace. She gripped his biceps, loving the way his muscles shifted with the touch. Moving her hands up his shoulders, she grabbed the back of his neck and toyed with the hairs on his nape.

That was obviously one of his erogenous zones because he sucked air through flared nostrils and groaned. Leaning forward, she brushed her lips across his forehead, his temple, to his jaw. The scratch of his five-o'clock shadow rasped through the quiet, and she closed her eyes. Her nipples formed stiff peaks at the contact with his chest, and she threw her head back.

His mouth latched on to her neck, sucking, nipping. Her fingers clenched in his hair and she emitted a full-body tremble as he moved to the other side, tracing the tendon with his tongue. Hot breath teased her jaw as he worked his way up to the shell of her ear. Tendrils of need wove through her until she couldn't remember her own damn name. His hands moved to her ass, kneading. Then, he rocked against her, and she lost it.

Fingers still fisted in his hair, she dragged his mouth to hers. Tongue and teeth. A war ensued over dominance and oxygen. Just as she thought she had the battle won, something vibrated her inner thigh.

She smiled against his lips. "You brought toys to the party."

With a low laugh that came out more like a groan, he fished in his pocket and withdrew his phone. He glanced at the screen and set the cell on her nightstand. "Even though they would've been all right overnight, Flynn took my dogs home."

"Does he know where you are?" One of her concerns was his family. Though they'd always treated her like one of their own, she worked for them. Friends and dating were two separate things.

"Yes." He tilted his head, tucking a strand of hair behind her ear. "My brothers are surprised yet encouraging of our new development." With a heavy sigh, he squeezed her leg. "Though I fear a certain part of me will be awake all night, I think we should go to sleep. I promised you that much."

"Exactly which part will be an insomniac?" She trailed a finger down his chest. "Do you mean the one below your belt—"

He grabbed her hand and twisted his body until they landed on their sides, facing each other. With her head resting on his upper arm and his thigh between hers, he stared at her. "I try very hard not to break my promises. Quit tempting me."

"How *hard* do you try?"

On a rugged, rough laugh that ended in a groan, he kissed her forehead. "Close your eyes. Sleep." As if by punctuation, he snapped his lids shut.

A light rain began to splatter against the windowpane.

"Okay," she said on a sigh. "But I'm only going to pick up this line of questioning in the morning."

Chapter 18

Drake awoke with his face buried in lavender-scented hair and a whippoorwill cooing just outside the window. Zoe's rearend was snug against his increasing happiness to her vicinity as he spooned her. His leg was draped over both hers as if, even in slumber, he'd been concerned she'd bolt, and his hand was splayed between her breasts.

Grinning like an idiot, he lifted his head. Heather had never been much for cuddling. After sex and when they'd first fallen asleep, sure, but by morning, they'd wound up on opposite sides of the bed due to her restless patterns. It appeared the only time Zoe pressed the pause button was while unconscious.

It had been some time since he'd slept with someone. Sunlight streamed through her blinds to create slanted patterns on her soft olive skin. Features relaxed, she looked like a fantasy with her lush mouth parted and dark lashes fanning her cheeks. Her hand rested over his, the other was tucked under her head.

Desire and affection and something he dare not name crashed around in his chest. Most of all, happiness tightened his throat. For years, he'd woken up with the mantra to get through another day. Rinse. Repeat. He almost didn't recognize the sensation of being anything other than numb.

The things she'd admitted last night tugged at him. Worse were the tears she'd shed while saying them. He'd had no clue she'd felt that way about him. He could count on one hand the number of times he'd seen her cry. She'd always been strong enough to will them away, the exception being the moment Heather had died and the resulting funeral.

But Zoe had opened a vein, had finally let him in, and he wouldn't make her regret it. He couldn't change the past, didn't want to, but he could do something about the future. Though he was scared to death of what the test would reveal, the results would be moot. It didn't matter when or where. He was going to take her. Like an oath. A promise. And he was keeping her. He'd told her repeatedly he didn't know where they were headed. He'd only wanted her to try. But that had been a lie. He knew from the second he'd kissed her where his feelings lay. Probably before, dating back to Cade and Avery's wedding. He just hadn't recognized it.

Falling for Heather had been a gradual glide until she'd been so embedded he never questioned his love. Thing was, Zoe had always been there. Thus, the descent with her had been a thirty-story drop with no cushion. Perhaps it was his upbringing with two loving parents who showered affection, or maybe it was just his genetic makeup, but he never shied from emotion or grew embarrassed to demonstrate feelings. What was the point in hiding?

Except Zoe had been walking through life like she'd been alone. She'd had her mom and her friends, but fierce independence and pride—and hurt—had kept her from openly expressing her needs. That ended today.

She stirred, and he kissed her bare shoulder over the adorable freckles, wondering where else she had them. He nuzzled her neck while she slowly awakened, and he grew harder as she shifted against him.

In slow motion, as if testing reality, she turned her head and glanced at him over her shoulder. She blinked and rolled to face him, those hazel eyes mossy in the morning light. Her gaze skimmed his features. "Hi," she said in a voice still husky from slumber.

He smiled to diffuse her confusion. "Hello. Do you have any idea how adorable you look when you sleep or how sexy you are when you first wake up?"

A tiny wrinkle formed between her brows. "You already have me in bed. There's no need to—"

Pressing his lips to hers, he kissed her to shut her up and because it was what he most wanted—right below breathing and above eating. Holding the back of her head, he deepened the kiss. She melted against him, all soft curves and even softer skin. Breathing got bumped to the bottom of the list when her hands settled on his chest and her nails raked their way down. *Lower, lower...*

Sucking air, he lifted his head. "You're feisty first thing in the morning."

Her lop-sided grin made him groan. "You started it. And I did warn you we'd continue my line of questioning from last night." She tapped her chin with a finger and teasingly pouted. "What was the word you used? Ah, yes. Hard. I see you were right about a certain appendage being an insomniac."

Her deft fingers trailed over his abs and wrapped around his—

"Sweet Christ." He rolled her beneath him. But that wasn't much help.

She crossed her legs behind his ass, cradling him against her heat. His eyeballs thunked the back of his skull. "Zoe." He said her name three more times and buried his face in her neck.

She laughed. A husky, smoke-filled sound that did nothing for his attempt at control. "Problem, Drake?"

"Yes," he mumbled against her skin. "I'm trying to take things slow here, but you smell good. And look good. And sound good. And feel good. Do I need to keep going?" He lifted his head, staring into her pretty eyes. "And taste good."

He kissed her, first her upper lip, then the lower. Tilting his head, he licked the seam of her mouth and was granted entry. Stroking his tongue against hers, he slid one hand under her head and let the other drift. Up her side, beside her breast. Such small, perfect breasts that would fit in his hands. He grazed his thumb across her peaked nipple and her mouth parted wider in a gasp.

Loving her responsiveness, he groaned. She arched under him, sliding her good parts against his until he was blind, deaf, and dumb to anything but her. Blood raged through his veins, pounded at his temples, roared in his ears. Her fingers teased his nape, clenched his short hairs, and heaven help him, he rocked his hips. Need tightened his muscles and put restraint just out of reach.

To draw a much-needed gulp of air, he kissed his way across her cheek and to her jaw. "Since we have softball today, and I'm assuming you want to visit your mom first, we should resurface."

Breaths uneven, she unhitched her legs from around his ass and dragged one heel up his back, grinding his erection more snugly with the motion. Mercy, she was nimble. Her fingers trailed down his sides, dipping into the waistband of his shorts and pausing. Meanwhile, her tongue and teeth worked his throat, sending his lungs into asthmatic fever.

"I cry uncle." Before he became incapable, he rolled off her and sat at the edge of the bed. The room spun. "I'm going to borrow your shower and crank it to deep freeze. I'll make you breakfast after."

Grinning, she stretched her arms over her head, causing her shirt to ride up her taut belly and thrusting her breasts toward the ceiling. "I don't eat breakfast."

He bit down another groan. "Coffee, then."

She yawned, and even that was cute. "My hero."

Kneeling on the mattress, he leaned over her. "By the way, we're going on a date tonight."

Her eyes popped out of their sockets. "What? Why?"

"I told you I wanted to date you."

She sighed. "Yeah, but—"

"Save your breath." He kissed her forehead. "I'll see you at the game. And I'll pick you up here at six."

Leaving her steamed and confused, he took a cold shower, fed her cat, started a pot of coffee, and headed out to relieve Flynn of his dogs.

By the time he made it to the field, he was dying to be near her again. See if she was still pissy and how many times she'd try to worm her way out of tonight. Seemed she was okay with inevitable sex, with sleeping with him, but dating was another story. Part of him couldn't blame her, not with her mother's condition hanging over her head. But if they were going to do this, they'd do it right. She deserved to get all the things on her list, and though she may have abandoned those dreams, he wouldn't.

Standing next to the dugout fence with Flynn and Cade, pre-game warm-up going on around them, Drake watched Zoe chatting with Jason, Parker, and Gabby by the third base line.

Some of the humidity had passed with the overnight rain, but the sun was hot in a cloudless sky. Off in the distance, fog at the base of the Coast Range was beginning to dissipate and sea salt hung on the breeze to mix with damp grass and pine. Not a bad day to play ball.

"What did she say about the test?"

Drake's gut sank with Flynn's reminder. "She hasn't done one. She's going to make an appointment this week."

Cade nodded. "Are you okay?"

"The better question would be is she okay." He rubbed his neck, unable to fathom Zoe declining like her mother. All that kept running through his mind was *not her, not her, not her.*

Flynn sighed and stared ahead. *"I don't know what I'd do if it was Gabby. You must be going out of your mind."*

That about summed it up. Finished with the conversation, Drake strode past the fence, looped an arm around Zoe's waist, and hauled her against his chest until her toes dipped off the infield grass.

"Excuse us, please, guys." He headed toward the bench.

She frowned as he carried her. "What are you doing?"

"This." He kissed her. Right there in front of God and the whole county. Long enough to turn heads, but swift enough no one had to blush or cover their kids' attention. He could all but feel two hundred sets of eyes on him from the bleachers.

Jason whistled behind them. "Does this mean I can't make innuendos about the size of my baseball bat anymore?"

Keeping his gaze locked with Zoe's, Drake shouted, "Yes."

"Well, okay. But I can't promise to keep Parker in check."

Drake assumed the snort in response came from the aforementioned sheriff. Drake kept walking, staring at Zoe. "No smartass remark?" Her droll expression was answer enough. "Would you listen anyway?"

"No."

"Just to be argumentative, we shouldn't be doing this. Everyone's watching." He glanced over her shoulder to the bleachers, his gaze locking with his mom's. She had a hand clutched to her chest and the biggest grin in damnation. Pressing her lips together, she nodded in approval. Drake shifted his gaze back to Zoe. "I disagree."

They wound up winning the game by one run when Gabby, of all people, bunted, allowing Cade to steal home. Congratulations went around, and Drake packed up his gear, ready to head out.

He caught up with Brent, Miles, and Zoe walking to the parking lot and slung an arm over her shoulders. "Good game. Nice homer in the sixth."

"My brilliance is to be expected."

Holding Brent's hand, Miles paused mid-step. "That was a great kiss pre-game." He smirked at Drake.

Brent fanned his face. "Totes agree."

"Don't encourage him." Zoe rolled her eyes. "And you are sweaty." She nudged Drake with her elbow. "So am I."

He grinned at her. "If you're able to pry the clothes from my body, you can have what's underneath."

A careening gasp from Brent turned several heads their way. "Oh my Gucci. Did you just…did you…?" He released Miles' hand and skipped toward the area near a popcorn stand where Drake's mom and two aunts were chatting. "Marie! Guess what."

Zoe crossed her arms. "I knew it. I *knew* he was in cahoots with the Battleaxes."

With a placating smile, Miles patted her arm. "Knowing is half the battle. I'll go wrangle my boyfriend before he does more damage."

"Aw. *Boyfriend.*" Zoe's full-cocked grin had Drake shaking his head and fighting his own.

Miles winked. "I hear we have you to thank for the suggestion he ask me out."

"Yep. You can reward me with shoe shopping and tequila shots."

"You're on." He kissed her cheek and followed Brent.

When Miles was out of hearing range, Zoe eyed Drake. "You're catching on to this flirting thing. Well done."

He slung his bag over his shoulder. "Wait until tonight. You haven't seen anything yet."

"Yeah. About that…"

"Pick you up at six."

Leaving her staring, slack-jawed, he drove home, showered, and ran his dogs ragged in the backyard. Then he fried some chicken, packed a basket with some other items, and tried fruitlessly to pass time until he could go pick up Zoe.

Christ. He hadn't been this excited or nervous in a decade. As he drove the back roads to her house, he shut off the radio and put down the windows, letting the wind fill the cab of his truck.

She answered within seconds of him ringing the bell and wore a… bathrobe. Short, silky, and black. Crossing her arms, she smiled. "I need to know where we're going in order to properly dress."

She could wear that for all he cared, but he glanced down at himself. He'd worn jeans and a T-shirt. "Casual is fine."

"Be right back."

As she disappeared down the hall, he kicked the door shut. Cotton wove around his legs. Drake gave him some attention and paced the living room with the cat purring in his arms.

Fifteen minutes later, she came out wearing skinny jeans, a loose swoop-neck blouse the same color gray as the speckles in her irises, and black sandals. She'd left her hair down, and he realized the purple color had faded to a barely noticeable violet. Silky waves fell around her shoulders. She'd done something insanely sexy with her eyes, too. Smoky. It made them seem even bigger.

He cleared his throat from across the room. "You look…very nice." She looked like a siren and he nearly swallowed his tongue.

Her brows raised at his pause, but she said nothing as she gathered her purse and walked to the door.

In the truck, he passed her a small bouquet of yellow Gerbera daisies. "For you."

"Thanks." She stared at them like no one had given her flowers before. Knowing her refusal to date, that might be the case. "These are close to my favorite."

Drake had to call Brent to learn that tidbit after striking out with Gabby. Brent had not made it easy for Drake to gather intel on something as mundane as flowers. "Good to know."

She was eerily and uncharacteristically quiet as he drove through town and to the outskirts. A quick glance her way, and he caught her still staring at the bouquet with a cross between a frown and confusion. Suddenly pissed off at her previous lovers, he sighed.

"Do I smell chicken?" She turned in her seat and eyed the basket behind him. "Is that your mom's fried chicken? Say yes."

He laughed. "Mom's recipe. I made it."

"Are we there yet?"

He laughed again. "Almost." Taking her hand, he kissed her inner wrist, successfully keeping her quiet the rest of the drive. Any amount of romanticism seemed to render her mute, so he made a note of that for when she started another battle with him over...anything.

Parking near the cove, he opened his door and grabbed the basket. "Wait here." He walked around the truck and opened her door. She stared at him, unblinking. "Well, come on."

"You said to stay here."

He ran his tongue over his teeth. "So I could open your door for you." Who knew he could teach her a thing or two about a proper date? At thirty-one years old, she should've had some semblance of chivalry, right? Apparently not.

"Huh." Taking his hand, she hopped down.

They walked across the gravel parking lot, through a short wooded trail, and down a set of stone stairs to a small strip of beach. Rocky bluffs jutted on both sides with an inlet area of the Pacific past the shore. Off in the distance, the Klamath Mountains peaked toward the fading daylight, surrounded by fog from the banks. The fisherman piers were off to the left. Huge boughs and masts bobbed in the water, proving the ships were docked for the night.

He loved this spot. Townsfolk knew about this area of the cove but, at tide, the cave next to the manmade staircase would flood, so most didn't venture this way late in the day. He'd checked the tide calendar, and they'd be good here until at least eight. Even then, they could sit on the steps after dusk.

Setting the basket in the sand, he laid out a blanket, the food, and turned to her. She was standing where he'd left her, on the bottom stair, and biting her thumbnail. His heart twisted in his chest at her nervous tell. One thing she should never be with him was anxious.

The mighty Zoe Hornsby, brought to her knees by a simple picnic.

"Come here." He held out his hand, waiting.

It took her a beat, but she toed off her sandals and moved in front of him. Her hair whipped around her face with a stiff wind. "This is the spot I painted last night."

He grunted. "That's what gave me the idea." He studied her expression, but she wasn't giving him anything to work with. "Think we'll find any crabs sword fighting?"

A ghost of a smile traced her lips, there and gone in a blink. She gathered her hair in her hand to keep it from blowing around and stared past him at the view. Knowing her artistic eye, she was probably mapping a painting. The longer she stood there, the more nervous he became.

"What are you thinking?"

With a breathy laugh, she shook her head. "Never ask a woman that question." She smiled. "Let's eat."

Chapter 19

He'd made fried chicken, potato salad, and sliced watermelon. Drake had even brought along her favorite peanut butter cookies from Sweet Tooth Bakery and a bottle of wine. A picnic. She still couldn't wrap her mind around it.

Zoe shook her head while sitting on the stone steps near the cove and gazed at the horizon. Tide was coming in, filling the small patch of beach with water. Dusk settled, casting the sky in pink and purple hues and turning the water black. Stars were beginning to wink overhead. With the rocky bluffs surrounding them, it felt like they were the only two people in existence.

Drake O'Grady definitely knew how to plan a date. She couldn't help but wonder if it was wasted on her. The future was uncertain and, let's face it, she was a sure thing. When he was ready to be intimate, she'd be there. All she could give him was now. Until she took the blood test and the results came in, they were suspended in a what-if state.

And yet her throat grew tight at his gesture. He'd bought her flowers and opened her car door and had even made food for a picnic. She'd known all her life Drake was a rare breed of gallant, but this exceeded expectations. How many times as a teen had she laid in bed dreaming of a date with him? How many stupid fantasies had rolled around in her head after Heather died for just one night with him?

From next to her, Drake poured the last of the wine in their glasses and set the empty bottle in the basket on the steps by his feet. "You're awfully quiet."

She took a sip to cool her throat and forced a smile. "How odd you would complain about it."

"I'm not complaining. I'm concerned."

"Don't be. I'm having a great time." Sighing, she rested her head on his shoulder. Those shoulders had carried such enormous weight through the years, and her gut ached that she might be adding to it.

"Me, too." He kissed the top of her head and spoke into her hair. "But it's not like you to be silent this long. Makes me wonder if the end of days is coming. Talk to me."

"About what?" If he knew what she'd been thinking, he'd get upset or, worse, convince her to backtrack.

"Anything. Nothing. I don't care."

Closing her eyes, she smiled and thought about the last time she'd been here. "Did you know that a great way to avoid consuming calories after nine p.m. is to eat a tub of ice cream at eight-fifty?"

His laugh ruffled her hair. "Is that your way of telling me you want ice cream?"

"No. I said the same thing to Gabby when we came out here one night a few years ago with a pint of mint chocolate chip. She'd gone on a date that went horribly wrong. She cried buckets, like Gabby tends to do, and we did some male bashing as therapy."

"And what great piece of advice did you bestow on our Gabby? Knowing you, there was some snarky opinion involved."

Setting her chin on his shoulder, she looked up at him. "Of course. But I can't break girl code to tell you."

"It all worked out anyway. Her and Flynn are... What does Brent say? Epic?" He took her glass and set it aside, doing the same with his own, then faced her once more.

In the low light, his brown eyes appeared black as midnight and were filled with such amusement, such affection, it stalled the breath in her lungs. Their faces were so close she wouldn't have to go far to kiss him. A wisp of a smile curved his mouth as he studied her. His gaze drifted over her hair, forehead, cheeks, chin, mouth, and settled back on her eyes. He seemed to be working something out in his head by the way his eyebrows drew ever so slightly together and his lips parted.

"Now you're the one being quiet. Are you thinking about our next date or preparing to run for the hills?"

"I don't run. And this date isn't over yet." He brushed his nose against hers. "I'm supposed to take you home and kiss you good night on your porch."

Her heart pounded so hard she was surprised he couldn't hear it. "No one would blame you for changing your mind." By the slight edge filling his eyes, he knew she wasn't talking about a kiss, but rather the whole idea of dating in general.

He stared at her an eternity and then cupped her cheek. "That's not going to happen. There's no changing my fucking mind, Zoe."

Damn, he could knock her off her feet with one sentence. Every time. Her skin heated and she trembled at the intensity in his expression. Desire colliding with irritation. "Then what are you waiting for? Kiss me."

A low groan rumbled in his throat. "We're not on your porch yet." His gaze dipped to her mouth and back up again. "Honestly, I don't want to drive you home."

"Where do you want to take me?"

Closing his eyes, he rested his cheek to hers, and when he spoke, his hot breath fanned her ear. "Everywhere." His lips caressed her neck. "Every damn where."

Her head rolled back as a full-body tremor coursed through her. Her core throbbed and her breasts ached and she was panting worse than a Cocker Spaniel at a Bullmastiff convention. Needy whimpers rose in her throat.

His lips grazed her jaw as he shifted to the other side of her neck. "You're not making this any easier with those sexy little sounds, honey."

"Sorry."

His tongue traced over her pulse.

"Okay, not sorry," she breathed. Swear to God, if he didn't take her home or right here on the steps, she was going to implode. Threading her fingers through his thick, black hair, she forced him to look at her. "How about a compromise? Your house. We can watch a movie and make out like teenagers on your couch."

Tension creased his brow. "I want you. But I'm trying really hard to prove I don't want only one thing from you."

She held his jaw, his outgrowth scratching her palms. "I know that."

And damn did she admire the hell out of him for it. But they weren't taking that ultimate physical step until he was ready and showed her, without a trace of doubt, that he truly was there. It had been four years since Heather died and, due to her illness, five since he'd been intimate. Plus, his wife was the only woman he'd ever been with. Except, the way he was behaving, it seemed like he was putting on the brakes more for Zoe's benefit.

Biting her lip, she debated what to say next. "You're nothing like other men, and I'm not asking you this to pressure you. Are you sure? It's been a long time since—"

"It's not as if I don't know what I'm doing, Zoe." Frustration bit his tone, but damn if there wasn't doubt in his eyes, making her suspect this all might be a lack of confidence. "I may not have your experience, but I know what I want. I just don't…" He sighed and pulled out of her grasp, pinching the bridge of his nose.

"What?"

He scrubbed his hand over his face. "I don't want the act of us sleeping together to be a reason for you to believe you're a rebound. I know what some people are saying and I know how guys have treated you." He reached up and touched a strand of her hair, rubbing it between his fingers. "You're not a catalyst for me to move on and I'm not using you as one."

God, this man. "I know that, too."

"Do you?" His penetrating gaze wouldn't allow her to look away when instinct was telling her to abort. "Understand me, honey. I'm with you because I want to be." He swallowed and laced their fingers together. "And yes. It's been a long time."

She blew out an uneven breath. "For the record, it's been just about as long for me." What a pair they made. "My offer stands. We should make out at your house. Slowly work our way back on the saddle or whatever."

He flashed a grin, exposing the dimple on his left cheek. "How about this? Spend the night with me and we'll see what happens." His smile slipped. "The conference in Portland is next weekend." He looked away, his expression indicating he wanted to say more.

After a silent crackling moment, she understood. He wanted to take the next step with her then, while they were far from everything and everyone they knew, making sex just about them. It made sense his first time with someone else should be away from home. An act rather than a pressure-filled decision.

She squeezed his hand. "Portland."

His gaze whipped to hers. Held. Emotions filled his eyes, too many to track. Finally, he nodded. Rising, he held out his hand.

An hour later, they were cuddling in his bed watching a violent action movie she couldn't remember the name of and making fun of the actors. Fully dressed and on top of the covers, they'd done nothing inadvertently sexual, and she was okay with that. This had been the best date ever.

Drake lay on his back, one arm behind his head. His other hand idly played with her hair while she rested her cheek on his chest. Their legs were tangled and she adoringly breathed in his scent of warm male. Comforting and arousing in the same breath.

Gunfire exploded on the screen and his chest vibrated with a chuckle. "I love how the bad guys are standing ten feet away and still can't hit their target."

She hummed. "Or how, in a fist fight, they go after the lead one at a time."

"Why are we watching this again?"

"You picked it. Besides, heckling cinema is my favorite pastime."

He laughed. "We could put on something else."

"Naw. I'm good." Very good. As in, she never wanted to leave this bed. She bit her thumbnail. "Is this awkward for you?"

"What? Us in my bedroom?" His hand stilled over her head. "No. Honestly, all I see in here now is you."

Crap. She set her chin on his pec and looked at him. "That wasn't my intention. If you want to redecorate again, we can."

He glanced around as if considering. "I don't want to change it. I like having traces of you in here. Besides, I have an original Zoe Hornsby on my walls. The trees are really cool."

True, but what happened if the blood test came back positive or they didn't work out? Then she'd be all he'd see in here and that wouldn't work either. He'd moved on from Heather, but he'd have to redecorate to move on from Zoe. She should've just left things alone.

Determined not to upset him, she let it go for now and focused on something else as the credits rolled on his flat screen. "I don't have anything to sleep in. Or a toothbrush."

He kissed her forehead and climbed out of bed. Opening a dresser drawer, he rummaged around and pulled out a white tee. He handed it to her and jerked his chin toward the adjoining bathroom. "I think there's an extra toothbrush in the cabinet. Have at it."

She stepped into the bathroom and closed the door. After washing her face, she changed into his shirt and checked the vanity. Not seeing a toothbrush, she opened a drawer and froze. A small stack of photos were neatly tucked next to toothpaste and shaving cream.

Grabbing the pictures, she sat on the toilet lid. The first was her and Drake dancing at Cade's wedding, followed by another of them retreating from the church after the ceremony. She paged through, finding a couple of her playing ball or painting. The last one was a shot of them kissing after the parade. He had to have downloaded it from the internet and printed it.

Hands shaking, she blew out the breath she'd been holding. Why did he have these? And in the bathroom? Had he stashed them quickly when their plans tonight had changed and she'd come over? She wondered if he planned to frame them and…put them in his bedroom.

Or maybe she was just being paranoid. Yes, it was strange, but he'd just redecorated and that could account for misplaced items.

Like photos of her. And him. And no one else.

Screw it. "Drake?"

He opened the door and poked his head in. "Find a toothbrush?"

"Not exactly." She stood and held up the stack.

Brows furrowed, he stepped deeper into the room and examined the pictures. A smile teased his lips at the last one. "Aunt Rosa gave me these a couple days ago. I had 'em in my pocket and forgot I dumped them in here." He met her gaze and his smile died after taking in her expression. "What's wrong?"

"Nothing." Everything. Damn it. "I just…jumped to conclusions."

Setting the photos aside, he wrapped his arms around her back. "What kind of conclusions?" When she didn't answer, he nodded slowly in understanding. "You thought I was going to go psycho boyfriend and put them all over my house?"

"Maybe."

A grin lit his eyes. "I already have pictures of you downstairs on my mantle. Those are staying, mind you, but the kissy couple ones can wait. Feel better?"

Embarrassed as hell, she dropped her forehead to his chest. "I'm sorry."

He pulled her in for a hug, setting his chin on the top of her head. "I know you feel uncertain, and until you take the test, that feeling isn't going to go away. No matter what, we'll go at our pace, Zoe. Not my family's or our friends' or what the town deems fit."

Before she could apologize again, he stepped away and grabbed the pictures. "I am pretty fond of this one." He held up the shot of them kissing at the parade and gave her an eyebrow waggle.

"Shut up." Laughing, she smacked his arm.

Sobering, he reached in the drawer and passed her a toothbrush. "I'm going to let the dogs outside. Take your time in here."

She understood loud and clear. Meaning, take whatever time she needed to get her head in order. He'd wait. He left, and she glanced around in an attempt to calm herself.

The bathroom was massive compared to hers at home and sported white tile floors, sage green in the whirlpool tub and surround, and a his and hers vanity. Glass doors to the corner shower stall were frosted with a leaf pattern. This room, too, had been altered after Heather had died. The first one in the house, done about two years ago.

She took a cleansing breath and brushed her teeth. Drying her mouth, she glanced at herself in the mirror and blinked. She'd grown accustomed to the purple hair color. As she fingered the strands, she realized it was time to dye it again. Not only because the color was fading, but because she was used to it. That was her pattern.

What next? Blue? Red? Green? Or…brown.

She stood, contemplating. They did have that conference next weekend.

Going back to her natural brunette color would be more professional and...
She sighed. It was time.

Out of a sense of preservation, self pity, and grief, she'd been hiding
behind a rainbow of box colors instead of facing facts. Mama wasn't going
to get better, but Zoe could still live her life and do what she loved. Time
might be at a minimum, but Drake had been right. She wasn't alone. If
that test did come back positive, she should snag every bit of joy before
the worst happened.

A calming sense of relief filled her. She might not have any control over
genetics or fate, nor could she promise Drake anything more than right
now, but she could take a corner of her life back.

Starting tomorrow, she was going to paint every day, and when Mama
got out of rehab, at least two hours a week. She'd also make plans to go to
Shooters with the gang once a month instead of every blue moon.

And she'd stop dyeing her hair.

Chapter 20

Lying in bed, Drake flipped through TV channels and waited for Zoe to exit the bathroom. It had been fifteen minutes since she'd run water or made a sound. He stared at the door as if that would make her come out faster. Worry twisted his gut.

Those pictures had obviously upset her. There was nothing he could change about that or her circumstances. Best he could do was be with her, offer support, and pray to all that was holy her genetic testing came back negative. Even if it didn't, he'd be here, where he'd always been.

Sighing, he set the remote aside. He had the sinking suspicion she planned to dump him if she got a positive result. She'd fought the idea of dating so adamantly before she had a clue if her mom's condition was even a factor. Knowing Zoe, she'd shut down, back off, and wait out the impending storm alone. Not that he'd let her.

The door clicked and she stepped out wearing his white tee. It fell to her knees, offered no hint at the curves beneath, but hell if his heart didn't pound. Nothing was sexier or more intimate than a woman in a guy's shirt.

She set her clothes by her purse on the chair and sat at the edge of the bed facing him. She stared at his chest, her throat working a swallow. He waited her out, but she said nothing, nor did she move. Perhaps tonight had been too much for her.

He sat up and covered her hand with his. "Do you want me to take you home?"

Her gaze flicked to his and away. "I can walk, if you prefer I leave. I just need to say a few things first."

Like hell he'd let her walk. And the pounding of his heart from moments before stopped so fast he flinched. "Stay."

Closing her eyes, she took a second as if to compose herself and then looked at him with gutting, visceral torment. Yep. She was preparing to rip the rug out from under him. There it was in her expression, plain as day.

He shook his head, pissed off as hell. "Is this the point where you tell me you're gone if that test is positive? You'll just walk away as if what we have together is nothing?"

"It's not nothing, and that's the problem." She ran a shaking hand over her forehead. "If you were in my place, wouldn't you do the same?"

Staring at her, he ground his molars. For her benefit, he thought it over. "No. You might think you're protecting me, but all you're doing is making decisions on my behalf. After Heather died, I didn't think about the months she was in bed hooked up to IVs. It was the years we had prior that I chose to recall. Our high school dances, our wedding, the time she had with you."

She bit her lip. "My condition wouldn't be months, but years, Drake."

"I understand that. And I'd rather have the chance for a few years with you together like this or as friends than none at all. You're trying to take the choice away from me."

"You're right." Her gaze locked on to his, potent and definite. "That's not fair to you. While in the bathroom, I made the decision to stop hiding. I'm going to hang out more with my friends and paint and not waste what time I might have left."

"You need to consider something else." He watched her, hoping he could break through. "You're basing a lot of this condition on your mother's case. Our circumstances are different than hers. If you do get sick and your memory regresses, who's there? Me. My brothers. Your friends. We go way back, Zoe. As in, all the way. I'll make sure you're not scared. If nothing else, you'll remember me."

Her expression softened. "I care about you so damn much. And you're the kind of man who goes all in. Before Portland, before this thing with us goes any farther, you need to seriously ask yourself if this is what you want. We have the opportunity to call it quits—"

"It's what I want. You're what I want." He searched her gaze, rammed home his point by not looking away. "You're correct about the all in part. I have been from day one." He took her hand, lacing their fingers. "Last week, when it dawned on me your true reason for keeping me at a distance, my first thought was *not her*. Not you, Zoe. My second was to get to you as fast as humanly possible. Be here with you. I can't and won't shut down that desire. Not as a friend or a potential lover."

Trembling, she studied him. She had the same look in her eyes as she did the day Heather had been diagnosed, the same agony as when his father had passed away. Helpless. Her lower lip quivered, and her teeth sank into it even as her eyes filled. Blinking, she quickly looked away with a nod.

He could tell she had other doubts, more roadblocks but, for now, she was submitting. At least she'd not only heard him this time, but listened. "Stay," he said again.

In an extremely rare gesture of weakness, she flopped onto the bed with her head in his lap, her fingers still clutching his. He paused in shock, then used his other hand to brush the hair away from her face. She was so damn beautiful his chest threatened to cave. This tender, soft side of her wrecked him every time it was exposed.

She stared, unblinking, at something across the room and released a ragged exhale. "I don't want to hurt you."

Christ. She slayed him. "Then don't."

He slid his arms under hers, laid on his back, and hauled her up his body so she was sprawled across him. For good measure, he pulled the blankets over them, creating a cocoon.

She wrapped herself around him like a bandage, burying her face in his throat. "What now?"

"The way I see it, we can do one of two things. Make out like teenagers as you suggested earlier, or go to sleep. I'm up for either but, given a choice, I take door number one."

She went utterly still, and then—thank Christ—she laughed, just as he intended. Hard enough to shake them and the mattress. Lifting her head, she stared down at him. "Once again, you are improperly dressed for bed. Since you're still wearing your clothes, I assume you don't want to sleep."

Smiling, he pushed her hair away from her face, loving the banter between them. "You would be correct. I'm not very subtle, am I?" He took in her huge hazel eyes, barely noticeable freckles on her nose, and pouty mouth. "You're quite beautiful, you know that?"

She blinked. Then blinked again. "You have got to stop with the reduce-me-to-puddle talk. Seriously, you had me with your body."

"I'll have you know, I was serious."

"So am I."

And before he could retort, her mouth was on his. No coaxing on her part. She just went right at him with deep strokes of her tongue, sending him from want to need in the time it took him to thread his fingers through her hair.

Her hands started to wander and his heart relocated ribs. Down his arms, across his chest, over his stomach… Fire licked his skin from her path. Unsure how far to take things, he settled his hands on her waist and squeezed. In retaliation, she shoved hers under his shirt and tugged the material up as if she wanted it off.

Jackknifing, he sat up, taking her with him, and she pulled the tee over his head. Then...hers followed, and hell, he didn't dare look anywhere but her face. Their chests crashed and they stared at one another, panting. "Boundaries," he rasped. He slammed his eyes shut. "I need to know boundaries, Zoe."

She brought her lips to his and spoke against them. "We agreed to Portland." His lungs refused to cooperate, not with her warm, soft skin against his, her breasts crushed between them, her lavender scent invading his nostrils, and her breathy voice. "Right now. What are the boundaries right now?"

Fingernails raked lightly down his back. "We can use our hands."

Dipping her head, she licked his neck. "And our mouths."

Sweet mercy. "Where?"

She nipped the other side of his neck and soothed the ache with her hot tongue. "Everywhere."

That was all the intel he required. He crashed his mouth to hers and grabbed her thighs. She ground against him until he was so hard he throbbed.

Quick as a flash, it dawned on him he was doing this. He was with someone other than... Hell. Other than Heather.

He'd talked this to death with Zoe, and his feelings for her were separate from what he'd had with his wife. Unique. New crashing with old. Friendship meshing with more. They were two completely different women in personality and physical stature, at two different periods in his life. Until right this very second, getting intimate with Zoe had been rhetorical. There was an instant heat, attraction, and chemistry, but also a bond. He tried to dissect deeper meaning and couldn't because nowhere amid his emotions were...

No guilt . No shame . No doubts. Being with her was...right.

"Are you okay?" She held his face, her gaze seeking. Her lips were swollen from his kiss and her cheeks were flushed.

"Yes." He wasn't merely okay. That term could be described as what he'd been the past four years. Zoe and his brothers had made sure of that with their actions and presence. But, over the course of a few weeks, she'd managed to make him much more than simply okay. He was happy again. "Definitely, yes."

His gaze dipped past her throat, collarbone, and to her breasts. Tiny. Perfect. Olive skin and dark, pert nipples. Breathtaking. He glanced up, meeting her eyes as he cupped her, and brushed his thumbs over the swells. Her breath caught and her fingers toyed with the hair on his nape. Watching her, he slid his hands past her belly to her red lace panties, tracing the waistband with his fingertips.

"You have a thing for lace." The yellow pair she'd worn the other night would be imprinted on his retinas forever.

Removing her hands from his neck, she fingered his nylon shorts. "And are you a boxers or briefs man?"

She gave him no time to respond. Pushing him to his back, she used that weapon of a mouth to suck, kiss, and bite his throat. Lower to his nipples, where she swirled the tip of her tongue. Lower yet across his stomach. And then... She tugged his shorts down his hips.

"Boxer briefs." She smiled up at him.

Immobile, he stared at her. Desire so potent he was dizzy spiraled through him. Stole his air. He tried to swallow and couldn't. Hell, now she was taking his briefs, too. His erection sprang free and he suddenly forgot what the hell he was supposed to do, where to touch, what to say. He clenched his fingers at his sides.

"Zoe," he rasped in a voice hoarse with need.

She tossed his clothing aside, set her palms on either side of his hips, and leaned on her hands. Without so much as a muscle twitch, she looked in his eyes. Calm. Assured. And, if he wasn't mistaken, as turned on as him. Silently, she asked him with her expression what he wanted. Yes or no.

Muscles shaking with curiosity and violent need, he lifted his head and wove his fingers through her hair. Lavender rose up to claim him and he nodded. Still, she waited a moment, then wrapped her fingers around his base and stroked.

His head slammed to the pillow and his hips involuntarily rose. When she got to his tip and added her mouth, his lungs emptied. To avoid hurting her, he unclenched his fingers from her strands and pressed them to the headboard instead.

Hot, wet mouth. Firm, deft fingers.

He groaned from a place so deep his throat burned. Lightning splintered his nerves. His lower back tightened and he arched off the mattress. He tried warning her he was close, but she didn't stop. Lifting his head, he looked down at her and got trapped by her hazel eyes locked on his, her red mouth wrapped around him.

And he was done for. Chasing the white light, he exploded with her name on his lips, and the release seemed to go on forever. Spasms. Tension. Insane fucking pleasure. He slumped, staring at the ceiling, panting like a man dying.

She crawled up his body as he caught his breath. Mind blown and thought obsolete, he wrapped his arms around her. And since that didn't seem like enough, he ran his hand up her back, into her hair, and kissed the shit out of her.

Smiling, she nuzzled her nose with his. "You seem very pleased." Running his thumb across her lower lip, he cleared his throat and fought the pressure in his chest. "You amaze me." And he'd reciprocate as soon as he knew what planet they'd landed on.

A grin lit her eyes as she leaned in to kiss him. This time, she started slow. A build up. More endearment than heat. But, in typical Zoe fashion, that swiftly catapulted into blinding desperation.

He slid his hands down the curve of her spine, under her panties, and grabbed her ass. Fingers kneading, he stroked her tongue with his, mimicking the dance he couldn't wait to do with her next weekend. She made those noises that drove him to delirium, and he rolled her beneath him.

For months, he'd wanted to kiss every inch of her, know what it felt like to have her beneath him, and the reality was almost too much. Completely unashamed of her taut little body, she wrapped her limbs around him, her hands tracing the contours of his where she could reach, and all while she kissed him with reckless abandon.

Resurfacing for air, he made his way over her collarbone and to her breasts. Sucking one hardened bead into his mouth, he fingered the other. She bowed to meet him, moaning and fisting his hair. By the time he moved to her other breast, he was hard as fieldstone again.

Inching lower, he swirled his tongue around her belly button and looked up at her as he got to her panties. She had one arm bent under her head, the other hand resting just below her wet breasts, and unadulterated passion in her eyes. Getting his answer, he slid her panties down her thighs and dropped them to the floor.

His gaze immediately landed on the tattoo on her pelvic bone. He got a better look this time, and emotion clogged his airway as he remembered that day. He traced the dandelion stem, the fluff, then the seeds drifting. And because he'd never get her memory for the ink out of his mind, he kissed her there. "I'll give you a hundred dandelions next time."

She went rigid under him. Slapping a hand over her face, she emitted a whimper. Belly quivering, she sucked a harsh inhale and shook her head like she couldn't deal.

Hell. While she still hid behind her hand, he called her name, praying he wouldn't find tears. She shook her head again, brows pinched.

"Zoe, honey. Look at me." When she finally did, her eyes were dry, but red-rimmed as if she'd let go any second. "A hundred of them. I swear to you."

Forehead wrinkled, she pressed her lips together. Her breath hitched.

To diffuse her, he kissed the tattoo again, then her inner thigh. Her expression smoothed in ease, and he moved his lips higher until he hovered over the dark triangle of neatly trimmed hair on her mound. Gently, he spread her thighs, keeping his gaze locked with hers, and waited. Only once her eyes radiated interest and not distress did he finally break the connection and look down.

Damn beautiful. Pink lips already wet for him and her little nub was hard. He kissed her there first, and with a quiet inhale, she closed her eyes. Refocusing on his task, he tasted her, using his tongue and fingers until she threw her head back. Her hips rose to meet him.

Even during pleasure she was vocal. Sounds and sighs and breathy whispers of encouragement. He was unaccustomed to it and found he liked it immensely, loved knowing what she craved. Wanting nothing more than to see her fall off the cliff, he groaned and increased the pressure as liquid fire flowed through his veins.

She didn't take long. With a cry and a shudder, she came, bowing off the bed. He brought her down slowly while she bit her lip, still trembling with flushed cheeks. Her arms flopped limply to the mattress as pride filled his chest.

He shifted to lie beside her and, eyes still closed, she turned to him. With her curled to his side, he covered them with a blanket and kissed her forehead. Damn amazing night. Exhausted, happy, and sated, he started to drift off.

She yawned and burrowed deeper. "You get back on the saddle pretty well, cowboy."

Chuckling, he dipped his head and kissed her. Long, languid, and trying to infuse every sentiment swirling inside him.

The next thing he knew, he was prying his eyes open to sunlight streaming through the balcony doors. He stretched and patted the bed beside him, finding the sheets cool.

With a frown, he sat up. A quick glance at the chair showed Zoe's purse and clothes were still there. Muffled voices rose from the lower level. He climbed out of bed, relieved his bladder and brushed his teeth in the bathroom, stepped into a pair of shorts, then headed downstairs.

His brothers sat at the kitchen island on stools, Zoe was at the stove wearing his tee from the night before, and four dogs were positioned obediently at her bare feet.

A yawn cracked his jaw as he stepped deeper in the room. "We have visitors."

Zoe glanced over her shoulder. "Yes, and explain to these two this isn't what it looks like."

Cade grinned. "Looks to me like you're wearing Drake's shirt, your hair is sleep tousled, and you're making breakfast in his kitchen."

Spatula in hand, she faced them. "Okay, it's kinda what it looks like."

Unable to help it, Drake laughed. He kissed her cheek. "Good morning."

Flynn's brows rose to his hairline. *"Speaking of morning. Since when do you sleep past seven?"*

Drake glanced at the wall clock. Almost eight. He couldn't remember the last time he'd zonked out that hard. Typically, he'd crash after midnight, get sporadic rest at best, and rise promptly at six.

He shrugged and poured himself a cup of orange juice. "Must've been tired."

"Or worn out," Cade muttered under his breath.

Zoe choked on her coffee.

Setting his drink aside and ignoring his brothers, Drake wrapped his arms around her and kissed her properly. He couldn't recall ever waking up so damn...satisfied either. Happy. While he waited for her heavy lids to open, he peeked at the stove. Omelets. Awesome. She blinked up at him, amusement in her eyes. He grinned, kissed her nose, and reclaimed his juice.

Zoe went back to the stove, the dogs following.

He stared at Tweedledee and Tweedledum over the rim of his glass. Both brothers looked like they'd been smacked upside the head with a golf club. "Problem?"

Eyes wide, expression flipped to stunned, Cade shook his head. "Zoe, come over here, yeah?"

She glanced at him. "Why?"

"Just do it."

She mumbled something about shoe ad slogans and walked around the counter while Cade kept his eyes on Drake. "What?"

"Closer."

She stepped beside Cade's stool.

Little brother grabbed her shoulders, smacked a quick kiss to her mouth, and pushed her back. "Thank you."

"Gah, Cade." Seemingly horrified, she wiped her mouth. "What the heck?"

"Thank you." He grinned at her as if in awe, pointing to Drake. "See that? Check him out. Thank you." He swiveled to face the island. "And be glad I'm happily married or I'd kiss you proper."

With a roll of her eyes, she went back to the stove. Flynn hopped off the stool and blocked her path. Her hands flew up to sign and speak simultaneously. "Oh, no. Not you, too."

Flynn held up his fist instead. After she bumped it, he hugged her.

Grinding his molars, Drake narrowed his eyes. "Stop touching her. Both of you. Why are you here anyway?"

Flynn and Cade headed for the back door, two of the four dogs in tow, and Cade turned. "We come bearing a request. Family dinner at Mom's tonight. She expects Zoe, too."

The guys left.

Zoe crossed her arms. "I'm totally tattling on him to your mom for kissing me."

Chapter 21

Sunday dinner at the O'Grady home front was a two-hour affair. Zoe played tic-tac-toe with Avery's daughter, Hailey, and then watched the guys chase the dogs around Gayle's yard with Gabby. The meal consisted of baked ham, mashed potatoes, and peas. No one dared make her eat the latter. The entire night, Drake's mom watched Zoe like a hawk, a smile permanently on her face and relief in her eyes. Zoe even managed to rat out Cade for kissing her, to which no one but Drake got angry about.

She'd had many family dinners at the house growing up, yet it was the first time Zoe was dating one of the boys. It wasn't uncomfortable by any means, but she didn't care for the hero worship from Gayle or Drake's brothers. Yes, he was finally moving on past his grief, and yes, he did seem happy and more like his old self. But if they knew her possible future, surely they'd think Zoe was as selfish as she felt.

As they all were getting ready to leave, she noticed the picture of Heather and Drake was missing from the mantle and replaced with one of him and Zoe. She hadn't seen this one before, but it had been taken at the softball game when Drake had dragged her away from Jason and Parker to kiss her.

Gayle stepped beside her. "You made him happy again."

Damn. Just…damn. She glanced at Drake, but he was talking to his brothers by the door. "Please put the photo of them back up. She was an important part of his life."

Gayle smoothed a hand down Zoe's hair. "It wouldn't upset you having it out?"

"No." God, no. "She was his wife and my best friend. Ignoring her is like pretending she never existed. If you want to display this one of us, that's great, but please keep the other picture as well."

With an endearing smile, Gayle nodded. "That's a very mature approach,

Zoe-bug. I'm not sure most women would think that way. How is it that just yesterday you were climbing trees and coloring with crayons, and today you're all grown up? I'm very proud of you. Your mom would be, too."

Feeling like the lowest species of life form, she hugged Gayle and fought the guilt clutching her stomach.

On Monday, Drake insisted on going to the doctor's office with her first thing in the morning for the blood test, even though it was just a lab visit. And since this was typically her day off unless the clinic was crazy-busy, she spent the rest of the whole day painting. What started out as a whim turned into a mission, and after work the next two days, she finished the four pieces.

By Thursday, she was crawling out of her skin to not only skip town with Drake, but to learn the genetic test results. Her doctor said the labs had to be sent out of state, so it might take up to two weeks to hear word. The findings were supposed to be mailed directly to her.

Ever since Mama's diagnosis, Zoe had teetered back and forth on whether to be tested. On one hand, knowing would bring relief on many levels. But on the other hand, how could she live with herself if it was positive? If she and Drake stuck, he'd be giving up the family he desperately wanted and they'd be counting the days until she cracked. The fallout after it happened would be disastrous. Mama's decline proved it.

Trying to get her mind off something she couldn't control, she glanced around the Animal Instincts break room late Thursday afternoon. Avery had closed shop early and pulled them into a meeting. They were waiting on Brent to return from an errand to get started. While the others chatted, Zoe mentally went through her packing list for Portland.

A few minutes later, Brent strode in.

"Finally," Gabby said. "You're late."

Brent took a chair beside Cade. "Sorry. My dentist was like, you need a crown, and I was all like, I know, right? A sparkly one." He waved his hand. "Anyway, what gives? We never had meetings before Avery came along."

Avery narrowed her eyes. "You never had a charting system, supply closet, or coded files either."

"I'd shut up or she'll make your life hell." Flynn grinned.

"Exactly." Avery tapped her iPad. "First up, Drake and Zoe's Portland conference. Check in is at three on Friday. There's a drink mixer at the hotel bar that night." She passed Drake a sheet of paper. "That's the schedule. I have our clinic brochures for you to take. They appear to have five workshops and two guest speakers on Saturday. And good thing I checked the itinerary because there's a formal banquet dinner that evening. Black

tie. Continental breakfast on Sunday, check out. Blah, blah, blah."
Drake laced his fingers and stacked them on his head. "Guess I'm
packing a suit."

"Squee." Brent clapped his hands. "Looks like Zoe and I are going
shopping tonight." He dropped his voice to a stage whisper. "We'll hit up
the lingerie store, too."

"Christ, man. TMI." Cade tossed a wadded piece of paper at him.

"Said the guy who kissed me yesterday." Zoe looked from Cade to Brent.

"My underwear drawer is quite sexy. You're already acquainted with it."

"Interesting. Thought you were going to a work conference." Flynn grinned.

"Shut up." Drake frowned and then focused on Zoe. "How would Brent
know what your panties look like?"

"He's in the know about such things." Gabby dropped her chin in her
palm. "Trust me."

Flynn eyed Brent. *"You are so lucky you're gay, else you might
be a dead man."*

"Miles agrees with you." Brent blew on his knuckles and swiped them
on his shirt, his face smug.

"Anyway." Zoe reached behind her chair and pulled out the eight-by-
ten paintings she'd made. "Speaking of Miles, are you two good? Is he
ready to kill you yet?"

Somehow, Brent managed to cock a hip while sitting. "Please.
We're fantabulous."

"Good. This is for you, then." She slid the painting across the table and
watched while he examined it. The piece wasn't like her usual surrealism
twist. None of the ones she'd completed this week were, in fact. The canvas
she gave Brent was him and Miles holding hands by the tree in the park,
twilight behind them.

Eyes wide, Brent waved a hand in front of his face. "Oh my
Cher. I f-love it."

"Awesome, Zoe." Cade looked over his tech's shoulder. "Why don't I get—"

Eyebrows raised, she passed him another canvas. And before the others
got pissy, she handed over Flynn's and Drake's, too. "I had time this week
and my muse showed her face again."

All three were set in the guys' backyards. Cade's had him in sunlight,
sitting in the grass with Hailey between his legs, and the dogs lying beside
them. Avery was behind him, kissing Cade's cheek. Flynn's was done by
the riverbed at dusk. He stood by the bank, Gabby on his back laughing,
with her cat and his dog running ahead. Drake's was painted at night
near the forest edge. He was tossing a ball for both his dogs, who she'd

captured mid-run.

"Jesus, Zoe." Cade glanced up at her, his eyes soft with emotion. "It's amazing."

Flynn dragged her in for a one-armed hug. He pulled away and signed, *"I'm glad you're painting again. I'm hanging this above the fireplace."*

As Avery and Gabby cooed, Zoe glanced at Drake. He was still staring at his, gaze determined, jaw set. She couldn't read his expression and grew a little nervous.

"Sorry to hijack your meeting." Zoe looked at Avery. "Wanted to pass those out before we left tomorrow."

"No worries." Avery brought up a few items like the supply room closet lock getting fixed, then looked down. "We only have one other thing to discuss, but it's important." She pulled a breath and looked at Cade. "We're pregnant."

Drake finally brought his head up and darted his gaze between Cade and Avery, lips parted in surprise.

The room went quiet as Cade grinned. "She's due in March. Sounds lucky to me."

"Oh my God." Gabby flew out of her chair and launched at Avery, nearly toppling them both with a hug. "That's the best news." And...the crocodile Gabby tears came as she focused on Flynn. "We're definitely doing a September wedding. She won't show too much and dress shoes will still be comfortable."

Flynn laughed. *"Whatever you say, sweetheart."*

As the others congratulated them, Zoe sat back in her chair, smiling like a fool. A little jealousy trickled inside her head, but she shoved it down. She'd resigned herself years before to the probable fact she couldn't have children. If her test was positive, she could pass the gene to her offspring, and that was a hell no. She'd dote on her friends' kids and it would have to be enough. It did her heart good to see them happy, though.

Avery's first marriage to Hailey's father had been disastrous. The prick never paid attention to Hailey and had cheated on Avery. When Cade—reformed playboy—had met her, he'd fallen flat on his face for both mother and daughter. They were perfect together.

"You're going to make the best dad." When Cade met her gaze, Zoe nodded confirmation. "You were raised by the best and you're already more of a father than Hailey has ever known."

"Hell." He cleared his throat. "I really needed to hear that, I think. I was a little nerve-wracked. Excited, but anxious."

"Don't be." Smiling, she winked at Avery.

Zoe could feel Drake's gaze on her, but she focused on everyone else until Avery finally adjourned the meeting. Grabbing her things, she followed Brent.

"Where are we going shopping and what, exactly, do you have in mind?" His grin resembled the Grinch in plot mode. "Naughty, naughty things, firecracker."

"I knew we were friends for a reason."

After two stores, she wound up with a gold slip dress that fell mid-calf, had spaghetti straps, and reminded her of the twenties-style flapper ensembles, minus the fringe. Black strappy heels completed the outfit, and Zoe hugged Brent as they parted ways. From there, she stopped by the drugstore for hair dye and headed home.

Later, she flopped in a recliner, once again a brunette, and sipped wine. Anticipation coiled in her belly for this weekend.

On and off, and for as long as she could remember, she'd wanted Drake. Other lovers had been good, some great, but after what she'd done with Drake last weekend, she knew no other guy would compare. He'd been generous and attentive and observant. God, his hands alone could elicit a bone-deep tremor of desire. Add in the emotional factor? She didn't even need to question if they'd be good. There was no doubt.

And she badly needed this trip. Not just for sex or to spend time with him. It had been years since she'd gotten out of Redwood Ridge, and though this was no vacation, she intended to treat it like one. Who knew when or if she'd be able to travel again.

Cotton jumped onto her lap and purred, begging for attention.

She ran her fingers through his soft, white fur. "You better be good for Uncle Brent while I'm away. He'll come by to feed you and play."

Meow.

"It's only a few days. No wild parties. Got it?"

Meow.

"I know. Brent is a bad influence, but just try to keep him in line."

Meow.

Her cell alerted a text. Grabbing it off the table, she checked the screen. Drake. Her pathetic heart puttered.

I'll pick you up between eight and nine, if that's okay.

She thumbed a response. *Works for me. I'll have coffee ready.*

The icon indicated he was typing. *I'm looking forward to this weekend.*

Grinning, she pressed her lips together. *Me, too.*

You left the office before I could thank you for the painting.

Rubbing her forehead, she stared at the screen. He hadn't given her any indication if he'd liked it or not.

I'll properly show you my thanks in Portland.

And still no praise. It wasn't as if she was a compliment whore or anything, but his opinion mattered to her. *Did you like it?* Biting her lip, she waited for his response.

Loved it. They were all amazing. Mine's missing something, though.

She hadn't thrown anything crazy in that set like she typically did. They'd been true-to-life renditions of the O'Grady boys and their significant others. She'd been torn on whether to put Heather in Drake's. However, she'd decided against it since he'd been trying to move on. Besides, he and Zoe were dating and it had seemed awkward.

Sighing, she typed a response, not sure she wanted to hear his answer if it would involve his dead wife. *What's missing?*

She loved Heather. Always had, always would. And though Zoe had no idea what to do about Drake, she so desperately wanted to claim this tether of joy while it lasted. But Heather had been his first love. The real deal. She was an impossible person to follow. No one else could compare. Truth be told, Zoe was, at best, a second choice, and a crappy one with baggage at that.

He hadn't responded, and her anxiety grew. Perhaps he didn't know how to tell her or he thought she might get upset with his answer. Quickly, she shot off a text. *I'll paint Heather in for you as soon as we get back from Portland.*

His reply was so swift she could feel his irritation from across the cellular void. *Heather is gone. You're what's missing.*

Crap. The only answer worse than Heather was that one. Her sinuses prickled and her throat tightened. And she was so stupid for being moved by his words. Always honest, forever plunging heart first, Drake was whittling her down sentence by sentence. Touch by touch. Action by action.

Zoe?

She sniffed. *I'm here.*

The icon whirled. *I asked you not to make decisions for me.*

Intuitive jerk. She closed her eyes and took a calming breath. He'd been correct about calling her out. She had no right to take his choice away. But she *could* do what was right for herself if it came down to it, and that probably meant letting him go if the test was positive. Her conscience was beating down the door already. Yet she'd promised him she'd try, and nothing was written in stone.

Obviously impatient with waiting, his reply pinged. *Don't give me a reason to come over there. I just saw you a few hours ago, and I'm already fighting the urge to make an excuse to see you again. Waiting until*

tomorrow sucks.
A rough laugh shot past her lips. *I'll make the wait worth it.*
A man can hope. What does your dress look like for Saturday night?
Smiling, she thumbed the screen. *It's a surprise.*
Doesn't matter. The only place it'll look better than on you is on the floor.
Her jaw dropped. *Are you sexting me, Drake O'Grady?*
LOL. Maybe I am, Zoe Hornsby. However, I'm going to quit while I'm ahead.
Two can play this game. *What a shame. I just took off my shirt. And I'm in bed naked. Good night. See you tomorrow.*
With a heavy sigh, she glanced at Cotton. "I never should've taught him how to flirt."

Chapter 22

Drake crossed his arms and waited for Zoe to answer the bell. Anxiety and excitement churned his gut, and they couldn't get to Portland fast enough for him. After years of numb autopilot, she'd awoken something in him, and scary as it seemed at times, he'd missed...living. The almost euphoric bubble of hope and happiness and possibility.

She swung the door wide and turned, jogging toward the kitchen. "I'm putting coffee in to-go cups now. Just give me a sec. My bag is right there if you want to take it to the car."

"There's no rush." He stepped inside and shut the door. Reaching for her bag, he glanced at her and froze.

She'd dyed her hair back to normal. Light brown with caramel highlights, it flowed in soft waves to her shoulders. His lungs went into hyper drive trying to keep up. Damn, she'd been beautiful before. Turn her natural and she was gorgeous. He had nothing against the ridiculous colors the past few years, but this was the real Zoe. The one he very much preferred.

She did a double-take. "It's not that heavy."

He glanced at her bag in his hand, not realizing he'd picked it up, and dropped it. "Come here." Never mind. He strode to her and caged her against the counter. "I like your hair."

She blinked her huge hazel eyes. "Um, thank you?"

Amused she'd turned her response into a question, he smiled. "I missed you."

"I missed you, too?"

Laughing, he let his gaze travel over her hair, her face. "Am I confusing you?"

She bit her lip. "A little bit. What's with the caveman thing? Stalking over here and trapping me—"

He kissed her and pulled away. Then framed her face with his hands and kissed her again. "Missed you."

"It's only been a day," she whispered.

"I meant in a general sense. Not that I didn't wish you were with me last night. But I was referring to your hair. I like the real Zoe better."

"Oh." She ran her fingers through the strands. "Thought it was more professional." Her gaze darted away. "And time to stop fearing what I can't control."

Christ. He was pretty sure he fell the rest of the way right there in her living room. Strong and outspoken, Zoe stood up for what she believed in. Smart and a spitfire, she could elicit a witty comeback and hold her own on any topic. Giving and empathetic, she'd taken care of his wife and her best friend in Heather's final months, and had given up nearly everything for her own mother, no matter how hard it had hurt. Affectionate and sexy, she could pull primal and basic responses from him in seconds. And then there was this side of her. The soft, tender parts most didn't realize were there, just below the surface.

How the hell was a guy to defend himself against one of those aspects, never mind all of them? Throw in her gorgeousness? Lost cause.

With a deep sigh, he stepped away. She wasn't ready for declarations, but if it took everything in his arsenal, he'd get her there soon.

"Ready?" He smiled to erase the concentration on his face.

With a nod, she eased around him.

When they were on the road, she called Pine Crest to check on her mom and, from what he could gather of the conversation, Cat was doing really well. Which was a relief because Zoe had been extremely concerned and, at times, crawling out of her skin. It killed him to see her that out of sorts.

"I don't know what to make of it." She shook her head. "I mean, I'm glad she's adjusting and really seems happy, but I can't help but feel guilty, you know? Why wasn't she that relaxed at home? I could barely get her to sit down, never mind eat. Taking her meds had become this ritualistic chore involving award-winning acting skill."

Reaching over, he clasped her hand. "She probably recognizes Pine Crest from working there for years, even if it's not cognitive memory. You are doing the best you can. Don't beat yourself up. It's not your fault. This disease is shitty and hurts those left behind the most."

She squeezed his hand and went silent for awhile.

The rest of the drive up to Portland went smoothly. They chatted about everything and nothing. She took over the radio and he pretended to be affronted. Truth was, he loved listening to her sing along to hard rock because she screeched the higher notes and her expression grew adorable at the lower ones. If a person ever claimed boredom in Zoe's presence, they didn't have a heartbeat.

Once they arrived at the hotel, he canceled the second room and they dropped their luggage off in the suite. Queen-sized bed, mini kitchenette, and a great view of the Willamette River with Mount Hood in the distance. Orientation was tedious, and by the time they walked into the bar for the drink mixer, he was vying for excuses to take her back upstairs.

Primal, basic, and fierce. Yet it wasn't only physical. Maybe that was the key. The emotional assault she rendered had all of him, every atom, firing on all cylinders.

She wore a white sundress with cherries on it, of all things, and her hair in a ponytail, exposing her regal neck. There were easily seventy people from the conference in the bar, mostly men, and at least half watched her entrance.

He glanced around at the sleekly polished wood, chrome, and green-shade lighting, and decided it resembled every other hotel bar in America. "Want a drink?"

"Sure." An evil grin lit her eyes. "I'll have sex on the beach. Or a fuzzy navel."

Leaning on the counter, he sighed. "You're only requesting that to hear me say the order aloud."

"Totally. I challenge you."

The bartender eyed them, his dark gaze darting back and forth between them and lips curved in amusement. He looked barely legal to buy alcohol, never mind serve it.

Drake shook his head. "She wants sex on the beach, and no, that's not an offer. I'll take a whiskey neat. Jameson if you have it." He'd need it to keep up with her and calm his nerves.

The bartender nodded and moved away.

Zoe hopped on a stool and faced him. "Bravo. You ordered with a straight face and managed to piss on your territory."

He ran his tongue across his teeth and skimmed his gaze over her outfit. "I can't tell if that dress is cute or hot."

"Hot," the bartender said, setting down their drinks. "Definitely."

Zoe grinned. "Give the man a big tip."

Without glancing at the nuisance, Drake held up some bills, told the kid to keep the change, and kept his eyes on Zoe. "How long do we need to stay down here?"

A rich laugh erupted from her red lips. "In a hurry?"

"Yes. And every Y chromosome-carrying human in here is watching you."

"Just the Y's?" She pouted. "That's disappointing."

Hell, he wanted her. Bad.

To distract them both, he slid the conference brochure toward her with one finger. "What workshops do you want to attend?" She took a sip of her fruity drink and opened the pamphlet. "Hm. There's only two catered for groomers. I think I'll do the first one early tomorrow morning and then play hooky. Maybe walk around the city."

Stepping behind her, he eyed the listing over her shoulder. None of them really appealed to him except, perhaps, the nine o'clock for a new surgical technique for cruciate ligament repair. They did a lot of those in the clinic. He leaned closer and inhaled lavender. "I'll attend this one"—he pointed to the workshop—"and then play hooky with you." He dipped his mouth close to her ear, earning a shiver. "We can get lunch and see a couple attractions, then arrive back in time for the banquet."

Turning her head, she eyed him, their faces so close he wouldn't have to strain to kiss her. "Are you sure? As our chief surgeon, aren't you supposed to be more of a presence?"

"No one will miss me. I'd rather be with you."

Her lips curved. "If that's what you want."

"I want." Christ, did he want. Thus, he resumed the spot at her side and slammed his whiskey, enjoying the burn. To avoid watching her lips wrap around the straw in her drink, he glanced at the attendees. A guy they went to college with was standing by himself near the exit. "I see someone I know. Will you be okay for a minute?"

"Sure." She batted her eyelashes and used her teeth to strip a cherry off a swizzle stick.

He groaned, shoving his hands in his pockets. "Five minutes. Tops."

As she laughed, he strode toward his former classmate. He and Zoe had attended the same college, but she'd been a graphic design major and he'd been in veterinary medicine. Ergo, Drake was confident Zoe didn't know Pete.

He said the guy's name and held out his hand.

Pete turned and grinned. "Drake. Long time, no see. Are you here for the conference, too?"

Drake's first thought was Pete didn't look much different. He still had a boyish face, very slim build, and red hair. He'd grown up in the Midwest and never really dropped that slight accent. His polo and khakis made Drake feel somewhat overdressed in charcoal slacks and a white button-down shirt. They made idle chit-chat about their clinics for a few minutes and then switched to personal crap.

"How's Heather? You guys must be hitched by now."

Drake cleared his throat. "We did tie the knot, but she passed away a few years ago."

Pete sobered. "I'm sorry. I hadn't heard." While Drake nodded, Pete sipped his ale. "Are you here alone or did one of your brothers come up?"

"I'm here with the woman I'm dating. She works at the office." Drake pointed to Zoe, who had three men surrounding her stool. He ground his teeth. Three minutes since he'd stepped away, and the hounds were circling.

"Is that…?" Pete snapped his fingers as if to conjure memory. "Zoe. That's her name. We had an English Lit class together freshman year. She got in a heated debate with our professor claiming Shakespeare's playwriting skills were minimalistic and based on miscommunication." He laughed. "I'll never forget it. She said his only redeeming quality was usually killing off a lead. Man, I wanted to ask her out, but never had the balls."

That sounded like her, all right. And she rarely went anywhere without drawing attention. "Let's go say hello. I'm sure she'd love to see you." Drake hoped not, but grinned anyway.

They worked their way through the crowd and Drake made it a point to wrap his arm around her waist. "Honey, look who I ran into. Do you remember Pete?"

"English Literature with Professor Dumbass." Zoe grinned.

Taking the hint, the other guys stepped away while Pete nodded. "Good memory. You look wonderful."

Thirty minutes later, Zoe and Pete were still talking about the class and Drake was on his second whiskey. He'd passed his social limit somewhere between Zoe's "remember that stupid tie he wore" and Pete's "he smelled like menthol cigarettes."

Downing the rest of his drink, Drake waited for an opening and pounced. "We have an early morning and you're probably tired from the drive."

With a smile for Pete, Zoe sighed. "That's code for I want to go upstairs. It was great seeing you again."

"You, too. I'll look for you both tomorrow."

Taking her hand, Drake walked her to the elevator and rode up in silence with a couple other passengers, keeping his focus on the numbers. In the tension-crackled silence, she lightly skimmed her fingers over his nape and he inhaled hard through flared nostrils. Her touch was a direct current to his southern hemisphere, and in five seconds, his arousal wouldn't be something he could hide. Judging by her mischievous little grin, she knew that. Out of the corner of his eye, he caught her tracing a path across the bodice of her dress, right over the cleft between her breasts.

He grabbed her hand and squeezed in warning. She chuckled under her breath. At their floor, he all but dragged her to their room and fumbled with the keycard while she laughed.

"Would you like me to do it?"

"No." He slid the card in, got a green light, and twisted the knob. She stepped in ahead of him, but he caught her around the waist before she went too deep in the room and pressed her back against the wall. "I thought we'd never get out of there."

He kissed her like he'd been dying to do all night. Pressing his body flush with hers, he got lost in the way their mouths mated, the way she could send him over the edge with one stroke of her tongue. Her slim, petite build against his taller one shouldn't fit so well together, at least not geometrically speaking, yet they did. Skimming his hands down her waist to her thighs, he traveled back up and under her skirt. He teased the skin of her hips around her panties and she moaned.

A thud hit the floor, and he realized it was her shoe. The second thud relocated his heart as anticipation collided with desire.

"Condoms are in my suitcase." She grabbed his hair by the fistful and climbed him, wrapping her legs around his waist.

Behind his fly, his erection thrust against her heat as he pinned her to the wall once more. So damn good. With a roar, he buried his face in her hair, his hands on her lace-covered ass and working their way under the flimsy material. Her heels dug into his lower back and more of those groan-inducing mewls filled his ear.

"I'm not taking you for the first time against the wall." Though he wasn't sure he could move ten feet to the bed, so his protest might be moot.

She nipped his jaw, sucked on his neck. "I don't care where you take me, just so long as you do it now." When her hot tongue traced the shell of his ear, he about collapsed.

Christ Almighty and all the angels…

"Zoe, I want to take my time with…" *Uhn.* She ground against him, using her hands and legs and mouth and tongue to make his brain flatline. "Never fucking mind."

Using one hand to push off the wall, he did an about face and carried her to the side of the bed, kicking off his own shoes on the way. One arm firmly around her, he dug blindly in her suitcase for the box of protection while she kissed him like a woman starving. His fingers met smooth cardboard. Grabbing the box, he tossed it on the nightstand, shoved the suitcase off the bed, and laid her out on the mattress.

Following her down, he covered her body with his, leaned on his forearms, and stared at her. Flushed cheeks, dilated pupils, heavy lids, even heavier breathing. Hell, a saint couldn't resist her.

"I don't want to rush." Thing was, even if she didn't have him at the razor's edge, it had been quite some time since he'd had sex. Chances were, he wouldn't last long.

Her gaze locked on to his, determined, aroused, while she slid the first button of his shirt undone. Then another. So slowly, he thought he'd expire. He groaned at her pace.

"That's what I thought." With a satisfied smile, she jerked the material apart, sending buttons pinging across the room, and urged it off his shoulders.

"Hated this shirt anyway." He brought his mouth down on hers and kissed her deep while struggling to free himself of the damn garment.

She tossed it across the room and fingered the snap on his pants. Teeth released from the zipper and, bringing her knees up, she toed both his slacks and boxers to his ankles. He kicked them off the rest of the way.

Her gaze swept over him, and he swore she was fantasizing things he couldn't imagine on a good day. Every time she looked at him, it was like she was seeing him for the first time. There was never any doubt she liked what she saw, that her attraction was genuine. It was enough to make a guy bat his chest or preen.

Then her mouth was back on his and hunger had a new name. Lifting his head, he gulped air and shifted to his knees, taking her with him. Gaze on hers, he dipped under her dress and grabbed her hips. "Stand up." Him guiding her, she stood on the mattress in front of him.

Gaze locked on hers, he slid her panties—green, like the stems on the cherries of her dress—down her legs and helped her step out of them. Then he searched her back for the zipper and released it. The dress pooled at her feet and he tossed it aside.

Hands on her thighs, he looked his fill. Narrow waist. Hourglass hips. Tiny, perky breasts. Long-as-hell legs. Smooth, satin skin. He could do nothing more than stare at her all night and be a happy man. He kissed her belly, her thighs, and then in between. Finding her already wet, he groaned his approval. Always when they'd played, she'd been slick with arousal. For him.

With a deep inhale, she wove her fingers through his hair, encouraging him.

Trying to resist rubbing his throbbing erection, he licked her hard nub and her knees locked. One hand on her hip to steady her, he glided his fingers through her slick folds and sank two fingers inside her. She seemed tight to him, and concern he'd hurt her banded his chest. She was petite in stature, waifish almost, and he didn't know how leashed his control would be after so long.

With a cry, she bucked. *Yes* and *please* and *Drake* fell from her lips as she thrust against his mouth. Her walls clamped around his fingers and her muscles clenched beneath his hand.

Christ, she could kill him alone with her responsiveness. It not only made it easy to know what she liked, that she enjoyed what he was doing, but he found her verbal foreplay sexier than sin. Lifting his head to watch her, he grazed his thumb over her clit instead, and she came undone. Head thrown back, lips parted, she shuddered.

When her legs gave out, he was expecting it. Grabbing her behind the knees, he spread them so she'd land on his thighs, straddling him. Before she got her breath back, he drove his hands in her hair, releasing the ponytail, and kissed her. Hard, desperate, their mouths mated.

Fire ravaged every inch of his skin where they met and he couldn't find enough places to touch. The slope of her ass, the curve of her spine, the giving flesh of her small breasts. Aftershocks still claimed her, and he was so damn turned on he thought he'd implode.

After a moment, she looked at him, her cheeks flushed. So hard, he fought the need to lay her out and plunge. She deserved better than that, but the longer her gaze perused him, the more difficult it became. Reverence and need and appreciation lit her hazel eyes.

Biting her lip, she settled her hands on his shoulders. Gaze dipping, it followed the path of her fingers as they trailed lower. She threaded them through the thin hair on his chest to his abs. His stomach concaved at her exploration and he tipped his face toward the ceiling, about to snap.

She leaned back and grabbed a condom from the box. With her teeth, she ripped it open, tossed the wrapper, and rolled the latex down his shaft. His hands fisted behind her back as air trapped painfully in his lungs. When her gaze landed on his once more and she rose over him, he realized her intent and grabbed her hips to stop her.

A subtle shift, and she laid out on the sheets. Her hair spilled over the pillow. Like he belonged there, she cradled him between her thighs and emotion rose in his throat. Taking her hands in his, he laced their fingers, pressing them into the mattress by her shoulders, and aligned himself. Utter shock that he was here with her battled with the feral need to claim her, to prove to them both this was not only inevitable, but right.

He nudged his hips forward and was surrounded by giving, soft heat. The breath expelled from his lungs in a whoosh and he dropped his forehead to hers. She kept her eyes on him, green and brown and blue swirling together in a haze of lust.

Halfway, he met resistance and gave her a moment before continuing. Unable to stand the exquisite torture, he pinched his eyes closed, lips parting over hers, and sank the rest of the way. Pausing, he panted against her mouth and realized her breathing was just as uneven.

"Are you okay?" he whispered, nearly unable to withstand the painful pleasure of her subtle walls. Or the fact she was under him. Around him. Inside him…as much or possibly more than he could be inside her.

"Yes." Her rich voice and lavender scent filled his head. She kissed his closed lids. "Are you?"

"No." He would forever and never be okay again. That was the kind of ludicrous contradictions she evoked. Safety and danger. Lust and love. Strength and tenderness. Shaking with restraint, his lungs uncooperative, he forced his eyes open. "I'm better than okay."

Her brows pinched in worry, her gaze seeking. "Drake." Her throat worked a swallow. "Please, I…"

And he knew. She sought assurance. Because she cared that much and put everyone—him most of all—before herself. Even now, while he was buried inside her and ready to snap, she thought only of his needs.

"Zoe, honey." He kissed her gently and repeatedly said her name so she'd have no doubt whatsoever he knew who he was with. The only woman he wanted. "I'm going to make love to you now."

Chapter 23

Eyes burning at his tender words, at the way he'd said her name with reverence, Zoe traced the hard planes of his body. The muscles in his back shifted as she worked her way down to his taut ass, over his hips, and around to where they were joined.

God, how she loved his body.

Closing his eyes, he inhaled. Tension and restraint coiled him, radiated off him in waves. His fingers of one hand clenched hers and released, only to cup her jaw while he slid his other arm between her hips and the mattress. The shift drew them closer, nudged him deeper, and she bit her lip.

His familiar scent of warm male wove around her, the fine hairs on his chest teasing her nipples. Every nerve became hypersensitive as he slowly withdrew. The thickness of his shaft glided along her walls and she felt every inch of him retreat. Oh, and he had a lot of inches. Not so huge he hurt her, but yeah...deliciously filling. When nothing but his tip remained inside her, she made a sound of protest at the loss.

He dipped his head and kissed her cheek. "Shh," he whispered coarsely against her ear. "I've got you."

Grabbing the back of her knee, he raised her leg and cinched it higher up his back, holding her thigh to keep it there. He thrust inside her, filling her again, and the new angle stole her breath. Every fluid stroke ground his pelvis against her clit, his shaft rubbing a tender spot inside her. Still sensitive from her previous release, she could barely withstand the satisfaction building, the graceful way he moved.

He opened his mouth over the tendon on her neck and increased the pace. She loved the quiet sounds of arousal he made, the way he sometimes held his breath as if unable to take the pleasure. His body grew more rigid and she assumed he was close. She wrapped her arms around him, holding her to him. But he wouldn't let go, was waiting for…her, she discovered. Close, she was so close. Warning tingles shot up her spine and she arched, taking him deeper. She hadn't expected much endurance on his part or to come again. Not after how long it had been for both of them. Time and frequency would take care of the rest later, but she should've known. He didn't just have a strong body, but mind as well, and he would not take from her without giving first.

The arm beneath her moved and he wrapped his fingers around her other knee, spreading her wider and…

"Oh my God," she breathed. "Yes, there."

She bowed, tensing for the onslaught while chanting his name. Harder, faster, he drove, all while keeping a rhythm meant to decimate. Fluent, graceful, his beautiful athletic body moved over hers. Tension knotted her belly and she gasped, straining on the cusp.

"You feel so damn good." He nipped her earlobe, and as if understanding what his low, hoarse tone did to her, he spoke against the shell of her ear again. "The things you do to me, Zoe. Come, honey." He let go of her legs and one hand fisted the pillow, the other tilted her chin to give him better access to her neck.

Tremors tore through her with each stroke of his tongue, mimicking what he was doing inside her. And she exploded. She cried unintelligible words and promises as the release went on and on and—*Oh my God*—on. Straining, she banded her limbs around him, clutching him to her, and riding out the current.

He barked a sharp cry against her skin and caged her head between two straining biceps. Rigid, he froze above her, then pumped with vigor before gently slowing.

Slumping, he kept his face buried in her hair, breaths soughing while she dare not move lest she shatter the moment. That was…that was…damn. Her brain was mush, her circuits fried.

He unfurled his fingers from the pillow, only to white-knuckle it again. "Sweet Christ." He groaned and turned his head to kiss her cheek, leaving his lips to linger. "Sweet fucking Christ."

A laugh built in her throat. Delirious, it escaped, shaking her chest. "My sentiments precisely."

Carefully, he pulled out, removed the condom, tossed it in the bedside trash, and looked down at her. She was still wrapped around him like a bandage and his weight was deliciously welcome. Satisfaction and traces of awed humor looked back at her. His dark eyes scanned her face while he stroked her jaw.

His lips parted like he wanted to say something, but he shook his head once and kissed her instead. Framing his face with her hands, she deepened the kiss. Sentiment and emotion poured through him as if he were claiming her, making a point. Days, years passed as it went on until she couldn't ever remember a time they weren't exactly as they were, together.

With a sigh, he pressed his lips to her collarbone and rested his head between her breasts. His fingers idly stroked her ribs while she played with the thick softness of his hair. Stretching her legs out, she settled in, content and warm and safe.

"Am I too heavy?"

Smiling, she hummed. "No. Stay where you are."

He went quiet for a beat. "There's so much I want to say to you right now."

"Is one of them good night? Because that orgasm did me in until sunrise." Her chest rumbled with his rough laugh, then he sighed.

Sensing he was at unrest, she rubbed his neck, his back. "What is it? You're thinking too hard."

He briefly smiled against her skin. "That's the thing, Zoe. I can think of little else but you." Lifting his head, he set his chin down and leveled his wary gaze on hers. "I have this awful feeling you don't understand there's no going back for me."

Air hissed between her teeth and she rubbed her eyes. "I do know." Or she'd suspected. No matter how they played out, there would never be anyone else for her either. Except he'd had his one true love already, but he'd always be hers. So many what-ifs hovered in the distance. "Hand to God, Drake. I'm doing everything in my power not to hurt you."

"And there's my other point. You'd never hurt me." He nodded when she looked at him. "You don't have it in you to cause anyone pain, especially me. Talk to me. Tell me why you're so intent on hurting yourself for the sake of supposedly protecting me."

They'd discussed this to death, and he knew her reasons. But she'd skirted around the underlying factors he was probably ignoring. "You want a family, and the potential for that was taken from you with Heather's death. There's still time, but not if we stay together."

With a frown, he rose onto his forearms. "What are you talking about?"

"DNA, Drake. If I carry that mutation dementia gene, I run the risk of passing it to my offspring."

He studied her a long beat, gaze penetrating. "Adoption, then."

"I'm thirty-one years old. Mama was in her late forties when she started exhibiting symptoms. They can present at any time. You really want to put a child through that? Because I don't." She sighed, her heart heavy. "I'm not having kids. And that's what you want most."

Closing his eyes, he rubbed his jaw. "Zoe." Staring at her, a war over his needs and her circumstances waged across his face. "You don't know what that test will say."

"And you need to quit living in denial and accept what the result might be." Swallowing the lump in her throat, she ran her fingers over the tension lines on his forehead and said the one thing she'd been holding back for too many years. "I love you."

His shoulders deflated. "Zoe—"

"Stop." She shook her head, knowing exactly what was coming next. "I love you and I know you inside and out. Don't you dare tell me nieces and nephews will be enough, that you'll adjust your dreams for me. Even if the test comes back negative, Mama is my responsibility. She'll be out of rehab soon. You've seen what she's like. That's no environment for a child." Her chest hitched. "Do you understand now? Do you get it? I'm not trying to be stubborn or pessimistic. I'm drowning in reality."

Chest rising and falling, jaw ticking, he stared at her through desolate eyes. The longer he stayed silent, the greater the sheen grew, until his eyes were red with unshed tears. He made a noise like a caged tiger and dropped his forehead to her breastbone. Fists clenched, he growled again. Huffing, he vibrated while obviously trying to get himself under control.

"I swear to you, I'll find a way around this." He lifted his head, set his palms on the bed by her shoulders, and hovered over her. "If I have to change your goddamn DNA myself, I'll fucking do it. Because I love you right back. I did not claw my way out of grief only to find you and have someone I can't breathe without taken from me again."

She squeaked in an attempt to pull oxygen into her lungs. Holy, holy cow. With his fierce alpha side barely in check, she almost believed he could bend time or shift space to his will. But the fact remained, no matter how badly they might want something, that didn't make it true.

But her childish pathetic heart latched onto what she'd always secretly dreamed he'd say. "You love me?"

His expression softened, smoothing the fear and rage from his handsome face. "Are you kidding me? Yes. I love you." His gaze darted back and forth between her eyes. "Now it's time for you to understand me. No test or anything else is keeping me from you. We will work this out together."

She almost believed him. Raising her head, she pressed her lips to his until the last of the strain in his body eased.

He brushed his nose with hers. "Tell me again, honey."

"I love you."

His thumb traced her lower lip as if he were trying to savor the feel of her words and not just the sound. "Then nothing else matters." Tilting his head, he kissed her until oblivion hung in the balance. His lips dragged across her cheek to her neck. "You." He moved to the other side. "And me." Open-mouthed kisses rained over her throat. "From now on."

"Them's fighting words." Arousal heated her skin, made her throb. His warm breath fanned her breasts as he laughed. "Damn right."

He latched onto her nipple and she gasped, holding the back of his head as if that would be enough to keep him with her. He shifted to the other breast and she moaned, dragging her heel up his leg to his ass.

Groaning, he reached for another condom, sheathed himself, and slid his arms behind her back. "Hold onto me."

She thought he meant metaphorically until he lifted her and she discovered he'd meant it literally as well. Cool air rushed her skin as he rose onto his knees, shifted his body to lean against the headboard, and brought her to a complete halt against his chest while she straddled him.

Gaze on hers, hands firmly on her hips, he paused. His tip nudged her opening and her lids fluttered closed. She sunk her fingers into the flesh above his pecs while he kept her suspended between heaven and hell.

"Drake, please."

His chest expanded as if that was exactly what he'd been waiting to hear. And in one breathtaking thrust, he filled her. A needy whimper raked her throat and she opened her eyes to find his locked on her. Heat and torment and promise shone through the depths. He moved his hands to her thighs, gradually sliding them toward where they were joined.

God, the way he touched her. Like he was learning and memorizing while seeking enjoyment.

She eased back to take him deeper and ground her hips. A tremor of need fizzled through her veins. No one made her ache, made her want like Drake. She explored his athletic body—the wide, strong shoulders, ripples of abs. A runner or swimmer's build. Perfection. His muscular thighs beneath her flexed, and she lifted her gaze to his.

Through hooded eyes dark with passion, he studied her in turn. As his gaze raked over her, his chest moved with rapid pants. "You're beautiful."

Throughout her life, she'd been told that many times over. Perhaps because of her gypsy heritage. But he was the first person to have her believe it or, at the very least, not question the words. She took his wrists and guided his hands to her breasts. With hers over his, she rocked her hips.

As if by instinct, he rose to meet her, and the connection was brutally breathtaking. She set a rhythm and he followed the dance, thrusting up as she came down over him. Tension built in her belly and she closed her eyes, tilted her face toward the ceiling. God, he filled her. Everywhere.

Even without looking, she knew he was watching her, and something about that heightened her response. An awareness crept into her, coiled, and sped her heart rate. Brows pinched, she parted her lips, whispering words of encouragement.

He moved one hand to her lower back, the other to where they were joined, and she imagined his intent gaze taking in how he drove inside her, how she rode him with abandon. Throbbing, her breasts grew heavy with desire.

His thumb circled her clit, and she cried out as her body splintered. Light and sound fractured. Time screeched to a halt while she all but convulsed with the violent release.

A groan, and he straightened. His chest crashed against hers. His arms wrapped around her back, hands holding her shoulders from behind. His mouth teased hers, open and poised as if in shock. And then he pulsed inside her, body rigid as he came, hips rocking to pull every drop of pleasure.

Dizzy, delirious, she wove her fingers through his hair and opened her eyes. His lashes fluttered, and she was met with dark chocolate. He stared at her, unwavering. Like he was lost and found, in agony and bliss, satisfied and hungry.

With a shaking hand, he cupped her cheek. "I can't breathe."

Her throat closed at his honesty. Because she knew the implication, what he'd meant. He'd said the same thing the night of Heather's funeral, and he was telling Zoe now. Somehow, he'd learned to function again after his wife's death, but now he was right back to square one.

Fighting to draw air.

Chapter 24

Drake scanned the semi-full banquet room a third time. Still no Zoe. Nauseated, anxiety-laden, he took a sip of whiskey and pretended to listen to Pete as he blathered about a workshop he'd attended.

People from the conference floated from table to table in the pre-dinner moments. It was like a jacked-up charity function with all the black ties and sequined dresses. White linen cloths and flower arrangements. An instrumental orchestra played annoyingly droll music in a corner. Drake would rather say screw it and head back upstairs. Strip Zoe down to nothing and lose reality inside her soft, hot body.

And never resurface.

When he'd awoken this morning, she had already been dressed and sitting by his hip in bed, holding coffee. She'd been so damn distant and aloof his heart had stopped. They'd attended separate workshops and then went out to lunch. Blessedly, from there, she'd begun to act more normal.

He'd taken her to Portland Art Museum because he knew her pretty eyes would wander everywhere and be happy. With a mix of Asian, American, and Native American pieces, she'd been in Zoe heaven. They hadn't much time after that, so they did a quick tour of the Japanese Garden where she'd claimed to get new painting inspiration. He'd have to bring her back to the city again when they had more chances to explore.

An hour ago, she'd insisted she would meet him down here for the banquet. Something about primping, but he suspected she needed some time alone. Adjusting his tie, he decided if she didn't show her gorgeous ass in the next three minutes, he'd go after her.

"The equipment they used wasn't half bad, though."

Drake grunted as if he'd been listening to Pete. He'd forgotten how talkative his former classmate could be. "Sounds like it was productive for you." Where the hell was she?

Pete laughed. "You haven't heard a word I said."

"Sorry. I'm distracted—"

Heaven help him. Across the room, Zoe stood in the doorway wearing a gold slip dress that clung to every subtle curve and stopped at her knees. Toned legs three states long and black heels. Her hair was up in some complicated twist and several strands fell around her face. Red lips, smoky eyes.

Oxygen backed up in his lungs as she glanced around, probably searching for him.

Pete laughed into his drink. "I can see why. She's one helluva distraction."

No shit.

Her gaze landed on Drake and a grin split her face. She made her way over and he groaned at her swaying hips, at the purely sexual way she moved. And he knew exactly the beauty that awaited him under that dress.

Pete chuckled. Again.

"Hey." She shook Pete's hand and kissed Drake's cheek. Her brow pinched at his lack of ability to speak, blink, or breathe. "What's wrong? Don't you like my dress?" She glanced down at the torture device in question.

"I need a minute." Since his voice sounded strangled, he cleared his throat. Like an idiot, he just kept staring. Funny how a guy could go his whole life knowing someone and never truly see them.

Pete, yet again, laughed, giving Drake the urge to punch the grin right off. "I'm going to find my seat. Zoe, you look lovely."

"Thank you." She eyed Drake. "Guess someone doesn't need time to flip a compliment."

When Pete strode away, Drake's fingers clenched his glass. "You don't look lovely."

Her lips flattened. "Well—"

"You look goddamn gorgeous and you're making it difficult to string consonants together to form syllables."

Her eyebrows pinged and her jaw dropped. "That'll do. Thank you."

"You're welcome." Stepping closer, he bent and kissed her forehead. Mercy, that lavender scent drove him insane. "We better sit. If we don't, I'm tempted to take you right back upstairs."

She sighed dreamily. "I'm good with either scenario."

Dinner was lengthy and tedious. Zoe had the salmon and Drake the tenderloin, and though he was sure both were delicious, he tasted nothing. All he could focus on were the male eyes on her, the way she slipped into conversation so easily as if he weren't there, and the damn laugh Pete kept dragging from her pouty red mouth. It was enough to make a man homicidal. During dessert, she moved her hand to Drake's thigh under the table and drew lazy patterns with her finger. Each little swirl brought her closer and closer to DEFCON Five. Leaning over, she whispered in his ear. "If you promise to stop killing conference attendees in your head, I'll scream your name later. After all, you're the only person I'm thinking about."

With a casual blink of her lashes, she smiled and resettled in her seat while he did everything he could to not growl. Or lay her flat on the table. Visions of her stripping out of that holy-hell dress and screaming his name forced him to shut his eyes or he'd wind up with a busted zipper. When he opened them, she was making love to a slice of lemon meringue pie with her mouth via a fork.

Drake slammed the rest of his whiskey. And her champagne.

Zoe smiled. "I'm going to the ladies' room. I'll be right back."

The guys at the table rose out of politeness. Drake didn't dare or he'd be expelled for indecent behavior. Napkin firmly in his lap to hide his erection, he stared at his plate and thought through the steps of neutering surgery. By the time she returned, the orchestra had started again and people were mingling about or dancing.

Smiling, she set her clutch purse on the table. "Pete, would you care to dance?"

Hell. He knew she was only being polite since Pete was here alone, but Drake's molars nearly cracked.

With a grin, Pete rose. "I would love to." He glanced at Drake. "So long as my face will not be rearranged when we return."

Unable to help it, Drake laughed. "Keep your hands where I can see them and you have a deal." Zoe rolled her eyes and, as they stepped away, he called her name. "That goes for your hands, too."

Mocking a pout, she sighed. "Damn." She smiled at Pete. "It was worth a shot."

Drake tracked their progress on the floor throughout the song, smiling at her vast expressions as she spoke, imagining the witty nonsense she was probably spouting. Never a dull moment with Zoe around.

After the first song, he met her on the dance floor and took her hand, tugging her to him and setting them in motion to an elevator version of *Just the Way You Are*. "Haven't danced with you since Cade's wedding. I think my heart pounded just as hard, but for an entirely different reason."

She smiled up at him. "And why was that?"

"First time it beat in years. You have a way of doing that, you know."

Studying him, her smile slipped a fraction. "You don't have to say sweet things all the time or be jealous. You're the only one I'm interested in."

"I speak truth." As for the other thing, he didn't think jealous was the right word. Being around her gave him an uncanny urge to beat his chest and growl *mine*, but that was more territorial than envy. "I'm not sure where the jealousy vibe comes from. I was never like that with Heather."

Her fingers played with the hair on his nape. "Probably because you guys started dating so young. Everyone kind of knew she was yours. Besides, she wasn't a flirt like I am."

True. He dipped his hands low on her back and urged her closer. "You two were very different in a lot of ways. From an outside prospective, it's surprising you were best friends."

"Yeah," she said quietly. Her gaze grew distant as she looked away, her expression indicating her thoughts had drifted into enemy territory.

"What is it?"

She shook her head. "She's just a tough act to follow."

His stomach bottomed out. He stilled their movement, utterly shocked this had been a concern on her part. "Are you worried I won't love you as much as her?"

"Of course, you won't." Her irritated, vulnerable gaze nailed him. "You two were epic. Storybook. I wouldn't ever expect us to compare with that."

Christ, he was an asshole for not seeing this sooner. "You're wrong." He set them in motion again, trying to find the words to explain while he breathed through the way she'd wrecked his gut with her admission. Worse, that she believed it. "I love both of you with the same heart, Zoe, just in different ways."

Since she'd lowered her head and rested her cheek on his chest, he couldn't see her face to read her expression. But she moved easily with him, despite the stiffening of her spine. Breathing in her lavender scent, he closed his eyes and picked apart his past, his present, and found answers he thought she needed.

He rested his chin on her head and caressed her neck, her back. "Heather was a calming presence in my life. She was a pleaser and very agreeable. She saw only the best in people. There was quiet passion and gentle readings of the mind. We could sit in silence for hours and not feel the need to talk. No demands or pressure, and I loved that most. The simplicity of just being with someone."

Sighing, he kissed Zoe's hair and left his lips to linger. "You both have huge hearts and giving natures and fierce loyalty to those you love. The two of you are dreamers and romantics. Family always comes first, whether that's by blood or friendship. Those shared traits are what I treasure, what drew me to both of you."

His arms banded tighter around her and he held the back of her head, fighting an emotional onslaught as memories shoved around in his skull. "You, Zoe, challenge me. When I want to sit idle, you force me to look at what's around me and participate. I'm constantly on my toes, wondering what you'll say next and causing my head spin to keep up. No one can make me laugh like you do. You see both sides of the coin, and you're not afraid to speak your mind in a world where most people would rather placate. You, honey, are a fighter."

Closing his eyes, he blew out an uneven breath. "Same heart," he repeated, "different ways to love."

She didn't speak or respond or falter in her steps as they danced. Both arms were still around his back and one hand was buried in his hair. Songs bled together. Partners came and went from the floor. He'd swore she'd left the premises if he wasn't holding her so damn tight.

After he didn't know how long, she slowly lifted her head and stared at his chest. "Drake…"

Enough. He took her hand, twirled her, and brought her back to him. "We're not upstairs yet. Don't start chanting my name. And by the way, you promised to scream it."

She breathed a husky laugh. "I'm a woman of my word. Let's go."

He held her hand in the empty elevator ride up, his gaze focused on the numbers. "What color panties do you have on tonight?"

"Who says I'm wearing any?"

His head thunked the wall. "That's exactly what I'm talking about. I never know what you'll say next." He paused. "Were you serious? About…"

Eyes ahead, she grinned.

Twenty, twenty-one… Finally, floor twenty-two.

She followed him to the room and he walked to the bed, flipping on a lamp and turning down the sheets. When he spun around, she was leaning against the wall, fully dressed, but with a pair of black panties dangling from one finger.

"Well, that answers that question." He ate the distance and kissed her. No finesse, no coaxing. Just devoured her whole as he pinned her in place.

She shoved his suit coat off his shoulders and it dropped to the floor. The tie was next before she got to work on the buttons of his shirt. Untucking it, she broke away to look at him as she parted the material. Sliding her hands up his pecs, one corner of her mouth curved. Then the shirt joined the other items on the floor and she kissed the dead center of his chest.

Closing his eyes, he threaded his fingers through her hair and loosened the pins holding her waves. Once free, he combed through the strands while she licked and nipped every square inch of his torso. Fire seared his skin and his shaft throbbed.

Then she reached for his back pocket. She pulled out his wallet, removed a condom, and tossed the leather aside. Fisting the foil packet, she got to work on his belt.

"How'd you know it was in there?"

Belt…gone. Fly…unzipped.

Her hand wrapped around him and stroked. He lost all sensory above his neck. Pressing his palms to the wall beside her head, he leaned into them. Thrusting into her sweet embrace, he looked into her eyes, about to come undone at the seams.

"You're always prepared." She nipped his jaw and he let a groan loose. "And you were a boy scout, after all."

Stilling, he shut his eyes, damning the thoughts invading at the most inopportune time. But she was stroking his aching shaft and kissing the hell out of his neck, so his brain detached from his mouth. "You usually prefer the bad boys."

She removed her hand from his pants and he nearly wept. Lifting her head, she stared at him. "Is that a concern of yours?" When he didn't respond, she blinked her hazel eyes. "It is, isn't it?"

He ground his teeth at the stupid insecurity. He'd thought he'd gotten over it, but apparently not. "Let's face it. I'm not the typical man you go for."

Releasing a shallow breath, she shook her head. "Exactly. You always do and say the right thing."

This conversation was quickly going south. And not the good kind below the belt. "No, I don't."

"Yes, actually, you do." She cupped his face, and the tender gesture had him curling his fingers against the wall. "You logically think through what to say before speaking in order not to hurt feelings. Every other sentence is a compliment intended to make me feel good. You'd lay down your life for your family and friends, and you love so hard you chronically tear a chunk of yourself away. Don't you see how rare that is? A man in tune with his emotions who's not afraid to act on them?"

He stared at her. Hard. Though he couldn't deny what she said, it didn't exactly answer his question. He might be genetically engineered to give a shit when most males were taught to bottle feelings, but that didn't mean his type was what she wanted.

She sighed. "Bad boys are fun, but that's all they are. I'm not here with them. I'm with you. Why do you think I fought us being together? My circumstances could erase happily-ever-after." With a frown, she swallowed. "I wasn't supposed to get you, so I went after the opposite."

Christ. More internal stitches would be required if she kept this up. But there was his answer. He never should've doubted her in the first place.

Removing his hands from the wall, he set them on her thighs, shoved her dress up her hips, and pressed her firmly back in place. She squeaked in surprise. Grabbing her perfect little ass, he lifted her until they were face to face and kissed the ever-living shit out of her. Maybe she'd understand what she did to him, the power she had over him, or maybe she wouldn't. But right now, he was going to take her like he'd been wanting to do all night.

She fumbled with his pants, shoved them down his hips, and tore the condom wrapper. Keeping her mouth plastered to his, she sheathed him and wrapped her legs securely around him. To hold her steady, he kept one hand on her backside and flattened the other on the wall. Then, he sank into her with a quick, desperate thrust.

Christ in Heaven. *Yes.*

Breaking away from the kiss, she threw her head back and let out a string of muttered nonsensical words. Moans, mewls, and panting. She clenched her fingers in his hair while he devoured her neck, throat, ear. Her heels dug into his ass, but he'd take the marks they were sure to leave behind. Let her brand him for all he cared. Encouraged by her reaction, he pumped harder, legs straining and back tight.

Judging by her erratic breathing and the way her soft walls held him in a vise, she was damn close. Burying his face in her hair, he drove into her for all he was worth. He'd never done this against the wall before, but Zoe was always so responsive, so vocal, he knew he was doing something right. Not that he had any complaints other than he might die right where he stood, balls deep inside the most amazing woman he knew.

She was devastatingly beautiful like this—cheeks flushed and defenseless to passion.

Without so much as a warning, her walls fisted him and yanked his release with shocking power and a side jolt of lights-out. A strangled sound shot past his throat. Lids tightly sealed and lips parted, she shuddered against him, rocking her hips. She arched and…sweet damn.

She did scream his name.

Chapter 25

After she'd changed out of scrubs and into jeans and a tee, Zoe sat on the edge of Avery's desk, waiting for her to finish a call. The morning had been hectic, but she got through it. The whole week had been pretty nuts. Zoe barely had time to visit Mama during breaks.

Avery hung up and smiled. "Done with clients?" Once Zoe nodded, Avery checked the schedule on her computer. "Not a bad way to end the week. A half day on Friday." She sighed. "Take me with you. Please? We have the Dawson twins coming in this afternoon with their Chow-Chows to see Cade. They cling to him like saran wrap, and I don't mean the dogs. I'm sure I'm going to need your amnesia stick by the time they leave."

Zoe laughed at the reference to her baseball bat skills. "How about I take you to lunch instead? I have something I wanted to talk to you about."

"Sure." Avery set out the be *back soon sign*, locked her PC, and rose.

They made their way across the street to the deli and grabbed a couple sandwiches, taking them outside to a cafe table. Rain had fallen last night, leaving the Ridge shrouded in fog and sticky humidity in the air. A cool breeze wafted down from the mountain to relieve the heat. Shoppers passed by on the cobblestone walk, chatting.

Avery took a sip of sweet tea. "When I first rolled into town, I thought I was in Silent Hill."

Zoe laughed. "You and your horror movies."

"Well, it was dark, foggy, the streets deserted, and it was snowing." Avery took a bite of her loaded ham and Swiss, speaking around her food. "So, Drake's grinning like a fool since you guys got back from Portland."

"What can I say? I rocked his world." More like he'd rocked hers. She set her turkey and cheddar croissant aside.

Avery laughed. "I'm glad. It's good to see him so happy." She wiped her mouth with a napkin. "What did you want to talk about?"

Zoe shoved the pickle around her plate. "It's really personal, my question. If I'm overstepping, just tell me. I didn't know who else to talk to."

"Hey, nothing's too personal around here." Avery clasped Zoe's hand, smile slipping. "Go ahead."

With a nod, Zoe chewed her lip. "Autism can run in the family, right?"

"Yes, it can in some cases. Since Hailey is a girl, the odds increase. I can't give you exact numbers, but there's some studies on it."

Zoe rubbed her forehead. "Does that worry you? Since you're expecting another baby, I mean."

An ah-ha widened Avery's eyes. "Cade and I did discuss the issue before we tried to conceive. But, to be honest, we both love Hailey and even if our next child winds up autistic, too, it wouldn't change our mind."

"She's a wonderful kid." Zoe had been expecting that answer, but she had to start talking about her concerns. Drake wanted a family so badly and her stomach was in a constant riot over the what-ifs.

"Is this about your mom's dementia? Did you get your results back?"

Zoe's gaze whipped to Avery's. "You know?" She hadn't treated Zoe any different. No pity stares or anything else.

"Drake was with his brothers when he connected the dots. Cade told me afterward."

"I haven't gotten the results yet. I'm expecting them any day." She hadn't been able to eat or sleep much the past week. Zoe was pretty certain their mail carrier thought she was stalking him. "Drake's always wanted children. I feel like a selfish bitch for what might be me stringing him along."

Avery squeezed her fingers. "You're the farthest thing from selfish. Drake loves you. Anyone with eyes can see that. Let him decide what he wants. Plans change."

"Yeah." She sighed. He shouldn't have to adjust for Zoe, though. "Thanks, Avery."

After lunch, Zoe headed to Pine Crest to visit Mama. Since she wasn't in her room, Zoe moved down the hall to the activity center and stopped short.

Among several tables and residents was her mom. Sitting in a wheelchair with her leg propped up, she laughed at something the elder woman across from her said. A checkerboard between them, they chatted. There was no trace of fear or apprehension on her face, nor tension in her posture. Aides walked around the room, helping patients, and she waved at them like she hadn't a care in the world.

This wasn't the first time Zoe had visited and found her mom calm. According to her chart, she'd been cooperative with meds, hygiene, meals, and bedtime. Her confusion was, as always, worse after sundown, but they were managing.

"She's doing really well."

Zoe glanced at the gentleman beside her. Donald Forester was the nursing home director and very good about keeping her up to date. Cocoa skin and shaved head, he was in his late fifties and had been a few years ahead of Mama in school.

She looked back at her mom, chest pinched and throat tight. Her eyes burned the longer she watched. The past few years, Mama had grown aggressive in her confused state and it had been a constant battle to get her to eat, rest, or even assure her she was safe. If not for the adult day center, Brent, or Drake, Zoe might've gone mad herself from the stress.

Hand to her chest, Zoe shook her head in awe. "She really does seem okay." More than okay. When the accident had occurred, she'd been utterly terrified moving Mama. But she was adjusting. And way better than she had at home with Zoe.

Guilt and shame coagulated in her belly.

Donald set a hand on her shoulder. "I understand things had been pretty rough at home. It's hard watching loved ones forget. They act out of character, do and say things they ordinarily wouldn't."

She nodded, already sensing what was best for Mama, even though it went against her original wishes and what Zoe had been determined to accomplish. God, this was so hard. "I'm going to go see her."

"Come by my office afterward, if you don't mind."

"I will." On legs made of lead, she walked to her mom's table and took a seat. "Hey, there. It looks like you're having a good game."

A confused expression dulled Mama's face, hollowed out her eyes. A look Zoe had seen too often. But instead of getting antsy or irritable, Mama... smiled. "I can't remember how to play. My friend here is beating me."

Friend. *Friend.* Zoe's chest hitched. It had been years since Mama had used that term with regards to Drake's mother or another soul. But the stranger across from her and the people here at Pine Crest had somehow become that very thing. Zoe did everything in her power to keep the tears from falling.

"That's wonderful."

She sniffed as a couple ladies walked by and asked her mom if she wanted to watch a movie tonight. Her tablemate said something about the coffee being good.

Mama agreed and absently pushed a checker piece in an illegal move. "Is that right?" Uncertainty wrinkled her brow.

Zoe bit her tongue hard enough to draw blood trying not to weep. "It's exactly right." Blinking rapidly, she breathed through the deluge of emotion. "Do you like it here?"

The woman across from her slid a checker piece, seemingly just as perplexed.

"Gosh, yes." Mama patted her dark brown hair, which someone had neatly combed. "This is the best job." She frowned. "Is it time to go back to work?"

Patting her arm, Zoe smiled reassuringly. "No. You have time yet." Lots of time. In a place where she was comfortable and well cared for. Gut-wrenching decision made, Zoe blew out a breath. "Would you like to stay here with your friends?"

Focused on the board again, Mama nodded. "Sure."

Wiping tears, Zoe pressed her lips together. "I love you," she whispered. "I'll visit all the time. I promise."

"Of course."

Zoe stayed another hour and then went into Donald's office. It took two additional hours to fill out paperwork and discuss financial concerns. Zoe didn't make enough to pay for the facility, but if she sold the house, she could swing it until county funds kicked in.

She cried the whole way home. Though the decision was the right one for Mama, Zoe couldn't help but think she'd let her down.

And when she walked in her front door and Drake rose from the couch, her chest cracked wide open. One look at her and he was across the room, holding her, rubbing her back. She buried her face in his chest, drenching his scrubs with tears and fisting her hands.

"Checkers...friends...smiling." She hiccupped as her raw throat burned and her head pounded.

His arms banded tighter and he hitched her up his body. Shifting to the couch, he sat with her in his lap. "You're scaring the shit out of me." Rocking, he kissed her temple. Shaking hands settled over her back, in her hair. "Tell me what happened, honey."

Unable to catch her breath, she wailed. "Mama doesn't...need me. She's...gone."

And it hit her. Mama *was* gone. Had been for a long time. All her memories, her strong personality—*poof.* As if she'd never been there at all. Zoe had been doing her damn best to honor the pact they'd made and keep her at home, but what she'd really done was selfishly looked past the signs that her mom didn't feel safe. What was best for her, Zoe couldn't provide. Wracked with guilt and denial, she'd ignored the truth.

Drake stilled, then cupped her face and stared at her. Wide brown eyes darted between hers with frenetic worry. "Is she…" He cleared his throat. "What do you mean gone?"

Oh God. She'd made him think Mama died.

Taking a calming breath, she closed her eyes. When she opened them, his unwavering gaze held hers. It took three attempts, but she told him about what happened at Pine Crest and her plan. With every sentence, he relaxed degree by degree until the strong body holding her was no longer rigid with fear.

He brushed the tears from her cheeks with his thumbs. "I know that must've been difficult for you but, for what it's worth, I think you did the right thing." He sighed, tender gaze sweeping her face. "She loved you so damn much, and I think it would kill her to know how bad things had gotten. She wouldn't want that for you."

Nodding, she rested her cheek on his shoulder. He'd tried to tell her the same thing before, but she hadn't been ready to hear it. They stayed quiet awhile until she got her bearings and no longer felt like a wet tissue run over by a salt truck.

Raising her head, she kissed him. "What are you doing here anyway?"

He smiled. "Thought I'd come by after work to see if you wanted to go out for dinner, but I think maybe we should stay in with pizza."

Sounded like an awesome plan to her. "Why don't you call? I'll feed the cat and check the mail."

After setting food down for Cotton, she went onto the porch and pulled items from the mailbox while Drake ordered pizza.

Kicking the door shut, she scrolled through bills and junk. Her gaze landed on a white envelope in the stack and… The rest of the mail fell from her numb fingers, scattering on the floor. Her hands shook. The blood drained from her head and she swayed.

"Zoe? What is it?"

Her stomach clenched. "It's from the lab," she whispered.

He strode over and stood in front of her. "Come sit down. We'll open it together."

Together. She rolled the word around in her head, but it didn't compute. This was it. All the maybes and what-ifs ceased right this second. Once she opened the results, her world either began or ended. Words on the address label swirled and blended in a blurry mass. She pressed a hand to her stomach to keep the measly half-eaten sandwich from lunch inside.

"Zoe, honey."

God, his gentle, deep voice.

"No, I…" Couldn't do it. She couldn't open it. Couldn't rip his world apart. Denial was so much easier. Safer. She had to…to…get out of here. Something. "I have to go."

"What?" He grabbed her shoulders, dipping his face to meet her eyes. "Go where?"

The same fear radiated in his gaze and stole her breath. How could she do this to him? After all he'd been through?

"Honey, come sit down."

She made a choked noise and pressed her lips together, shaking her head. "I'll be right back. Just… I don't know. I'll be right back." Pulling from his grasp, she opened the door.

"Zoe!"

But she was running and didn't stop to listen. It was all she could manage. To run. Toward, away, from, to… It didn't matter. Panic clawed its way to the surface and shredded her. Lungs burning, thighs cramping, she ran. Across her subdivision, through the outskirts of town, past a wrought iron fence, over damp grass until finally halting by…Heather's grave.

Collapsing, she leaned against the stone marker and heaved air. Sweat beaded down her face, dampened her shirt. Her skin hot, her insides cold, she clutched at her chest and realized the envelope was still in her hand. Unable to look at it, she shoved it in her back pocket and lay sideways on the rain-drenched grass, staring at her best friend's grave.

Wife. Daughter. Friend. May angels lead you home.

Outlandish, bone-jarring tears wracked her body. "I miss you."

Pressing her face into the grass, she let loose. Her cell rang and her shredded heart bled and her phone rang some more.

But she lay there long after the sobs quieted and dusk came and went. Crickets chirped and fireflies blinked in the distance. A light breeze crackled leaves over her head. The faint glow from streetlights lit part of Heather's stone, and Zoe sighed. What she needed most was her best friend.

"I miss you," she said again as if Heather were right there with her. "You died and left us all devastated." She didn't realize how angry she still was, but it wasn't as if Heather was at fault.

Swallowing, she rested her head on her arm. "I have a confession. Drake and I have been seeing each other. For the longest time, I fought my feelings, thinking you'd be so mad at me." A rough laugh shook her. "But you don't get mad, even when you should. You knew, didn't you? That day you died, you made us both promise to take care of each other. That was your subtle way of giving us permission if we ever moved past friendship. It took me four years, but I figured it out."

She ran her fingers over the lawn, threading the short blades, breathing in damp earth. She told Heather about Mama and the clinic and the damn meddling Battleaxes. "I swear, sometimes I conjure that serene voice of yours telling me to simmer down and not get arrested for battery. You used to say that all the time, remember? *Simmer down, Zoe.*"

And because she needed to, she rolled over and talked. Stars winked overhead and her phone blew up and Zoe kept right on talking. About Cade and Avery and Hailey. About Flynn and Gabby. About Brent and his new guy, Miles. Evening waned and her eyes grew heavy.

"I missed this most of all. Staying up all night gossiping." A yawn cracked her jaw. "Tell me I'm doing the right thing, Heather. Promise me I'm not hurting the guy we love by being with him."

Drained, exhausted, she closed her eyes.

Something vibrated under her hip and her lids flew open. Sunlight seared her retinas and she covered her face with her arm.

Wow. Okay, she'd fallen asleep in the cemetery. Moaning, she sat up and scrubbed her hands over her face. Damn, she was stiff. As a whippoorwill cooed in the distance, Zoe unpocketed her phone. And grimaced.

Twenty missed calls from Drake and Cade. Two texts from Gabby, one from Flynn, and fifteen from Brent. Crap. She scrolled through all the *where are you's* and *call me's*. Guilt twisted her gut. She hadn't meant to worry anyone.

She ran her hands through her hair. "We pulled an all-nighter, H. And not even a decent hangover for the effort."

Quickly, she shot off a group text to everyone letting them know she was okay and she'd see them at the softball game soon. Then she bit the bullet and checked Drake's messages.

Yeah, she'd scared the shit out of him. Once she got through the panicked voicemails, she pulled up his texts and fisted the phone. Air wheezed past her lips.

We met on a meteor.
We sailed across the sky.
I can't recall the day.
I know not how or why.

Zoe clapped a hand over her mouth, reading the next text.

We met on a petal,
A piece of dandelion fluff.
We floated on a breeze of wishes.
Foolish me not to recognize love.
We met on a crowded ballpark,
The thrush of humanity passing by.

And we were at a standstill,
Not even a breath in my lungs to sigh.
"Holy crap, H. He wrote me poetry." Shaking, she scrolled down and realized the next part was about Heather's funeral.

We met in an empty room.
Two broken souls among the fray.
Years and distance and regret between us,
And with one call, you stayed.
Tears burned her eyes, even though she should be irrevocably dehydrated by now. His last text said: *If you want the last verse, come find me.*

She'd tattooed memories on her body and he'd captured them with poetry. Some hers, some his. Mary Mother, that man.

Stark reality smacked her upside the head. It didn't matter if she was sick or not. He wanted her. She'd always wanted him. They should be together, however much time was allotted.

Blinking repeatedly, she set the phone aside and pulled the lab results from her pocket. With a sudden burst of courage and shaking hands, she ripped into the envelope, quickly scanned the page, and let out a wail. Fisting the paper, she allowed the rest of her tears to tumble and then rose to her feet.

She blew Heather a kiss. "Love you."

Chapter 26

Drake paced his living room, staring at the group text Zoe had sent moments ago. A fucking group text!

I'm okay. Sorry to worry everyone. See you at the game. xoxo

He was going to ring her scrawny neck with his bare hands until her pretty eyes popped out of her beautiful face. Right before he killed her and after he kissed her. Then probably repeat the process. Twice.

"Maybe you could quit climbing the walls now that we know she's all right, yeah?"

Drake sent Cade a blithering glare and continued pacing. His brother shrugged from the chair he was slumped in and rubbed his eyes.

When she hadn't returned last night after an hour, Drake had gone batshit. Storming the castle, howling at the moon, put him in a padded cell, batshit.

He'd posted Gabby at Zoe's, Avery at Cade's, Flynn at his own house, and Cade at Drake's while he and Brent had scoured the town for Zoe. They hadn't found a damn trace of her. Not at Shooters, the nursing home, the ballpark, and even the cove, or the fifty other locations they'd checked. She hadn't returned to her house or answered so much as one of his three-million and twenty-four texts or calls. According to Gabby's updates, Zoe's car was still in the driveway at home.

Worry ate away at the lining of his gut until his ulcers had ulcers. Christ, the way she'd stared at that envelope. Face drained of all color. Swaying on her feet. Shaking uncontrollably. Worse, was that the news had come right on the cusp of her longtime forthcoming meltdown over her mother. It fucking killed him dead watching her fall apart. For years, she'd held him together, and to see her lose it was the equivalent of running his heart through a meat grinder. And then she'd just taken off. Left him standing there holding his jaw and scratching his head.

And she... Did. Not. Come. Back.

"We're going to be worth spit in today's game." Cade yawned. "I'm not even sure I can move. Haven't pulled an all-nighter since college." Drake rubbed the ache in his chest. "Thanks for being here." If not for his brother, he might be in a straightjacket.

"Anytime." Cade eyed him warily. "She'll be okay, man. Zoe's made of grit and iron."

And tissue paper and toothpicks. Most didn't know how very fragile she could be under all that strength. "Thank you. Again."

His cell rang and he all but dropped it trying to answer. His chest deflated when he saw who was on his screen. "Hi, Mom."

"Hey. I forgot to tell you I stopped by your place yesterday when you were at work. I left something on your dresser."

Digging his fingers into his eye sockets, he nodded. "I haven't been up there, but I'll go look."

"I noticed the painting from Zoe on your fireplace. It's truly amazing. It got me all misty-eyed."

"Yeah." He'd hung the one she'd made of him and his dogs above the mantle. "She's talented, that's for—" He stopped breathing for the fiftieth time in twenty-four hours when his gaze landed on said painting. "I have to go."

"Sure. I'll see you at the game. And, Drake? About what I left for you? It was time you had it, that's all."

Confused, gaze still locked on the painting, he muttered an *okay* and hung up. He walked closer and stood in front of the fireplace. When the hell had she done this? Last he'd checked, the piece was of him and his dogs.

But now, Zoe had been added at the bottom, lying in the grass, watching him with that come-hither smile of hers. And that wasn't all. Heather was there, too, iridescent as a ghost and sitting on a cloud. Her finger was paused in a swirling motion, aimed toward the ground, where two dandelion seeds floated down. Like she'd conjured two wishes. Stars shone through her semi-transparent form.

"Holy hell." He rubbed his chest, but the damn ache wouldn't abate. Hadn't all night. It just kept spreading and growing and expanding. His sinuses prickled and he inhaled. Hard.

"Takes a special breed of woman to not only accept the deceased wife, but to embrace her." From his side, Cade stared at the painting. "I'd say it was because she was her best friend, but that's not giving Zoe enough credit."

Drake couldn't survive this a second time. He just...couldn't. He was one lucky bastard to have found two true loves in his lifetime, but if Zoe walked or wound up sick, he'd flat out die himself.

The front door opened and closed with a quiet click.

He whirled, and there—thank Almighty—was Zoe. Still wearing the same clothes from yesterday, her hair a knotted mess, and dark circles under her eyes, she bit her lip.

Most beautiful sight he'd ever laid eyes on. So he growled at the reminder of how she'd eviscerated him last night.

"I'm sorry I worried everyone."

"Right. Well, I'm going to go." Cade pointed to the door and raised his hands in surrender. He side-stepped to the exit as if fielding landmines. "Zoe, glad you're fine. Drake, remember she has a helluva left hook, yeah?"

Zoe tracked Cade until he was gone and then she stared at the floor. Rubbed her forehead. Blew out a sigh.

Screw this. "First of all..." He strode toward her and kissed her into next week. Let her walk away from that. "Second, where the holy fuck in all damnation have you been? I can see you weren't lying dead in a ditch. Which I blame my mother for putting that visual in my head."

Her mouth opened and swiftly shut.

Sweet blessed grief, it was hard to hold on to angry through all the relief. "Were you pole dancing naked? Standing on the Eighth Street Pier debating jumping? Saving the homeless? Drinking yourself into a coma? Held hostage by a team of Smurfs? Because I assure you, all those scenarios streamed through my head. And worse."

"Uh, no." She fisted a piece of paper in her hand. "Though being held hostage by tiny blue people would—"

"Then where, Zoe? Because you had me scared to damn death."

She pulled a deep breath and looked at him through fathomless eyes. "I was with Heather."

Shit. *Shit, shit, shit.* He was an asshole. And that was the one place he'd never thought to look when it should've been the first. Of course—*of course*—she'd go to the cemetery and be with her best friend.

Closing his eyes, his shoulders deflated right along with his chest. "Zoe, honey." He hauled her against him, shaking from an adrenaline crash. "I'm sorry. I love you and I'm sorry for yelling."

Pulling away, she shook her head. "No, I'm sorry. I freaked out." She held the balled up paper. "You wanted to do this together and—"

He took the thing from her and ripped it to shreds, then dropped the pieces so they rained down like confetti. "That's what I think of the damn test. I don't care what it says. I only—"

"It was negative."

Every hair on his body stood erect. "Wh..." He cleared his throat. "What?" "Negative. In uppercase and bold print. They ran it twice." His lungs refused air exchange and something sharp jabbed his chest from the inside. Hope, maybe. It had been so long since he'd recognized it. "So, you're not...?"

"Not a carrier." Her lip quivered. "Fifty-fifty odds, and I beat them. Never had a lucky day in all my life. But I'll take it, just this once." Her voice caught. "I think Heather had a hand in it. Said a good word for me or something. This also means we can have children someday."

Twenty. They'd have twenty kids. Hell, a hundred. It didn't matter. She was okay. That was the important thing.

He cupped her face, shaking his head in disbelief. "Thank Jesus." Because there was nothing else to say, and grateful didn't cover it, he kissed her. Long, deep, and righting his upturned world again.

"Speaking of Heather. I saw the updated painting." He'd never get over that. "I love it."

She brushed her nose with his and her uneven breath skated across his lips. "She belonged with us." Lip bite. Adorable smile. "I should've said yes when you asked about pole dancing. That couldn't have been too tough a visual for you."

Laughing, he kissed her again. Optimism blossomed and, for the first time in years, stuck. Grew. Cultivated. "I love you. And I think you should show me said dancing skills. Right now."

She smiled against his mouth. "I love you, too. And I totally would, but we have a softball game in under an hour. I need to run home and change."

Fine, later. Forever. Always. "I'll meet you there." He stepped back. "And you're coming home with me after."

"Duh. You owe me the last verse of a poem." Gaze softening, she smiled. "I loved it, by the way."

He shooed her out or they'd never make the game, then ran upstairs to change. Nylon shorts and jersey on, he turned to leave and glanced at the dresser. A little red box was placed near the candles Zoe had bought. Walking over, he lifted the lid and dropped on the bed in shock.

His mom's wedding ring. The diamond was princess cut and surrounded by small pink tourmaline gems, which was Mom's birthstone and Zoe's. The gold band had an inlaid swirl design he didn't remember it having before. It was pretty and just artistic enough to not be ordinary.

Dad had still been alive when Drake had proposed to Heather. Cade and Flynn hadn't the heart to ask Mom for her ring when they'd found their loves. It seemed too right, too perfect, that it should go to Zoe. Her mother had been his mom's best friend, and they did share the same birthstone.

He fingered the ring, heart in his throat. After he'd lost Heather, he never thought he'd recover, never love again. And then Zoe had swooped in like a tsunami, reminding him he still had life yet, even when her future was uncertain. She'd loved him as a girl, as a friend, and a woman. He couldn't ever recall a time he didn't love her either, no matter what capacity.

He'd meant what he'd said to her. He didn't care what the result was, he only wanted her. But with her test negative and her mother safe in a home, thriving better, there was nothing standing between him, this ring, and Zoe. A family was possible now, too.

His mind fired on all cylinders, plotting. Planning. Thinking. And with a curve of his lips, he rose, shoved the box in his pocket, and drove to the game.

Sunshine broke through the slight cloud cover as mid-morning fog dissipated. Rainstorms had finally dropped a smidgen of the heat two days earlier, leaving the temperature hovering in the mid-seventies. Players warmed up on the field as Drake slung a bag over his shoulder and walked to the dugout fence.

Gabby and Flynn had Zoe sandwiched in a hug. When they parted, Brent gave her a talk-to-the-hand and then hugged her also before sauntering to the bleachers. Packed house. Good weather would've done that alone, but their games always drew a crowd.

Cade stepped up beside him. "Looks like it all worked out. No bloodshed." He grinned. "And I hear the test results were favorable."

Christ, Drake nearly wept just hearing it again. "Between you and me, I don't know what I would've done. The very thought of losing her, too, was unfathomable."

Sobering, Cade faced him. "Listen to me. We all died a little the day Heather did, you most of all. Take this second chance with both hands and don't look back. Zoe's perfect for you, and no one deserves happiness more."

Since he rarely left an opportunity on the table, Drake grinned. "You know I love you, right?" He scratched his jaw. "I mean, I love Avery more, but you'll always be my brother."

Cade laughed. "Understood. And I love you, too."

Drake focused on the field, thinking about where he'd be if he hadn't had his parents' marriage as an example of how to love properly, without bounds. Sure, they'd fought and didn't always see eye to eye, but there was mutual respect and adoration. He and his brothers had grown up knowing they were loved unconditionally and taught that showing so was the only way to live.

Zoe's laugh brought his attention to her near the third base line. Parker and Jason flanked her and were grinning like dipshits. Didn't matter. She was coming home with Drake. Regardless, he called Jason over.

"What's up?"

"Question." Drake jerked his chin toward the mound. "Who's pitching today?"

"Funny story. Parker sent that douche Rick back up north to the precinct where he came from, which leaves me." He shrugged. "Why?"

"I'll keep you off the Battleaxes' matchmaking radar for six months if you throw Zoe a pitch she can knock out of the park in her last at bat."

Jason narrowed his eyes. "You do know she'd probably homer off me without help?"

"Consider it insurance."

"Huh." Jason adjusted his hat. "Sure, okay. You're on."

As he strode away, Flynn eyed Drake. *"What are you up to?"*

Happy endings, but he smiled and said nothing.

And Cade had been right about sucking today. They played like comatose sloths, but the game was tied one-one in the bottom of the ninth. Bases empty, two outs, Zoe took a practice swing and stepped up to the plate.

Jason slid Drake a glance and wound to pitch.

Zoe watched it sail right over the plate for a strike. "What was that? The ladybug colony in my backyard can throw harder than that."

With a sigh, Jason nailed Drake with a thanks-no-thanks glare and refocused on her. "Zoe, baby. I'm hung over and sweating Jagerbombs. Give a guy a break."

She narrowed her eyes and took her stance. "Your funeral."

Wind up. Pitch.

Her bat connected with a smack and the ball sailed over left field somewhere into the next zip code. She dropped her bat and took a bow, then jogged to first base. The stands roared in cheers and whistles.

Drake laughed. "That's my girl." With a nod of thanks to Jason, he ran onto the field.

Accepting high-fives, she rounded third and skidded to a halt between the bag and home. Jaw slack, her wide—growing wider—gaze took in Drake on one knee blocking the plate, ring in his outstretched hand.

"Holy crap," she breathed.

The park and stands were so quiet Drake could hear cumulous clouds drifting in the atmosphere. And he owed Zoe a last verse. Ignoring every set of eyes on him but hers, he laid his entire soul at her feet.

"We met just moments ago,
The blinding instant you set me free.

A blip in the fragment of time,
If not for all you meant to me."

Hand on her chest, she gasped. "I know what my next tattoo will be."

He raised his brows. A tendril of anxiety curled his stomach. "What's that?" She tapped her hip, a mirror position to the spot where the dandelion was inked. "A baseball. Right here."

Laughing, he scratched his jaw. "Is that a yes?"

"Are you serious?" She took a faltering step forward, then another. Still too far away, but he waited. "I...I..."

Jason cleared his throat. "Zoe, baby. You gotta touch home plate for the run to count. And save the guy from misery, would you? The rest of us can mourn your non-single status later."

"Yes." She breathed a watery laugh. Shook her head. And ran. Toward Drake. "Yes."

He had just enough time to rise, step back, and catch her as she stomped the plate and launched at him. Cheers erupted and his eardrums would never be the same, but he had all he needed.

Grinning, he kissed her. "To make it official, would you marry me?"

"Yes." She pressed her lips together, eyes shining. "The ring is beautiful."

Setting her on her feet, he removed the ring from the box and slid it onto her finger. "It was my mother's. Dad proposed to her right over there under the bleachers." He grazed his thumb over the gems, thinking it looked perfect on Zoe's hand.

"Really?" She glanced at the stands and back to him. "What would you have done if I hadn't hit a home run?"

Hilarious woman. "When have you ever *not* homered in a game?"

With a solemn nod, she pursed her lips. "This is true. I am awesome."

Laughing, he tucked a wild strand of hair behind her ear. "And gorgeous and smart and funny and talented."

"Don't forget yours." Her gaze swept his face as she swallowed. Gone was the uncertainty and apprehension and guilt he'd born witness to the past few months. "Don't forget, I'm yours."

"Never." Cupping the back of her neck, he drew her to him and kissed her. His lips moved over hers—a claim. Proof. A promise. As the crowd cheered anew, or maybe still, he eased away and spoke against her mouth. "I'll never forget."

Don't miss another great Lyrical Press release!

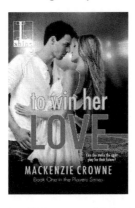

To win the game, they'll have to risk losing their hearts . . .

When a bizarre child custody stipulation pits popular sports blogger Gracie Gable against football superstar Jake Malone, losing the battle for her twin nieces isn't the only thing Gracie has to worry about. Forced to live for three months under the same roof as the sexy tight end, will she fall prey to his flirtatious pursuit? Or worse, will the skeletons in her closet destroy her chance for the love and family she so desperately wants?

Neglected by his parents as a boy, Jake doesn't believe in happily ever after. Yet living with Gracie and the twins might be enough to change his mind—and his womanizing ways. But when the press unearths a scandal from Gracie's past, will he lose the one woman he was ready to open his heart to?

Visit us at www.kensingtonbooks.com

Chapter 1

Like pure, walking sin, Jake Malone closed the distance in a deceptively lazy saunter. Gracie Gable fought the nearly overwhelming urge to take off running. Clenching her jaw, she lifted her chin. Without knowing her true identity, the various press publications flooding her blog's inbox with requests for interviews had been stymied in their attempts to track her down physically. How the hell had Jake?

And oh, God, why now?

A horrified groan rumbled deep in her chest. Having no idea what was in Pete's will, she couldn't afford to do anything to jeopardize her guardianship of the girls—like going toe-to-toe with the Manhattan Marauders' *Outlaw Tight End* right here on her brother-in-law's front lawn. She shot a worried glance down the historic farmhouse's long driveway, relieved to find it empty. With a little luck, Pete's attorney would be delayed long enough for her to deal with the famous all-pro's justified, but still overblown ego. She'd promise him anything—apologize profusely for insulting his integrity, offer him a bribe, whatever would get rid of him before Anthony Spinoza arrived.

Six foot five, with a fallen angel's face and the body of a god, Jake continued to approach. Gravel crunched beneath the heels of his boots, marking his long-legged swagger, as his thigh muscles flexed and stretched under faded blue jeans. A worn and battered leather bomber jacket rode his yard-wide shoulders. His trademark black Stetson and snakeskin boots completed the image of the Outlaw who held his own against opposing defensive lines and cast him in countless feminine fantasies. Hers included. She'd enjoyed more than her share of secret imaginings concerning the Marauders' number one tight end.

Though his nasty insults during their disastrous exchange on her blog the other day should've dealt a death blow to her foolish infatuation, the two-dimensional image she'd admired on her TV screen couldn't have prepared her for the flesh and bone temptation that was Jake Malone. Dismay crowded panic as every double X chromosome in her body quivered with giddy, XXX delight.

The X girls danced with anticipation, and the erratic thump of her heart increased with every fall of his size fifteen feet. *Down, girls. He may look like every woman's deepest sexual fantasy, but those boots are more likely to stomp us into the ground than end up under our bed.*

As angry as he must be to have taken the trouble to discover her true identity *and* find her, she could clearly imagine him grabbing her with those meat hooks he called hands and shaking her until her bones rattled. *Try it, buster. If you think the press is in a frenzy now, wait till I'm done with you.*

The silent threat boosted her flagging confidence. She angled her chin a bit more defiantly. At five ten, she was used to looking most men in the eye, but despite the added height from her three-inch heels, her gaze fell even with the sharp blade of his nose. Dark stubble shadowed the solid line of his jaw and upper lip, the same blue-black as the silky locks falling below the brim of his hat to brush his collar in the shaggy hairstyle popular among the ranks of pro football these days.

Disturbed at how badly her fingers itched to shove the hat from his head and stroke the glossy strands, she curled her hands into fists, and met his gaze. Blatant curiosity sparkled in eyes as verdant green as the needles of the pine trees lining the drive at his back. A slow smile curved his cleanly cut lips.

Huh? A sneer or even a dismissive smirk she could understand, but a smile? Where was his anger? She blinked when, instead of snatching her up, and shaking her like a dirty rag, he spoke in an easy, Texas drawl.

"You don't look like any Anthony I've ever met."

"Excuse me?"

"Anthony Spinoza. I'm supposed to meet him here."

Meet Anthony Spinoza? Why would Jake be meeting with Pete's lawyer, and why pretend ignorance of her identity? Why the pretense? Her temper simmered as logic provided a nasty explanation. Jake Malone had powerful connections and was famous for his ability to strategize. How many times had she applauded his knack for finding his opponents' weaknesses and using them to his advantage? Somehow, he must have found out, not only who she was, but her reason for being here today. She wouldn't put it past the seasoned predator to play her, acting as if he didn't know who she was, then pouncing when she relaxed her guard.

Like hell!

She bared her teeth in a tight smile. "Do you have business with Mr. Spinoza?"

"Of a sort." He didn't expand on the cryptic comment, crossing his arms, and raising an inquisitive brow. "Are you his assistant?"

Oh, he was good. The question contained the perfect amount of curiosity to make it believable. "No, I'm not. I'm supposed to meet him as well."

"Oh, yeah?"

Speculation replaced curiosity in his dark green eyes. Starting at the top of her head and moving down with a slow thoroughness, his gaze traveled her body, pausing momentarily at her chest. Her nipples immediately pouted in response. She fought the urge to slap her palms over them and prayed her fitted winter coat provided the necessary camouflage. Biting her bottom lip, she attempted to calm the girls by picturing him a good foot shorter with scrawny arms and nerdy glasses perched on a bulbous nose.

The vision refused to form.

His steady inspection continued down over her slim skirt. Winged eyebrows lifted at her leather half boots, and his smile slid toward a smirk. He examined her calves beneath the sheer protection her panty hose provided before his gaze made the return trip to her face.

"I should have known."

She bristled at both the disdain in his eyes and his snide drawl. "What, exactly, should you have known?"

"Sorry, sweetheart. You're a looker, but you're a little young, even for an old hound dog like Pete Thompson."

Hound dog? The derogatory description made no sense when attached to the loving older man her sister, Sarah, had adored, but then the rest of his comment registered. The insinuation quieted the remnant whispers of feminine awareness. Indignation strangled thoughts of crushes, walking sin, *and* expediting his departure.

She matched his stance, crossing her arms. Over the years, Sarah had done her best to break Gracie of her quick temper. When her sister's efforts had failed, she'd predicted one day, the personality flaw would get Gracie into more trouble than she could handle. Today was shaping up as that day, but the possibility didn't stop her from reacting to the insult his speculation represented.

She pinned him with a narrow-eyed stare. "Pete Thompson happens to have been my sister's husband."

His dark brows shot up. "No shit?"

She cleared her throat. "No shit."

He startled as though having his words tossed back surprised him. After studying her in silence for a long moment, the legendary charm for which he was famous made an appearance. Matching dimples popped in his cheeks with his unrepentant smile. "My apologies."

Whether the apology was for his implied insult or her familial connection to Pete, she couldn't tell. Before she could ask, he stuck out a hand and doubled down on his ruse of having no clue of her identity.

"Why don't we start over? Hello, I'm Jake Malone."

She should call him out, of course, demand he tell her what he was up to, but she couldn't resist the opportunity for a little tit for tat. She unfolded her arms to place her hand in his. "Gracie Gable."

"Nice to meet you, Gracie."

Despite her supple leather gloves, the tingling warmth of his large, bare fingers reached hers. She tugged back her hand, relieved when he let go. Equilibrium shaky, she sucked in a stealthy breath, crossed her arms once more, and cocked her head to study him. She tapped a fingertip to her bottom lip in mock concentration.

"Jake Malone? Isn't there a semi-famous...um, *soccer player* or something with the same name?"

His wry grin said he clearly recognized her slight for what it was. "Famous football player, actually. I play for the Marauders."

She repaid his slow inspection with one of her own, sliding her gaze from his dark hat to the tips of his booted feet. At two hundred forty-seven hard-muscled pounds, there was a lot of territory to cover. All of it radiated the superbly conditioned perfection of a pro athlete. Her pulse picked up a notch as her gaze roamed over powerful thighs, past trim hips, and over a flat stomach to a broad chest and impossibly wide shoulders. By the time she reached the chiseled line of his jaw, she'd forgotten how to breathe. She needed every bit of concentration to offer him a smirk instead of licking her lips.

"I should have known."

As paybacks went, repeating his insult was lame, but it was the best she could manage. He surprised her by laughing a full-throated, head thrown back, rumble of male approval. His eyes twinkled with appreciation when he lowered his head and winked. Despite the disturbing fluttering in her belly, she didn't try to disguise her satisfied smile.

"Touché, Gracie Gable." Hip cocked in a seemingly relaxed pose, he glanced away to look up at the house for the first time. "So, the old man was married?"

"Pete?"

Rolling his shoulders, he tucked the fingers of both hands into the front pockets of his jeans and nodded. She frowned at the unmistakable tension in the tight line of his mouth. What was that about? Her future was at stake here, not his.

She followed his gaze. Steady and welcoming, the familiar weathered shingles and pitched roofs of Thompson Farm brought a pang of grief to her heart. As always, whenever she visited the Long Island home Sarah and Pete had shared, Gracie was reminded of the promise she'd given her sister before she died. A promise neither had expected to come due this soon.

"To my sister. She died three years ago." Even after three long years, the words left the foul bite of burnt ash on her tongue.

"I'm sorry." He turned, his eyes full of sober intensity.

The erratic whip of emotions, from panic at why he was here, to helpless feminine interest, and back to suspicion made her dizzy. Enough already. If he was going to cause a scene, she wanted their confrontation over and done with while they were still alone. "Why are you here?"

Thick lashes lowered at her bald demand, shuttering the green of his eyes. He shrugged. "Damned if I know."

Confused, she opened her mouth to demand a better answer when the distant crunch of gravel announced the arrival of two vehicles bumping down the drive. She stifled a self-disgusted groan. He'd managed to sidetrack her, and she was out of time.

Outmaneuvered by a pro…with killer dimples.

A dark sedan stopped behind Jake's SUV. A sleek yellow sports car rolled to a halt several yards away. The door swung open and a petite, redheaded woman rose from the small high-performance machine. The bold, red-woolen power suit covering her curvy frame should've clashed with her mane of rusty curls, but somehow didn't. Bright and vibrant, her steady blue gaze roamed the face of the house and surrounding property before landing on Jake. She lifted a slim hand in a flirty, fingertip wave and beamed a smile.

Gracie disliked her on sight.

A thin, older man emerged from the second vehicle. Only the pale oval of his face beneath a classic fedora relieved the steady black of his heavy overcoat, conservative business suit, and wingtips. He clutched a briefcase in one gloved hand. Crossing to the woman, he greeted her in a short exchange. They turned together and headed up the walkway.

"Lawyers." Jake grumbled at Gracie's side. "They usually have a slick, plastic look. Figures this one resembles an angel of doom."

Her head whipped around at his odd comment, but his gaze was locked on the approaching couple.

She turned and eyed the woman. "The redhead doesn't resemble any lawyer *I've* ever seen."

He chuckled and cast her a slight smile. "I'm sure she'll be happy to hear that. Her name is Victoria Price, and she isn't a lawyer. V is my publicist."

His publicist? Am I about to be double-teamed?

She braced for disaster as Anthony Spinoza and the vivacious "V" arrived.

"Mr. Malone." The black-clad lawyer greeted Jake then smiled at Gracie. "Miss Gable, I'm Anthony Spinoza. Thank you for coming."

Gracie nodded and shook his offered hand.

"I see you've met Mr. Malone. Miss Price is acting as his representative this morning."

Okay, what the hell is going on?

Obviously Jake was here for some reason other than to have it out with her over their blog spat, but what the reason was, she couldn't imagine.

"Call me V, please. Everyone does. Nice to meet you, Miss Gable."

Gracie shook the publicist's hand, noting the Texas accent similar to Jake's. "Likewise."

"It appears we're all here." Anthony lifted a hand toward the front door. "Shall we proceed?"

Gracie's gaze flew from face to face, desperate to discover why Jake Malone and his publicist would be sitting in on the reading of Pete's will. No plausible explanation presented itself.

Well, crap. I've slipped down a rabbit hole.

Meet the Author

Bestselling author **Kelly Moran** gets her ideas from everyone and everything around her and there's always a book playing out in her head. No one who knows her bats an eyelash when she talks to herself, and no one is safe from becoming her next fictional character. She is a Catherine Award Winner, Readers Choice Finalist, Holt Medallion Finalist, and earned one of the 10 Best Reads by USA Today's HEA. She is also a Romance Writers of America member. Her interests include: sappy movies, MLB, NFL, driving others insane, and sleeping when she can. She is a closet caffeine junkie and chocoholic, but don't tell anyone. She resides in Wisconsin with her husband, three sons, and two dogs. Most of her family lives in the Carolinas, so she spends a lot of time there as well. She loves hearing from her readers. Please visit her at authorkellymoran. com, twitter.com/authorkmoran, or facebook.com/authorkellymoran.